# The Way Back to Us

Sarah Park

Published by Sarah Park, 2024.

This is a work of fiction. Similarities to real people, places, or events are entirely coincidental.

THE WAY BACK TO US

**First edition. September 8, 2024.**

Copyright © 2024 Sarah Park.

ISBN: 979-8227805836

Written by Sarah Park.

# Chapter 1: A Chance Encounter

I've always believed that life has a way of bringing people back into your orbit when you least expect it. My name is Mia Caldwell, a successful author living in serene Charleston. I thrive in my little world of words and deadlines, where my characters' dilemmas are just as tangled as my own ever-evolving plotlines. But as I walked through the grand doors of the opulent venue for tonight's charity gala, I felt a stirring in my chest that had nothing to do with my latest manuscript.

The event was held at the historic Ashworth Mansion, its candlelit ballroom awash in the warm glow of chandeliers. I marveled at the transformation of the old estate, from its usual state of quiet grandeur to a lively hive of socialites and philanthropists. The mingling of hushed conversations and clinking glasses created a soft symphony of elegance, but beneath the surface, I could sense the faintest tremor of anticipation. It was as if the air itself was charged with the promise of something unexpected.

As I made my way to the silent auction tables, my gaze swept over the crowd. I was drawn to the silent auction's art pieces, their frames reflecting the ambient light like little stars. My mind was preoccupied with the latest addition to my book series, but tonight was supposed to be a break from the relentless tick of the clock and the swirl of deadlines.

And then I saw him.

Standing near a display of antique vases was Ethan Martinez. My heart skipped, and time seemed to fold in on itself. The years had been kind to him. He still possessed that same magnetic charm and the easy smile that had once been the highlight of my teenage years. He was dressed impeccably, a deep navy suit that accentuated his broad shoulders and the relaxed grace of his presence. He looked just as I remembered, yet somehow, impossibly more. The memories of him rushed back with an intensity that took my breath away.

I felt the weight of those years, the space that had grown between us. We had been so young, so in love, and then life had taken us on different paths. It was as if all the years between our last goodbye and now had compressed into a single, palpable moment. My fingers tingled with the sudden urge to reach out, to bridge the chasm of time with a simple touch.

I hesitated, caught in the swell of nostalgia and curiosity. What had he been up to all these years? How had his life unfolded? The questions were endless, but before I could gather the courage to approach him, he turned and his gaze locked with mine.

For a fraction of a second, there was no room for words. The connection was immediate, visceral, and incredibly vivid. It was as though the years hadn't existed, and we were back in that small town, our lives intertwined by fate's whimsical design.

Ethan's smile widened, and he took a step towards me. "Mia," he said, his voice a rich, deep timbre that sent a shiver down my spine. It was both familiar and foreign, a reminder of what once was and what might have been.

"Mia Caldwell," I replied, forcing myself to sound composed. "I didn't expect to see you here."

His eyes, the same warm brown that used to be my solace, searched mine. "Neither did I. It's been a long time."

The warmth of his gaze was both comforting and unsettling. I wanted to lean into it, to bask in the shared history, but I also felt a pang of the unresolved issues that had been left hanging between us. "Yes, it has," I said softly, the words barely escaping my lips.

There was an awkward silence that followed, filled with the subtle hum of the gala's ongoing festivities. Ethan cleared his throat, a gesture so familiar it almost made me laugh. "You look incredible, Mia. I'm glad you could make it."

I could see the sincerity in his eyes, but I was acutely aware of the delicate dance we were about to engage in. The intimacy of our past clashed with the formality of the present. It was a fragile, almost surreal moment. "Thank you, Ethan. It's good to see you."

We fell into step beside each other, wandering through the gallery of auction items. Each piece seemed to blur into the background as we spoke, their stories insignificant compared to the one unfolding between us. We exchanged polite small talk, but underneath it all, the old, familiar tension crackled like static electricity.

Ethan was the same, yet different. His laughter had a deeper resonance, his eyes held stories I could only guess at. The ease with which we fell into conversation belied the complexity of our shared history. There were questions unasked and answers unspoken, but for the moment, the simple act of being in each other's presence was enough.

We reached the balcony, where the evening breeze offered a brief respite from the ballroom's heat. Ethan leaned against the railing, his gaze fixed on the city lights below. "Do you ever think about those days?" he asked suddenly, his voice tinged with nostalgia.

I looked out at the sprawling city, at the vast expanse of possibilities and memories. "Sometimes," I admitted, "but it's strange how time changes everything."

Ethan's silence was a testament to the weight of his own reflections. We stood there, two people bound by a shared past and uncertain futures, letting the moment stretch and linger.

We lingered on the balcony, the city lights flickering like stars fallen to Earth. The breeze was cool, brushing against our faces and carrying the distant sounds of the gala inside. It was as if the world had shrunk to just the two of us in that moment, the years we had spent apart dissolving into the night air. I caught myself stealing glances at Ethan, the way he shifted against the railing as though he was trying to find comfort in a familiar, but distant, place.

"I read your latest book," he said suddenly, his voice cutting through the gentle hum of the city below. "It's amazing, Mia. You've really found your voice."

His compliment was genuine, the kind that came from a place of understanding rather than mere politeness. It took me by surprise, a reminder of how well he knew me. "Thank you. It means a lot, coming from you," I replied, trying to sound nonchalant while my heart fluttered at the mention of my work.

Ethan turned to face me, his expression softening. "I remember those late-night writing sessions you used to have, trying to finish your stories. You were always so dedicated."

His words wrapped around me like a comforting embrace. I could almost see the image of my younger self, hunched over a desk in a cluttered room, lost in the world of my characters. "And you were always there to listen to my rants and celebrate my small victories," I said with a smile.

For a moment, we fell into a comfortable silence, reminiscing about a time that had been filled with dreams and promises. But the past wasn't just a series of warm memories; it was also a tapestry of unresolved emotions and unspoken regrets.

"How have you been?" I asked, my voice barely more than a whisper, afraid to shatter the fragile cocoon of nostalgia we had built around ourselves.

Ethan's gaze grew distant, as if he was searching for the right words in the vast expanse of his own memories. "I've been... managing," he said finally. "Life has a way of taking you on unexpected journeys."

I nodded, sensing the weight behind his words. Ethan had always been a man of few words, but those few had a way of carrying deep meaning. "What about your career?" I asked, trying to steer the conversation to safer waters.

He smiled, a hint of pride in his eyes. "I'm actually working on a project that's pretty close to my heart. It's been a lot of hard work, but it's rewarding."

I was curious, but I didn't want to pry. Instead, I let the conversation flow naturally. "I'd love to hear more about it sometime. Maybe we could catch up over coffee or dinner?"

The offer hung in the air between us, both a hopeful invitation and a tentative step towards rekindling our connection. Ethan's eyes met mine, and for a moment, I saw a flicker of something that resembled the warmth we once shared. "I'd like that," he said softly.

As the evening wore on, the gala inside became a distant memory, the sounds of laughter and music blending into the backdrop of our conversation. We talked about everything and nothing—our favorite books, the places we'd traveled, the little things that made life beautiful. It was as though no time had passed at all, and yet every moment was laden with the complexity of our shared history.

The stars above seemed to shine a little brighter, and the city lights below sparkled with a new kind of promise. It was an intoxicating mixture of nostalgia and possibility, the kind that makes you believe in second chances and the magic of unexpected reunions.

Eventually, the night grew late, and the cold began to seep through the thin fabric of our evening attire. I shivered slightly, and Ethan noticed. Without a word, he removed his jacket and draped it over my shoulders. The warmth of the garment was a tangible reminder of his presence, of the connection we had once shared.

"Thank you," I said, my voice tinged with gratitude.

He nodded, a soft smile playing on his lips. "You look cold. I'd hate for you to catch a chill."

The gentle, caring gesture was a reminder of the Ethan I had known—thoughtful and attentive. It was a stark contrast to the tumultuous end we had faced years ago. It made me wonder about the person he had become, about the life he had built for himself and whether our paths had diverged in ways that could ever be reconciled.

As we stood there, wrapped in the quiet embrace of the night, I couldn't help but feel a mixture of hope and apprehension. The past had a way of haunting you with what could have been, but it also held the potential for what might still be. The unresolved feelings between us were like an open wound, but the possibility of healing them was too compelling to ignore.

Ethan took a deep breath and glanced at me. "Mia, I know this might sound strange, but I'm glad we ran into each other tonight."

I smiled, the warmth of his jacket spreading through me like a comforting fire. "Me too, Ethan. It's been a long time, but it feels good to reconnect."

He nodded, his gaze steady and earnest. "Let's not let another decade pass before we see each other again."

As the evening drew to a close, we exchanged a lingering look, one that spoke volumes about the emotions we had yet to explore. With a promise of future conversations and a shared sense of nostalgia, we parted ways, each of us carrying a piece of the night's magic with us into the unknown chapters of our lives.

As I walked away from the gala, my mind was a whirlwind of thoughts and emotions. Charleston's cobblestone streets felt unfamiliar under my feet, though they had once been the backdrop to my youth and dreams. The night air was crisp, carrying the faint scent of the sea mixed with the distant aroma of southern magnolias. It was a sharp contrast to the warmth and nostalgia I'd just experienced with Ethan.

The conversation we had was a bittersweet reminder of a time when everything seemed simpler. Yet, now, every word we exchanged felt like a delicate dance around the deep and unresolved feelings that had lingered long after our parting. The laughter we shared, the stories we revisited, it all seemed to hint at the possibility of healing old wounds, but also at the complications that came with reopening them.

As I reached my car, I paused for a moment, taking a deep breath to steady myself. The sight of Ethan's face, the sound of his voice, it all seemed too vivid, too real to be just a fleeting encounter. The charm of the evening had left a mark on me, one that was both exhilarating and unsettling.

Once inside my car, I turned on the engine and let the comforting hum of it fill the silence. I drove slowly through the city, reflecting on how effortlessly Ethan had slipped back into my life. It was as if no time had passed at all, yet every moment we spent together was laden with the weight of our past decisions. My heart ached with a mix of longing and apprehension, the kind of feeling that makes you question whether you're moving forward or merely retracing your steps.

The lights of Charleston seemed to blur as I drove, lost in thought. I couldn't shake the image of Ethan, standing there on the balcony, his eyes full of the same warmth that had once made me fall for him. But there was also a shadow in his gaze, a sign of the struggles he'd endured since we last saw each other. I wondered how much he had changed, and if the person I once knew was still there beneath the surface.

When I finally arrived home, I could hardly muster the energy to do anything but collapse onto my couch. My mind replayed every moment of the evening, each word, each glance, as if trying to piece together the meaning behind our encounter. The familiar ache of longing resurfaced, mingling with a new sense of hope.

I thought about the way Ethan had looked at me, the way he had spoken. It was clear he had his own demons, his own scars. But he had also carried a spark of something—something that hinted at a possibility of rekindling what we once had, or at least understanding what went wrong.

I picked up my phone and stared at the screen, tempted to reach out to him, to continue the conversation we had started. But I hesitated, unsure of what to say or how to say it. Our conversation had left so much unsaid, so many questions hanging in the air.

My fingers hovered over the keys as I considered what to write. The draft of a message seemed to form in my mind: an invitation to meet again, a query about his life, a way to bridge the gap between our past and the present. But I hesitated, caught between the fear of opening old wounds and the hope of finding closure or perhaps even something new.

In the end, I set my phone aside and tried to focus on the calm of my surroundings. The familiar comfort of my home was a stark contrast to the emotional turbulence I felt. I wanted to believe that everything had a reason, that our paths had crossed again for a purpose. But the uncertainty of what that purpose might be left me feeling more unsettled than ever.

I eventually fell into a restless sleep, my dreams filled with fragmented images of Ethan and the life we might have had. The night seemed to stretch on forever, each moment filled with a longing to make sense of the emotions stirring within me. It was as if my subconscious was trying to piece together the puzzle of our encounter, hoping for clarity where there was none.

The next morning arrived with a quiet dawn, the first light of day offering a fresh perspective. I awoke with a renewed sense of determination, a desire to face whatever came next with courage. The past was a part of me, but it didn't have to define my future. If Ethan and I were meant to reconnect, then perhaps it was worth exploring, even if it meant confronting old ghosts.

I sat down at my writing desk, the familiar sight of my manuscripts and notes offering solace. Writing had always been my refuge, a place where I could make sense of my thoughts and emotions. As I began to work, I realized that the story of my life was far from over. It was still unfolding, with new chapters waiting to be written.

And so, with a mix of apprehension and hope, I resolved to embrace whatever came next. If Ethan was a part of my story again, then I would face it with an open heart, ready to navigate the complexities of our shared history and the possibilities of our future. The chance encounter we'd had was just the beginning, and I was prepared to see where it would lead.

# Chapter 2: Echoes of the Past

The days following the gala felt like a blur. I found myself lost in thought, my mind wandering back to the moment Ethan and I had shared. The city, once vibrant and bustling, seemed quieter now, as if holding its breath, waiting for me to make sense of the encounter. The memories of our time together played on a loop, mingling with the present and creating a cocktail of emotions I wasn't quite ready to handle.

It was a gray afternoon when Ethan called, asking if I'd like to meet for drinks. My heart fluttered with a mix of anticipation and nervousness. I agreed, partly out of curiosity and partly because the idea of seeing him again was something I couldn't shake from my thoughts.

When we met at a cozy, dimly lit bar in the heart of downtown Charleston, I was struck by how familiar and foreign Ethan seemed at the same time. The bar's soft lighting cast a warm glow over his face, making him appear timeless, like a character from a storybook I had once loved. His deep-set eyes, the same ones that had once captivated me, still held that intense warmth that drew me in.

We chose a secluded booth, the kind with high backs that offered a sense of intimacy. As we settled in, I could feel the gravity of the moment, the unspoken acknowledgment of the years that had passed between us. Ethan's voice, smooth and rich with its familiar timbre, cut through the silence as he spoke, recounting anecdotes from his life since we had last met.

"I never thought I'd see you again," Ethan began, his eyes meeting mine with a sincerity that made my heart skip a beat. "But here we are, and it's like no time has passed at all."

His words were a double-edged sword, a reminder of the distance that had grown between us while simultaneously bridging that gap with the warmth of our shared history. I found myself laughing, the sound of it almost foreign but comforting. We reminisced about our youthful escapades, the stolen kisses in dimly lit corners, the endless dreams we had spun together. Each memory was a bittersweet reminder of a time when everything seemed possible.

Yet, beneath the laughter and easy conversation, there was an undercurrent of something deeper, something that both of us seemed to acknowledge but were hesitant to voice. There was a palpable tension in the air, a sense of regret for the time lost and a curiosity about what might have been if circumstances had been different.

I watched as Ethan's expression shifted, a flicker of vulnerability crossing his face as he talked about his recent past. "Life has a funny way of moving on," he said, his gaze drifting to the window. "Sometimes, you look back and wonder what you would have done differently."

I knew the feeling all too well. The decisions we made in our youth seemed so clear at the time, but looking back, it was easy to see the paths we had not taken. It was as if we were both trying to piece together a puzzle of our shared past, searching for meaning in the choices we had made and the lives we had built separately.

As the evening progressed, the conversation shifted to more personal topics. We spoke of dreams and regrets, of the people we had become and the paths we had followed. Ethan's eyes held a depth of emotion I hadn't seen in years, and it was clear that he had faced his own set of challenges since we last saw each other.

"I've often wondered how you've been," Ethan admitted, his voice softening. "What your life has been like without me in it."

His words struck a chord, opening up a space I hadn't fully explored. I realized that, despite the time apart, the impact of our relationship still lingered. The decisions I had made, the person I had become, were all tied to our shared history in ways I had only begun to understand.

"I think about you too," I confessed, my voice barely above a whisper. "About the what-ifs and the paths we didn't take."

There was a moment of silence between us, a pause filled with the weight of our unspoken feelings. The connection we had once shared was still palpable, a thread weaving through our conversation and pulling us closer despite the years that had passed.

As we finished our drinks and prepared to leave, the air was charged with a new understanding. The night had revealed that while time had moved us in different directions, the echoes of our past were still very much alive. Ethan and I had both changed, but the core of what had drawn us together remained intact.

Walking out of the bar, I felt a mix of melancholy and hope. The encounter had stirred up old feelings, but it had also opened the door to new possibilities. As Ethan and I parted ways, I couldn't shake the feeling that our paths had crossed again for a reason. The echoes of our past were calling, urging us to explore the chapters that might still be waiting to be written.

The night air was cool against my skin, a soothing contrast to the emotional intensity of the evening. I walked home with a sense of anticipation, wondering what the future might hold and whether the echoes of the past would lead to a new beginning or simply serve as a poignant reminder of what once was.

The days following that evening felt heavy with unspoken questions and unfinished conversations. I tried to distract myself with my writing, the rhythmic tapping of my keyboard a poor substitute for the clarity I sought. My characters were growing restless, their stories unable to compete with the vivid replay of Ethan's smile, his laugh, and the way his eyes had searched mine for answers.

It was during one of these solitary moments, while I stared blankly at the cursor blinking on the screen, that my phone buzzed with a new message. Ethan's name flashed on the screen, and a jolt of anticipation shot through me. I hesitated only for a second before opening the message, as if bracing myself for a tide that might sweep me off my feet.

"Hey Mia, I hope you're doing well. I've been thinking about our conversation the other night. Would you like to meet up again? Maybe we could talk more about... everything."

The simplicity of his words was a stark contrast to the emotional whirlwind they stirred. I took a deep breath, my heart racing as I typed a response. "Hi Ethan, I'd like that. How about we meet at the same place tomorrow evening?"

As the day passed, I found myself growing increasingly anxious. My thoughts circled around our last encounter, replaying every nuance of our conversation, every glance. What was it about Ethan that pulled me in so deeply, despite the years that had passed? The unresolved feelings seemed to have a life of their own, growing more intense with each passing hour.

When I arrived at the bar the next evening, the familiar setting felt different somehow. The dim lights and soft music were now a backdrop to a scene that held far more significance than before. I waited at our usual booth, my fingers nervously tracing patterns on the table. The anticipation was palpable, a tangible thing that made my pulse quicken.

Ethan arrived promptly, his presence filling the space with a warm, familiar energy. He greeted me with a soft smile and a gentle kiss on the cheek that sent a flutter through me. We sat down, and for a moment, there was a comfortable silence as we each gathered our thoughts. The air between us crackled with the weight of our past, the unspoken words hanging like a fog.

"I'm glad you agreed to meet again," Ethan said, his voice steady but with a hint of vulnerability. "I've been reflecting on our conversation. It's funny how sometimes the past has a way of resurfacing just when you think you've moved on."

I nodded, feeling a lump form in my throat. "I know what you mean. Seeing you again has stirred up so many memories. It's like I've been transported back to a time when everything was so different."

Ethan's eyes softened, a trace of sadness mingling with the warmth I had always loved. "Do you ever wonder about the paths we didn't take? The choices we made and how they led us here?"

The question was like a gentle probe into the core of my heart. I thought about the dreams we once shared, the future we had envisioned together. "All the time," I admitted. "I wonder what could have been if we had stayed together. But life took us in different directions, and I suppose we've both grown in ways we never imagined."

He leaned back, his gaze distant but thoughtful. "I've often thought about the way things ended between us. There were so many things left unsaid, so many feelings that were never fully explored."

The conversation drifted to our lives since that time, the experiences that had shaped us. Ethan spoke of his career, his travels, and the relationships he had formed. Each detail was a brushstroke painting the picture of the man he had become. I found myself admiring his growth, his resilience, and the way he spoke with such honesty about his life.

When it was my turn to share, I talked about my writing, my achievements, and the quiet satisfaction I had found in my solitude. I spoke of the moments of doubt and the triumphs, the simple joys of daily life. There was a catharsis in opening up to him, a release of emotions I hadn't fully acknowledged until now.

As the evening wore on, the conversation took on a more personal tone. We spoke of regrets, of the things we wished we could change. Ethan's eyes met mine with an intensity that made my heart ache. "There's something about you that's always stayed with me," he said softly. "Even after all these years, I find myself thinking about what might have been if we had chosen differently."

The raw honesty in his words was both painful and beautiful. I felt a tear slip down my cheek, a solitary token of the emotions I had kept hidden for so long. Ethan reached out, brushing it away with a tenderness that spoke volumes.

"I've missed you," he said quietly. "More than I realized until now."

The acknowledgment of our past, the recognition of the bond we had shared, was a balm to the wounds I had carried for years. It was clear that while time had altered our lives, it had not erased the connection we once had.

As we parted ways that night, the echoes of our past seemed to fade into a hopeful silence. The unresolved feelings, the regrets, and the curiosity about what might have been were now part of a larger narrative. Ethan and I were both on new paths, but the intersections of our lives had not been erased. The echoes of our past had merely resurfaced, inviting us to explore the possibility of what might still lie ahead.

The days following our heartfelt conversation seemed to stretch endlessly, each moment wrapped in a cocoon of reflection. I went about my routine with a distracted air, my thoughts frequently drifting back to Ethan. His words had stirred a storm of emotions, each one a reminder of the love we once shared and the pain of our parting.

One afternoon, as I sat in my favorite café with a manuscript spread before me, the hum of conversation and clinking of coffee cups felt distant, almost surreal. The once comforting environment now seemed to emphasize my solitude. I sipped my coffee absently, my mind replaying our last meeting, the way Ethan's gaze had lingered on me, filled with a mix of hope and uncertainty.

My phone buzzed, pulling me from my reverie. A message from Ethan. I hesitated before opening it, a mix of excitement and apprehension swirling inside me. His message was brief but warm, inviting me to join him at a local art exhibit that weekend. I read the words several times, each repetition heightening my anticipation and anxiety. I agreed quickly, not trusting myself to overthink it.

The evening of the art exhibit arrived, and I found myself standing before the grand entrance of the gallery, dressed in a simple yet elegant dress that I hoped conveyed the right blend of casual and refined. The air was crisp, carrying with it the faint scent of rain. I took a deep breath, steeling myself for the emotions that might surface.

Ethan greeted me with a warm, genuine smile that melted away the last of my apprehensions. His presence was like a comforting embrace, familiar and yet laced with the complexity of our history. He looked dashing in a dark suit, his eyes lighting up as they met mine. We exchanged pleasantries, and I noticed the subtle ease between us, as though the years had done little to erode our connection.

We walked through the gallery, the art pieces displayed like fragments of a world we were just beginning to explore together. Ethan's enthusiasm for the art was evident; he spoke passionately about each piece, his insights painting a vivid picture of his perspective. I listened, fascinated not only by the art but by the way his eyes sparkled with genuine interest, revealing a side of him I hadn't seen in years.

As we moved from one exhibit to another, our conversation shifted from the art to more personal topics. Ethan spoke about his travels, his voice tinged with nostalgia as he recounted tales of distant lands and unforgettable experiences. There was a certain warmth in his storytelling, a yearning for connection that mirrored my own.

When we stopped in front of a particularly striking piece, a painting of a stormy sea under a darkened sky, Ethan's expression grew contemplative. "This painting reminds me of how tumultuous our lives have been," he said softly. "How sometimes, despite everything, we still find ourselves drawn to what we once had."

I studied the painting, its dramatic swirls of color reflecting the chaos I felt inside. "It's true," I replied. "Even when we think we've moved on, there are parts of us that remain tethered to the past, to the people who shaped us."

Ethan nodded, his gaze lingering on me. "I've been thinking about that a lot lately. About how our paths diverged and how we ended up where we are now. I keep wondering if there's still something left between us, or if it's all just echoes of what once was."

His words struck a chord deep within me. The echoes he spoke of were not just remnants of our past but a persistent reminder of the love that had once been so vibrant. I felt a pang of longing, a desire to explore what might still be there.

As the evening progressed, we moved to a quieter corner of the gallery, where a small jazz ensemble played softly in the background. The ambiance was intimate, and the soft lighting cast a gentle glow over Ethan's face. He reached for my hand, his touch electric against my skin. The simple gesture was both comforting and stirring, igniting a familiar warmth that I had tried to ignore for so long.

We talked more openly now, our words laced with the vulnerability that had been absent from our earlier conversations. Ethan shared his fears, his hopes, and his regrets, each revelation bringing us closer to the heart of our shared history. It was a delicate dance of confessions and understanding, each step revealing a bit more of who we had become.

As the night drew to a close, I felt a mix of exhilaration and melancholy. The evening had been a beautiful exploration of our past and present, a tentative step towards understanding what might still lie between us. We walked out of the gallery together, our conversation a gentle hum as we strolled through the city streets, the cool night air a soothing balm to our heightened emotions.

When we finally said our goodbyes, there was a lingering sense of something unfinished, a question that remained unanswered. As I drove home, I couldn't shake the feeling that this was just the beginning of a journey that would lead us to places we had only begun to imagine. The echoes of our past had become a powerful force, guiding us towards a future that was both uncertain and tantalizingly full of possibilities.

# Chapter 3: Rekindling Old Flames

The cozy aroma of freshly brewed coffee hung in the air, mingling with the subtle scent of baked pastries as I walked into the café. The place was a small, charming nook in Charleston, with its vintage furnishings and warm, inviting ambiance. I spotted Ethan seated at a corner table, his posture relaxed yet attentive, as though he were waiting for a significant moment. He stood up as soon as he saw me, his smile broadening, and my heart fluttered in response.

"Hey, Mia," he said, his voice carrying a note of genuine happiness. The way he said my name, with that same warmth and familiarity I had remembered, felt like a touch of comfort in a world that had become increasingly unpredictable.

I slid into the chair opposite him, feeling the weight of our past settling between us like an old friend. We exchanged pleasantries, the initial awkwardness of reuniting melting away as we settled into easy conversation. Ethan had always had a way of making everything feel effortless, and today was no different. He spoke animatedly about his recent projects, his eyes lighting up as he described the intricate details of his architectural designs. The passion he conveyed was contagious, and I found myself captivated by the way he spoke about his work.

"There was this one project in San Francisco," he said, leaning forward with enthusiasm, "where I got to design a rooftop garden. It was all about blending nature with urban life. Seeing it come to life was one of the most fulfilling experiences I've had."

His hands moved expressively as he talked, painting vivid pictures of his adventures. I could see the man he had become—a successful architect with a vibrant career and a world full of experiences. Yet, as I listened, I couldn't shake the feeling that the boy I once knew was still somewhere within him, just beneath the surface.

"Wow, that sounds amazing," I replied, my admiration evident. "You've really accomplished so much."

Ethan's smile was both proud and humble. "I've been lucky," he said. "But enough about me. Tell me about you. How's the writing going?"

His question was sincere, and it sparked a conversation about my career, my novels, and the journey I had taken to get where I was. I spoke about my latest book, the challenges I faced in writing, and the joy I found in creating stories. The conversation flowed effortlessly, each topic leading naturally into the next, and I began to feel that old connection reemerging.

As we talked, I noticed how easily we fell into our previous rhythms. The banter we used to share, the way we could finish each other's sentences, all felt as though no time had passed. It was as though we were picking up from where we left off, only now with a deeper understanding of who we had become.

"So, how do you manage to balance your work and personal life?" I asked, genuinely curious. "It seems like you've got such a demanding career."

Ethan's expression grew thoughtful. "It's not always easy," he admitted. "There are times when I feel like I'm barely keeping up. But I've learned to prioritize what really matters. And sometimes, it's the little things that keep me grounded."

He reached for his coffee, taking a sip before continuing. "Like this," he said with a smile. "Moments like these, where I get to catch up with old friends and just enjoy the present."

I found myself smiling in response, touched by the sentiment. The conversation had a way of making me feel both at ease and electrified, as if the space between us was charged with a potent energy. It was clear that despite the years apart, there was a magnetic pull between us, a spark that had not only survived but seemed to have grown stronger.

As the afternoon sun streamed through the café's windows, casting a golden glow over the room, I could feel the undeniable tension building between us. It was a mixture of excitement and trepidation, a recognition of the unresolved feelings that had been buried for so long. Each glance, each touch, seemed to carry a weight of possibility, making the air around us hum with potential.

Ethan's laughter rang out, genuine and infectious, and I couldn't help but join in. It felt so natural, so right, to be sitting here with him, sharing these moments. The familiarity was comforting, but it was also paired with a sense of newness—of rediscovering a part of myself that had been dormant for too long.

As our conversation wound down, Ethan suggested taking a walk along the nearby waterfront. "I'd love to show you a place I've been working on," he said. "It's not far from here, and the view is supposed to be incredible."

I agreed, feeling a rush of excitement and curiosity. We left the café together, the warmth of our conversation lingering like a soft glow as we walked side by side. The sun was beginning its descent, painting the sky with hues of pink and orange, and the world seemed to hold its breath in anticipation.

The waterfront was beautiful, the gentle lapping of the waves creating a soothing soundtrack to our stroll. Ethan guided me to a newly designed park area, where lush greenery and thoughtfully placed benches created a serene space amidst the bustle of the city. As we walked, I could see the pride in his eyes, and it struck me how much this place represented not just his career but also his heart.

The evening grew darker, and the stars began to twinkle above us, casting a soft, ethereal light over everything. Ethan turned to me, his gaze searching mine with an intensity that made my breath catch. "I'm really glad we did this," he said quietly. "It feels like old times, but better. More real."

I nodded, feeling the weight of his words and the depth of the emotions they stirred. The air between us crackled with an undeniable chemistry, and I couldn't ignore the growing realization that our connection was far from over. The old flame between us was not just a memory; it was a living, breathing force, waiting to be explored.

We walked along the waterfront, the sound of our footsteps muffled by the soft rustling of the grass and the distant murmur of the waves. The park Ethan had been working on was a testament to his skill and vision, a blend of modern design and natural beauty. As we approached a particularly striking overlook, Ethan stopped and gestured to the view before us. The city lights began to flicker on, casting a warm glow across the water, and for a moment, everything else seemed to fade away.

"I've always loved this view," Ethan said, his voice low and reflective. "There's something about seeing the city from this angle that makes it feel both alive and peaceful at the same time."

I nodded, taking in the panorama. The blend of shimmering lights and darkening sky created a stunning contrast, one that mirrored the complex emotions stirring within me. I could feel the familiar pull between us, a magnetic force that seemed to bridge the gap of time and distance.

We leaned against the railing, our shoulders brushing ever so slightly. I tried to focus on the conversation, but my thoughts kept drifting back to the years we had spent apart. Ethan was as captivating as ever, and as he spoke about his work and his life, I couldn't help but be drawn back into the warmth of his presence.

"It's funny," I said, breaking the silence. "I used to come here with my friends when we were in high school. We'd talk about our dreams and what we wanted to do with our lives. I remember you always had this incredible sense of purpose. Like you knew exactly where you were headed."

Ethan chuckled, a sound that was as rich and resonant as I remembered. "I don't know about knowing exactly," he said, "but I definitely had a lot of ambition. Sometimes I wonder if I was just stubbornly pursuing a dream, or if I really had a clear vision."

I turned to him, meeting his gaze. "I think it was a bit of both. You always had this way of making things happen, of turning dreams into reality."

There was a pause as we shared a moment of mutual understanding, a connection that seemed to transcend the years and experiences that had separated us. The magnetic pull I had felt earlier was now undeniable, intensifying with each passing second. It was as if the universe had conspired to bring us back together, only to see what would happen next.

"I've missed this," Ethan admitted quietly, his eyes reflecting the starlight. "I didn't realize how much until we started talking again. It's like finding a piece of yourself that you didn't know was missing."

His words resonated with me, echoing my own feelings. The sense of familiarity and the depth of our connection were both comforting and exhilarating. I felt a rush of emotions, a mixture of excitement and apprehension as I faced the possibility of rekindling something that had once been so important to me.

"I've missed it too," I said softly. "There's something about being here with you, talking like we used to, that makes me feel like I'm rediscovering a part of myself I had forgotten."

Ethan's expression grew serious, his gaze steady and intense. "Mia, I know we've both changed a lot since high school. Life has a way of doing that. But there's a part of me that still feels like I'm exactly where I'm supposed to be when I'm with you."

The honesty in his voice was both moving and unsettling. It was clear that our feelings for each other had not vanished with time, but rather had evolved into something deeper and more complex.

The thought of exploring this rekindled flame was both thrilling and daunting.

We continued to talk, sharing stories and memories that spanned the years. The conversation flowed effortlessly, with each revelation drawing us closer. I found myself opening up in ways I hadn't expected, revealing vulnerabilities and dreams I had kept guarded for so long. Ethan listened with genuine interest, his responses thoughtful and empathetic.

As the evening wore on, the park began to empty, leaving us alone with our thoughts and the soft glow of the streetlights. The air was cool, but the warmth between us provided a comforting contrast. Ethan reached out and gently brushed a stray lock of hair from my face, his touch sending a shiver down my spine.

"Mia," he said softly, his voice almost a whisper, "I don't want this to end. I want to see where this goes, to explore what's between us. But I also know that it's complicated. We've both changed, and there are things we need to figure out."

His words were a mixture of hope and uncertainty, reflecting the same emotions I felt. The prospect of reigniting our relationship was both exciting and fraught with challenges. I knew that moving forward would require navigating the complexities of our past and present, but the potential rewards were too tempting to ignore.

"I want that too," I said, my voice steady despite the whirlwind of emotions inside me. "I want to see where this can go. But we need to be honest with each other and ourselves. We need to confront our past and figure out how it fits into our present."

Ethan nodded, his expression a mix of relief and determination. "Agreed. Let's take this one step at a time, and see where it leads us."

As we stood there, the city lights reflecting in the water below, I felt a sense of both resolution and anticipation. The spark between us was undeniable, and despite the uncertainties, I was ready to explore the possibilities that lay ahead. With Ethan by my side, I felt a renewed sense of hope and excitement for what the future might bring.

The coffee shop was a cozy haven, with its soft lighting and the rich aroma of freshly brewed coffee hanging in the air. We chose a corner table, tucked away from the bustling crowd, where the world felt both intimate and distant. As we settled in, I couldn't help but notice how comfortable it felt to be in Ethan's presence again. The years had passed, but some connections felt timeless, and this one was no exception.

Ethan's eyes, always so expressive, seemed to hold a thousand stories as he spoke of his adventures. He talked about the high-rise buildings he'd designed in New York, the ancient ruins he'd explored in Rome, and the serene landscapes he'd marveled at in Kyoto. Each story was more fascinating than the last, and I found myself captivated by his passion and enthusiasm.

"It's strange," he said, leaning forward with a thoughtful expression. "I used to think that achieving my dreams would be the ultimate satisfaction. But now, I realize that it's the experiences and the people I've met along the way that matter the most."

I nodded, stirring my coffee absentmindedly. "I get that. I've had my own share of experiences, too. My writing has taken me to some unexpected places, and I've met some incredible people. But there's something about revisiting old connections that feels different, more profound."

Ethan's gaze softened as he looked at me. "You've always had a way with words, Mia. I remember how you could turn the simplest things into something magical. It's one of the things I admired most about you."

His compliment sent a warm flush to my cheeks, a reminder of how deeply I once felt for him. I could still recall the days when we would spend hours talking about our dreams and aspirations, our hopes for the future. Those conversations had been filled with promise, and it was both exhilarating and daunting to feel that same spark reignite.

As we continued to talk, the conversation naturally flowed from the past to the present. Ethan shared stories of his challenges and triumphs, his hopes for the future, and his reflections on life. There was an openness to his words, a vulnerability that made me feel closer to him than I had in years.

"I've been thinking a lot about what really matters," Ethan confessed, his eyes meeting mine with an earnest intensity. "Success and achievements are great, but they don't mean as much if you don't have someone to share them with. I've realized that having the right person by your side makes all the difference."

His words resonated deeply with me. I had spent so much time focused on my career and personal growth, often feeling like something was missing. The thought of rekindling our connection brought a mixture of excitement and apprehension, as if I was on the verge of discovering something profoundly meaningful.

"I've felt the same way," I admitted, my voice barely above a whisper. "There's been a part of me that's always wondered about what might have been, about the possibilities we never explored. Seeing you again has brought those feelings to the surface."

Ethan reached across the table, his hand brushing mine gently. The touch was electric, sending a jolt of warmth through me. I looked up at him, our eyes locking in a moment of silent understanding. The magnetic pull between us was undeniable, and it was clear that our connection went beyond mere nostalgia.

"Maybe this is our chance to explore those possibilities," Ethan suggested softly. "We've both changed, and we've both grown. But the foundation of what we had is still there, and it feels like it's waiting for us to build something new."

His words filled me with a sense of hope and possibility. The idea of starting anew, of exploring a relationship that had once been so significant, was both thrilling and daunting. I knew that there would be challenges ahead, but the prospect of rekindling something meaningful was too enticing to ignore.

We spent the rest of the afternoon lost in conversation, our laughter and shared stories creating a sense of intimacy that felt both comforting and exhilarating. As we parted ways, I couldn't shake the feeling that this was only the beginning of something significant. The spark between us was undeniable, and the possibilities were endless.

As I walked back to my car, the cool breeze brushing against my skin, I couldn't help but reflect on the day's events. The chance encounter, the coffee date, and the rekindled connection all seemed to be leading toward something greater. The future was uncertain, but I felt a renewed sense of hope and anticipation.

Ethan's reappearance in my life had stirred up old memories and unresolved feelings, but it had also opened the door to new possibilities. As I drove home, I found myself eagerly anticipating what the future might hold, and the thought of exploring this renewed connection with Ethan filled me with both excitement and trepidation.

The journey ahead would undoubtedly be filled with challenges and uncertainties, but the chance to rekindle an old flame and explore what might have been was a prospect I couldn't ignore. With each passing moment, I felt more certain that this was a path worth exploring, and I was ready to embrace whatever came next.

# Chapter 4: The Unspoken

Despite the laughter and warmth that lingered from our coffee date, a silent tension hung between us, an invisible thread that pulled taut whenever our eyes met. It wasn't something we spoke about, this unspoken weight, but it was there, a subtle reminder of the distance and pain that once defined our relationship.

The weeks that followed our reunion were filled with moments of quiet intimacy and unspoken questions. We met for dinner, took long walks through the city, and shared occasional texts that carried a warmth but lacked the depth of our earlier conversations. Each encounter felt like a dance around the heart of what had once been. While the chemistry between us was undeniable, there was a cautiousness in our interactions, as if we were both afraid to tread on the fragile ground of our past.

One evening, as we sat on a bench overlooking the Charleston harbor, the sunset painting the sky in hues of orange and pink, I found myself staring out at the water, lost in thought. Ethan sat beside me, his presence a comforting weight, but the silence between us was heavy, laden with unspoken words.

"What's on your mind?" Ethan's voice broke through my reverie, his tone gentle and inquisitive.

I turned to him, searching for the right words. "It's just... sometimes I feel like there's so much we haven't addressed. We've jumped back into this connection so effortlessly, but it feels like we're both skirting around the real issues."

Ethan's gaze was steady, his expression thoughtful. "I've felt it too," he admitted. "There are things we haven't talked about, things that shaped us both and left scars that aren't always visible. I want to understand what happened, what changed, and why."

The honesty in his words struck a chord within me. I had been grappling with my own emotions, trying to reconcile the person I was then with the person I am now. The wounds from our past were not easily forgotten, nor were they simple to heal.

"I think," I began slowly, "that we're both carrying pieces of our past with us. We've changed, grown, and moved on, but those changes don't erase the history we share. It's like we're trying to build something new on a foundation that's still uneven."

Ethan nodded, his gaze fixed on the horizon. "We have a history that can't just be swept away. I've made mistakes, and I know you have too. We need to acknowledge those mistakes if we're ever going to move forward."

His words were a balm to the part of me that had been aching for understanding. I knew that confronting the past was necessary, but the prospect of doing so was daunting. Our history was filled with moments of passion and joy, but also with hurt and regret. The idea of revisiting those memories was both frightening and necessary.

"Do you ever wonder," I asked hesitantly, "if we're doomed to repeat our mistakes? Or if there's a way to learn from them and create something better?"

Ethan's eyes met mine with a vulnerability that mirrored my own. "I think we have to believe that we can learn from our past. It's not about erasing what happened but about understanding it and using that understanding to build something stronger. We can't change the past, but we can shape our future."

The sincerity in his voice offered a glimmer of hope. It was a reminder that while the past had shaped us, it didn't have to define our future. Our journey was as much about healing as it was about rediscovering what we had lost.

As the evening wore on, we continued to talk, delving into the complexities of our past and how they had influenced our present. Each word we shared felt like a small step towards understanding, a way to bridge the gap that had formed between us. It was an uncomfortable but necessary conversation, one that laid bare the vulnerabilities we both carried.

By the time we parted ways, the tension between us had not disappeared entirely, but it had shifted. There was a newfound openness, a recognition of the need to confront the unspoken truths that had lingered for so long. The conversation had not solved all our problems, but it had paved the way for a deeper connection, one that acknowledged the past while looking forward to the future.

As I walked home, the cool night air was a stark contrast to the warmth of our conversation. I felt a mixture of relief and apprehension, knowing that the path ahead would not be easy. But for the first time in a long while, I felt a sense of clarity and hope. The unspoken had been acknowledged, and in that acknowledgment lay the possibility of healing and growth.

Ethan and I were navigating a delicate balance, trying to reconcile our past with our present. It was a journey fraught with challenges, but it was one I was willing to undertake. The road ahead was uncertain, but the willingness to confront our shared history and work through the unresolved issues was a crucial step towards finding a way forward together.

The days after our heart-to-heart by the harbor were filled with a mix of hopeful anticipation and guarded restraint. Each time we met, whether for a casual lunch or an evening stroll, there was an unspoken understanding between us, a recognition of the delicate balance we were trying to maintain. We were like tightrope walkers, each step measured and cautious, acutely aware of the height and the risk of falling.

The air was often thick with the things we didn't say, the memories and regrets that hovered between us like ghosts. Our conversations danced around the deeper issues, skimming the surface of our past with a politeness that felt almost artificial. The familiarity of his presence was comforting, but the shadows of our history lurked just beneath the surface, threatening to disrupt the fragile peace we were trying to build.

One crisp autumn afternoon, as we sat in a cozy corner of our favorite café, I found myself staring into my cup of coffee, the swirling steam offering a brief respite from the tangled thoughts in my mind. Ethan sat across from me, his gaze occasionally flickering to the window, where the world outside moved with a quiet bustle. The café was a familiar place, one that held its own memories of our younger days, and yet it felt different now—charged with an energy that neither of us could fully define.

"I've been thinking," I began, my voice soft, "about how much has changed since we last saw each other. Not just the obvious things, but the way we've changed, how we see the world differently now."

Ethan's eyes met mine, a mix of curiosity and concern in his expression. "I've been thinking the same thing. It's strange, isn't it? How we can pick up where we left off in some ways, yet feel like strangers in others."

There was a moment of silence, filled only by the muted clatter of dishes and the occasional murmur of other patrons. The silence was both comforting and unnerving, a space where our unspoken thoughts seemed to echo louder than words.

"I remember how easy it was back then," I continued, "how everything felt so natural and uncomplicated. But now, it's like we're navigating through a fog, trying to find our way while carrying the weight of what we've both been through."

Ethan nodded slowly, his fingers tracing absent patterns on the rim of his coffee cup. "I know what you mean. It's like we're carrying the baggage of our past with us, even though we've tried to move on. There's a part of me that's still caught in those old memories, and I think part of you is too."

The acknowledgment was both a relief and a burden. It was as though we were finally allowing ourselves to face the reality of our situation, the complexities and contradictions of our relationship. Yet, the very act of naming these issues made them all the more present, more daunting.

"You know," Ethan said after a moment, "I've been thinking about the decisions we made back then. The ones that led us here. I wonder if we ever really understood the impact of those choices, or if we were just too young to see the consequences."

His words struck a chord deep within me. I had spent countless nights replaying those decisions in my mind, trying to make sense of the reasons behind them and the way they had shaped our lives. It was a process of continuous self-examination, of attempting to reconcile the person I was then with the person I had become.

"I think we were," I replied softly. "Too young and too impulsive. We acted on what we felt in the moment without fully considering how those actions would affect us in the long run. And now, we're left with the aftermath, trying to piece together something that was shattered a long time ago."

Ethan's expression was contemplative, his gaze fixed on the swirling pattern of his coffee. "I don't know if we can ever fully understand everything that happened. Some things are just too complex, too intertwined with who we are. But maybe what matters now is how we move forward, how we address the unspoken things that have lingered between us."

There was a quiet resolve in his voice, a determination to confront the past with honesty and courage. It was a sentiment that I shared, even if the road ahead was fraught with uncertainty. We both understood that to build something meaningful together, we had to face the ghosts of our past and address the issues that had remained unresolved for so long.

As the afternoon sunlight filtered through the café windows, casting a warm glow over our table, I felt a sense of cautious optimism. The conversation had not resolved everything, but it had opened a door to a deeper understanding. It was a step towards acknowledging the unspoken, towards confronting the issues that had shaped our past and were now influencing our present.

Ethan and I were embarking on a journey of rediscovery, navigating the complexities of our relationship with a new awareness. The unspoken had been brought to the surface, and while it was daunting, it also held the promise of healing and growth. The path ahead was uncertain, but as we continued to face our past with honesty and openness, I felt a glimmer of hope that we could find a way to move forward, together.

Our days began to fall into a rhythm, a delicate dance of proximity and restraint. The afternoons were often spent wandering through Charleston's cobblestone streets, the vibrant hues of autumn providing a picturesque backdrop to our tentative reconnection. Each shared glance and half-spoken word seemed to carry the weight of our history, a silent dialogue that spoke louder than any explicit conversation could.

There were moments when I'd catch Ethan lost in thought, his eyes clouded with memories, and I would wonder what was playing behind those deep-set eyes. It was as if he were grappling with ghosts of his own, shadowy figures that haunted the corners of his mind, much like my own.

We visited the places that once held significance for us—our old favorite bookstore, the park where we'd first confessed our feelings. Yet, these locations, now suffused with the patina of time, felt different, tinged with a bittersweet nostalgia. They served as markers of our past, reminders of the love that once was and the pain that had followed. The comforting familiarity was underscored by a new layer of complexity, a realization that we were not the same people who had once wandered these streets hand in hand.

One crisp evening, as we settled into a quiet corner of a dimly lit bistro, the ambience seemed to amplify the unspoken tension between us. Ethan's laughter, though genuine, sounded tinged with a certain sadness. It was clear that beneath the surface of our easy conversations lay an ocean of unresolved feelings. We had started to delve into deeper conversations, but there was always a hesitance, a careful avoidance of the raw edges of our past.

"I sometimes wonder," Ethan said, his fingers tracing the condensation on his glass, "if we're trying too hard to recreate something that's no longer possible. Maybe what we had was a product of a different time, a different us."

His words struck me with unexpected force, as if he had voiced a thought that had been lingering in my own mind. I nodded, feeling a lump form in my throat. "I've been thinking that too. It's like we're trying to fit a square peg into a round hole. We're older now, and our lives have changed in ways we didn't anticipate."

The honesty in his voice was both refreshing and painful. It was a rare glimpse into the vulnerability he had been hiding behind his composed exterior. We were both acutely aware of the distance that had grown between us, a distance that couldn't be bridged simply by rekindling old habits or visiting familiar places.

We talked about our careers, our successes, and the changes we had each undergone. Ethan spoke of the architectural projects that had taken him around the world, of the cities he had explored and the people he had met. His stories were fascinating, but they also revealed a life that had moved forward without me. It was clear that his journey had been shaped by experiences and choices that were separate from mine, creating a chasm that was difficult to cross.

"I suppose it's only natural that we'd have different paths," I said softly, my voice betraying the melancholy I felt. "We've both grown in ways we might not have imagined back then. Our lives have taken us in different directions."

Ethan's gaze was intense, as if he were trying to read the depths of my emotions. "I think about what we might have been, what we could have achieved together. But then I wonder if we're clinging to an idealized version of the past, one that doesn't align with who we are now."

His words echoed my own fears. We were grappling with the duality of our situation—the pull of nostalgia and the reality of change. There was a deep sense of longing mingled with the awareness that some things were irretrievably lost. Our conversations had started to reveal the chasm between our past and our present, a chasm that neither of us knew how to cross.

As the evening wore on, the conversation shifted to lighter topics, but the underlying tension remained. We were both aware that our attempts to rebuild what we once had were fraught with difficulties. The shadows of our past loomed large, and the gaps between us felt more pronounced with each passing moment.

When the check arrived, Ethan reached for it with a casual ease that belied the heaviness of our discussion. As we walked back to the car, the crisp night air was a welcome relief from the weight of our conversation. The city lights twinkled in the distance, casting a gentle glow over the streets, but the sense of unresolved tension lingered like a cloud.

Our relationship was a fragile construct, built on the foundation of our shared history but tempered by the realities of our present. We were navigating a new phase, one that required patience and understanding. The unspoken between us was both a barrier and a bridge, a reminder of our past and a challenge to our future. As we moved forward, it was clear that we would need to confront our shared history and come to terms with the fact that some things might never be fully resolved.

# Chapter 5: Confronting Old Hurts

The evening air in Charleston was cool, carrying the crisp scent of the sea mingled with the subtle fragrance of blooming jasmine. As we strolled down the familiar cobblestone streets, the rhythm of our footsteps was the only sound that punctuated the silence between us. The city, with its historic charm and timeless beauty, felt like a living memory, a backdrop for the conversation we both knew was inevitable.

Ethan and I had chosen this quiet moment to confront the heartache of our past, a necessary step in understanding how we had arrived at this point in our lives. The setting was idyllic, but the weight of our conversation was heavy. We had navigated the small talk and light-hearted banter for weeks, but now, beneath the surface, there was a growing urgency to address the unresolved feelings that lingered between us.

As we reached a small, secluded park that overlooked the shimmering water, I could see the tension in Ethan's posture. His shoulders were slightly hunched, his hands buried in his pockets. He stopped at a wrought-iron bench and motioned for me to sit. I hesitated for a moment before taking a seat beside him, the old wood creaking softly under our combined weight.

"So," he began, his voice low and tentative, "I've been thinking a lot about what happened between us. It feels like there's so much we left unsaid."

I nodded, the ache of old wounds making my heart tighten. "I've been thinking about it too. There were so many things that we didn't talk about, so many reasons why things fell apart."

The silence that followed was thick with the weight of unspoken truths. The street lamps cast a soft, golden glow over us, and the distant murmur of traffic seemed like a world away. It was as though we were in a different time, a suspended moment where only our past mattered.

Ethan turned to face me, his expression one of vulnerability I hadn't seen in years. "I guess we should start with why we drifted apart. It wasn't just one thing. There were so many factors that contributed to our breakup."

I took a deep breath, feeling the sting of old memories. "I remember feeling like we were growing in different directions. I was so focused on my career and my ambitions, and I felt like you were constantly pulling away. It was like we were on different paths, and I couldn't find a way to bridge the gap."

Ethan's eyes softened, and he looked away, staring out at the darkening water. "I didn't know how to balance everything. I was trying to build my future, and I didn't realize how much I was neglecting our relationship. I thought I could juggle it all, but in the end, I ended up dropping the most important thing."

His words struck a chord deep within me. I had felt abandoned, as if the person I had once been so close to had become a stranger. "It felt like you were always busy with work and other commitments. I was trying to understand, but it was hard. I felt like I was losing you, and I didn't know how to reach out."

Ethan's face was etched with regret, his voice trembling slightly. "I should have been more present. I was so caught up in my own struggles that I didn't see how much you were hurting. I was selfish, and I didn't appreciate what we had until it was too late."

The honesty in his voice was both painful and refreshing. It was a reminder of the depth of our connection, but also of the mistakes we had made. "I guess we both made mistakes," I said softly. "We were young and inexperienced. We didn't know how to handle the pressures that life threw at us."

Ethan nodded, his gaze returning to me with a mixture of sorrow and hope. "We've both grown a lot since then. I think we're different people now, but the past is still part of us. It shapes who we are and how we relate to each other."

I couldn't deny the truth in his words. The years apart had transformed us, adding layers of complexity to our interactions. We had both experienced growth and change, but the scars of our past remained. "I've learned a lot from what happened between us," I admitted. "I've grown stronger and more self-aware. But there's still a part of me that wonders what might have been if things had been different."

Ethan reached out and took my hand, his touch warm and reassuring. "Me too. I wonder about the life we might have built together. But I also know that we have to acknowledge the past and understand it if we want to move forward—whatever that might look like."

As we sat there, hand in hand, the enormity of our shared history and the complexity of our emotions felt more manageable. This conversation was a step toward healing, a way to confront the old hurts that had shaped our relationship. It was a reminder that while we couldn't change the past, we could acknowledge it and learn from it.

The night deepened, and the city lights flickered like distant stars. Our conversation had been cathartic, but it was only the beginning of a journey to understand how we could find a path forward together. As we rose from the bench, I felt a tentative hope, a belief that maybe, just maybe, we could navigate the echoes of our past and find a way to build something new.

The dimly lit streets of Charleston seemed to embrace us in their historic charm as Ethan and I walked side by side, our footsteps echoing softly against the cobblestones. The picturesque houses and the distant murmur of the sea provided a soothing backdrop to our conversation. The city, a blend of old-world elegance and modern vibrancy, felt like a canvas on which our shared history was being painted once more.

Ethan glanced at me, his face a mixture of apprehension and resolve. "It's strange how walking through these old streets can bring back so many memories. It feels like we're retracing the steps of our past, doesn't it?"

I nodded, feeling a mix of nostalgia and unease. "Yes, it does. It's as if the city itself is whispering our old stories. It's hard not to get caught up in what used to be."

We stopped in front of a quaint, ivy-clad house that seemed almost frozen in time. I could imagine us walking these very streets years ago, lost in youthful dreams and promises. The sight brought a pang of longing. I wondered how much of our past was still alive within us, waiting to be acknowledged.

Ethan took a deep breath, his hands stuffed in his coat pockets. "Do you remember the summer after graduation? We had such big plans. I was supposed to go to architecture school, and you had your writing. It felt like we had the whole world ahead of us."

I smiled, though it was tinged with sadness. "I remember. We were so full of hope and ambition. It was like nothing could stand in our way. But life... it had its own plans."

The conversation took a somber turn, and I could see Ethan's eyes clouding with regret. "I never expected how hard it would be to balance everything. I thought I could manage it all, but I ended up letting the most important things slip through my fingers. And you—"

His voice faltered, and I could see the weight of his words pressing down on him. "And you were left feeling abandoned, I know. I was so focused on my career, on proving myself, that I didn't see how much I was hurting you."

My heart ached at his admission. "It wasn't just that you were busy, Ethan. It was like you were shutting me out. I felt like I was losing a part of myself, and I didn't know how to reach you. I tried to understand, but it was so hard."

He nodded, the regret in his eyes deepening. "I wish I had seen that sooner. I wish I had been there for you, instead of being so wrapped up in my own world. I was selfish, and it cost us everything."

We walked in silence for a moment, the gravity of our past weighing heavily on us. The old streets seemed to hold our secrets, the echoes of our laughter and arguments blending into the night. I could almost feel the ghost of our younger selves, still hopeful and in love, walking beside us.

Finally, Ethan broke the silence, his voice barely above a whisper. "I've thought a lot about how we ended things. I know I hurt you deeply, and I'm sorry for that. I never meant for things to end the way they did."

I looked at him, my emotions a turbulent mix of old pain and newfound understanding. "I've had a lot of time to process what happened, too. I realized that we were both at fault. We were young and inexperienced, and we let our problems become too big to handle."

His gaze met mine with a mixture of sorrow and hope. "We've both grown so much since then. I think we're different people now, but the past is still part of who we are. It shapes how we see each other and ourselves."

I could feel the depth of his words resonating within me. It was clear that we had both undergone significant changes, but the scars of our past were still visible. "I've learned a lot from what happened between us. I've become stronger, more resilient. But there's still a part of me that wonders about the 'what ifs'—what if we had been able to make it work?"

Ethan's hand brushed against mine, a touch that was both comforting and electrifying. "Me too. I wonder about the life we might have had. But I also know that we have to confront our past to understand how we move forward."

The evening had deepened, and the city lights reflected off the water, creating a shimmering mosaic of color. Our conversation had been raw and revealing, a necessary step in coming to terms with our shared history. It was a moment of reckoning, a chance to lay bare the hurts and regrets that had lingered between us.

As we continued our walk, hand in hand, there was a sense of tentative hope. We were acknowledging our past, understanding its impact on our present, and beginning to chart a path forward. The road ahead was uncertain, but this moment of honesty and vulnerability was a significant step toward healing.

The city, with its blend of history and modernity, seemed to mirror our journey. It was a place where old wounds could be addressed and where new beginnings might take root. As we walked through the streets, I felt a glimmer of optimism, a belief that perhaps, amidst the echoes of our past, there was a chance for something new and meaningful.

We reached a small park near the harbor, where a few old benches overlooked the water. The moon cast a soft glow over the scene, illuminating the gentle waves and the distant lights of the city. Ethan and I sat on one of the benches, the silence between us heavy with unspoken thoughts. The cool breeze rustled through the trees, adding a sense of serenity to our intense conversation.

Ethan took a deep breath, his gaze fixed on the water. "I've been thinking a lot about what we talked about. About how things fell apart and the pain we both felt."

I turned to him, feeling a mix of sympathy and residual hurt. "It's strange, isn't it? How talking about these things can make them feel so fresh again, yet so distant. Like we're reliving the past, but from a place of understanding."

He nodded, his expression thoughtful. "Yeah. It's like we're seeing everything in a new light. I've realized how much I took for granted back then. I was so focused on what I wanted to achieve, I didn't see how I was neglecting the most important part of my life—our relationship."

I reached out, placing my hand gently over his. The touch was tender, an unspoken comfort between us. "And I was so caught up in feeling abandoned that I didn't understand what you were going through. We were both struggling, but we didn't have the tools to deal with it."

The honesty in his voice was disarming. "I wish we had been able to communicate better. Maybe if we had talked more openly about our fears and frustrations, things might have been different."

I sighed, my thoughts drifting back to the arguments and misunderstandings that had driven a wedge between us. "It's hard not to dwell on the regrets. I think about the times I tried to reach out, but it felt like you were always just out of my grasp."

Ethan's eyes met mine, full of regret. "I know. I see now how my silence must have hurt you. I was dealing with my own insecurities and fears, but instead of opening up, I shut you out. And that was a mistake I deeply regret."

The weight of his words hung between us, heavy but liberating. For so long, we had been stuck in a cycle of hurt and misunderstanding, but this moment of raw honesty was breaking through those barriers. It was as if we were finally able to see each other clearly, without the haze of past grievances clouding our vision.

"There were so many moments I wanted to reach out, to find a way to fix things," I said softly. "But I felt so alone in the struggle. It was like I was fighting for us by myself."

Ethan squeezed my hand gently, his voice filled with genuine sorrow. "I wish I could go back and do things differently. I wish I could have been there for you, instead of letting my own fears and ambitions come between us."

We sat in silence for a while, the gentle lapping of the water against the shore providing a soothing backdrop to our introspection. The stars above seemed to twinkle with a kind of quiet approval, as if the universe was acknowledging our efforts to heal the wounds of the past.

Finally, Ethan broke the silence with a voice that held a mixture of hope and apprehension. "Maybe we can't change what happened, but we can learn from it. We can use this understanding to build something new, even if it's just a new chapter in our lives."

I looked at him, feeling a glimmer of hope amidst the lingering pain. "I want to believe that. I want to believe that we can take what we've learned and use it to make something better, whether it's together or apart."

Ethan's expression softened, and he leaned closer, his voice barely above a whisper. "I'm willing to try, if you are. I want to make things right, to be the person I should have been back then."

His words touched me deeply, and I could feel the old spark between us reigniting, though it was tempered by the understanding of our shared past. The path forward was uncertain, but this moment of connection felt like a step toward healing, a chance to rewrite our story with the wisdom of our experiences.

As we sat there, the night growing colder, I felt a sense of peace settling over me. The echoes of our past were still present, but they no longer felt like chains holding us back. Instead, they were reminders of how far we had come, and of the potential for a new beginning.

We stood up, our hands still entwined, and began walking back through the historic streets of Charleston. The city, with its blend of old and new, seemed to mirror our journey—an evolving landscape where the past and present coexisted, offering a chance for renewal.

As we walked together, the silence was no longer filled with unresolved tension, but with a quiet understanding. The road ahead was uncertain, but for the first time in a long time, it felt like a road worth traveling.

# Chapter 6: Finding Common Ground

The weeks that followed our heart-to-heart conversation felt like a slow, deliberate dance as Ethan and I worked to rebuild our connection. The streets of Charleston became our playground once more, each stroll a testament to the renewed effort we were both making to understand one another. Our interactions were no longer shadowed by the weight of our past mistakes but instead filled with the tentative excitement of rediscovering each other.

One sunny afternoon, we decided to visit the Charleston City Market, a place that had once been a favorite of ours. The vibrant stalls and the aroma of fresh coffee mingled with the hum of conversation created a warm, inviting atmosphere. As we wandered through the market, our conversation naturally veered away from the pain of our past to the lighter, more enjoyable aspects of our present lives.

Ethan's eyes lit up as he spotted a vendor selling handcrafted wooden puzzles. "Do you remember how we used to spend entire weekends working on those? I always got so frustrated when we couldn't find a piece."

I laughed, a genuine sound that felt good after the weight of our earlier discussions. "Yes, and I remember you getting so intense about finding the last piece. It was like the puzzle was a matter of life and death."

His smile was contagious, and it felt like a familiar warmth wrapping around us, dissolving some of the distance that had lingered between us. "Well, I guess some things haven't changed. I'm still pretty determined when it comes to puzzles."

As we continued to explore, we stumbled upon a small booth selling artisanal chocolates. The rich, sweet scents were irresistible, and we found ourselves discussing our favorite types. The conversation was easy, almost effortless, as we shared stories of our lives since we last saw each other.

"I've been experimenting with different recipes lately," Ethan said, handing me a piece of dark chocolate. "It's a new hobby of mine. I've discovered that cooking can be quite therapeutic."

I accepted the chocolate with a grateful smile, savoring the taste. "Cooking has always been a passion of mine, too. I've been working on perfecting my grandmother's old recipes. It's funny how some interests never fade, even after all these years."

The revelation was like a bridge spanning the gap between our past and present. We found ourselves engrossed in a lively discussion about our favorite recipes and culinary experiences. The shared enthusiasm was palpable, and it was clear that despite the years apart, some of our core interests had remained remarkably consistent.

The day was filled with small moments of rediscovery, each one adding a layer to the evolving picture of who we were now. We discussed our favorite books, music, and even our travel experiences. It was like piecing together a jigsaw puzzle, each conversation filling in gaps and revealing more of the person we had both become.

Yet, as our connection deepened, it became apparent that our current lifestyles were not without their differences. Ethan's career as an architect had introduced him to a world of high-stakes projects and international travel. His stories of bustling cities and ambitious designs contrasted sharply with my more grounded life as a local author.

We sat in a quaint café, sharing a pot of tea and reflecting on the contrasts in our lives. "It's strange," Ethan said, stirring his cup thoughtfully. "I've been so caught up in the whirlwind of my career that I've hardly had time to appreciate the simple things."

I nodded, understanding the sentiment. "I get that. My life has been more settled, more routine. It's not that one is better than the other; it's just different. But it's made me appreciate the little moments, the quiet times that many people overlook."

Our conversation shifted to our dreams and aspirations, and here we found a more profound common ground. Despite our different paths, our core values and long-term goals aligned in surprising ways. We both cherished the idea of making a meaningful impact, whether through architecture or writing. Our dreams of creating something lasting, something that mattered, were intertwined in ways that felt deeply resonant.

"It's incredible," Ethan mused, "how even though we've taken different routes, we still end up with similar dreams. It makes me wonder if there's something more to this connection than just nostalgia."

I met his gaze, a spark of excitement in my heart. "Maybe it's not just about where we've been but about where we're going. If we can embrace the differences and focus on what brings us together, there's a lot we can build."

The promise of possibility hung between us, a thread of hope weaving through the fabric of our renewed relationship. We were learning to navigate the complexities of our current lives while holding onto the shared values that had once drawn us together.

As we left the café, the sun setting behind the historic buildings of Charleston, it felt like we were walking into a new chapter of our story. The past was still there, a part of our history, but it was the present and the future that held the most promise.

We lingered in the soft, golden light of the Charleston sunset, the streets awash in hues of orange and pink. It was as if the city itself was celebrating our renewed connection, offering us a backdrop that was both comforting and exhilarating. We ventured into the heart of the city, where cobblestone streets and historic homes whispered tales of the past, blending seamlessly with our own story.

Our talks ventured deeper into personal terrain as we walked, our pace relaxed but our conversation charged with the energy of rekindled curiosity. Ethan shared anecdotes about his travels, recounting experiences from cities that were now etched into his memory. He spoke of Parisian cafes where he spent hours sketching designs and the vibrant street markets in Tokyo where he discovered new culinary delights. Each story was told with a passion that was both endearing and infectious.

"Do you ever miss it?" I asked, watching his eyes light up with the memory of a place he clearly loved.

"Sometimes," he admitted, a nostalgic edge to his voice. "But I think it's less about the places and more about the experiences. Those moments of discovery, of stepping into a new world and feeling like anything is possible—that's what I miss."

I smiled, feeling a pang of recognition. "I understand that. It's like the thrill of writing a new book, the excitement of exploring uncharted territory. Each story feels like a new adventure."

As we continued to walk, I couldn't help but reflect on how our lives had diverged since our last days together. Ethan's career had taken him across the globe, while my journey had kept me rooted in Charleston. The contrast was stark, yet there was something comforting about how our core values had remained intact.

"Tell me about your life here," Ethan said, his curiosity evident. "How have you been spending your days?"

I hesitated for a moment, then began to share the details of my daily routine, from the quiet mornings spent in my study to the community events that had become a regular part of my life. My stories were interspersed with moments of reflection on how I had grown, how the small, steady rhythms of my life had shaped me into who I was today.

"It sounds peaceful," Ethan remarked, a note of admiration in his voice. "I've always admired how you've been able to find joy in the simple things."

"It's been a journey," I said, thinking about the challenges I had faced along the way. "There were times when I struggled, but Charleston has a way of grounding you. It's the kind of place that makes you appreciate the little things, the quiet moments."

Our conversation turned to our future aspirations, and here, our shared dreams became apparent. Despite the different paths we had taken, we both harbored ambitions that were deeply intertwined with our core beliefs. We spoke of creating something lasting, something that would make a meaningful impact, whether through Ethan's architectural designs or my written words.

"There's something profoundly fulfilling about leaving a mark," Ethan said, his voice filled with conviction. "It's not about fame or recognition; it's about knowing that your work has touched lives, that it's made a difference."

I nodded in agreement. "Exactly. It's the idea of contributing something positive, of leaving behind a legacy that speaks to who we are and what we value."

As we reached the edge of the historic district, we found ourselves at the docks, where the gentle lapping of the water and the distant sound of seagulls created a soothing atmosphere. We leaned against the railing, watching the sun dip below the horizon, the sky painted in deep shades of violet and gold.

"It's moments like these that make me realize how much I've missed this place," Ethan said, his gaze fixed on the water. "I forgot how much I loved the tranquility of Charleston."

"I missed it too," I admitted, feeling a deep sense of contentment. "It's good to have you back, even if just for a while."

The silence that followed was comfortable, a quiet acknowledgment of the connection that had been rekindled between us. It was clear that, despite the differences and challenges, there was something profoundly genuine about what we shared. Our renewed bond was tested by the complexities of our current lives, but the foundation of our relationship was built on a shared understanding and respect for each other's dreams and values.

As we walked back towards the city, the evening air cool and crisp, I felt a sense of hope and possibility. Our conversations had shifted from past regrets to the potential of what lay ahead. The path we were navigating was still uncertain, but there was a reassuring sense of common ground beneath our feet, a mutual desire to explore where this renewed connection might lead.

As the weeks unfolded, Ethan and I continued to explore this new chapter of our relationship, our days blending into a comfortable routine of shared moments and honest conversations. We found solace in each other's company, savoring the simple joys of rediscovering who we had become and how our paths had evolved.

One crisp autumn afternoon, we decided to visit a local art gallery that had recently opened its doors in Charleston. The gallery was nestled in a quaint corner of the city, a blend of modern architecture and historic charm that seemed to capture the essence of our growing connection. As we walked through the exhibits, the artwork on display sparked a range of discussions—ranging from the philosophical to the personal.

"Isn't it fascinating," Ethan mused as we stopped before a striking abstract piece, "how art can convey such complex emotions and ideas without a single word?"

I studied the painting, its bold colors and erratic shapes resonating with me on a profound level. "It's true. Art has a way of tapping into the core of our experiences and translating them into something tangible. It's like finding common ground in a language that doesn't rely on words."

Ethan's gaze met mine, and for a moment, the unspoken understanding between us felt almost palpable. "Exactly. It's as if we're both searching for ways to articulate what we've been through, what we've learned, and what we hope for."

We moved through the gallery, our conversation drifting to the different pieces and the emotions they evoked. It was an unexpected yet delightful exploration of our artistic tastes, revealing layers of ourselves that we hadn't fully examined before. It was in these moments, amidst the art and the shared silence, that I felt a deepening connection, a sense of being seen and understood in ways that transcended the ordinary.

Later, as we strolled through the nearby park, the cool breeze rustling the fallen leaves around us, our conversation shifted to our future aspirations. Ethan spoke of his latest project, an ambitious architectural design that aimed to blend sustainable practices with aesthetic beauty. His enthusiasm was evident, and I found myself captivated by his vision, impressed by how his dreams had evolved since we last knew each other.

"It's incredible," I said, genuinely admiring his passion. "I love how you're not just designing buildings but creating spaces that reflect your values and vision for a better world."

Ethan's eyes lit up with a smile that spoke volumes. "Thank you. It's been a journey, figuring out how to merge my professional ambitions with my personal beliefs. But it's rewarding to see the ideas take shape, to know that they might have a positive impact."

I couldn't help but draw parallels to my own writing, to the stories and characters that had become my way of making sense of the world. "I feel the same way about my work," I confessed. "Each book is a reflection of my experiences, my hopes, and my fears. It's a way to connect with others, to share pieces of myself in hopes of finding a common thread."

As we continued our walk, we explored more of our shared dreams, finding solace in the fact that despite the different paths we had taken, we were still driven by similar values. Our conversations revealed a mutual desire to make a meaningful impact, to create something lasting and beautiful. We discovered that while our lifestyles had changed, the core of who we were—our passions, our hopes, our beliefs—remained strikingly aligned.

The days turned into weeks, and with each passing moment, the sense of ease between us grew stronger. We found ourselves falling into a rhythm, our interactions marked by a comfort that spoke of old familiarity and new possibilities. Our connection, once fraught with the weight of past hurts, now felt like a delicate tapestry woven from threads of understanding and shared aspirations.

Even as we navigated the complexities of our differing lifestyles—Ethan's global career and my rooted existence in Charleston—we managed to find joy in the intersections of our lives. Whether it was sharing a quiet evening at a local café or engaging in spirited debates about our favorite books, there was a sense of balance and harmony that we both cherished.

One evening, as we sat on my porch, the city lights twinkling in the distance, Ethan took my hand in his. The gesture was simple, yet it conveyed a depth of emotion that words couldn't capture. "I'm grateful for this," he said softly, his gaze fixed on the horizon. "For this chance to reconnect, to find our way back to each other."

I squeezed his hand, feeling a profound sense of contentment. "Me too. It's been a journey, but I think we're finding something special—something worth holding on to."

In that quiet moment, surrounded by the gentle hum of Charleston's night, I realized that our renewed bond was more than just a rekindling of old flames. It was a testament to our growth, to the strength of our shared values and dreams. And as we faced the future together, I felt a renewed sense of hope and possibility, knowing that we were navigating this path with an understanding and appreciation that had grown from the echoes of our past.

# Chapter 7: Cultural Challenges

The first time I stepped into Ethan's world outside the confines of our recent rekindled romance, I felt a mixture of excitement and trepidation. We had been navigating our newfound connection with ease, but the deeper layers of our lives were waiting to reveal themselves. The cultural divide between us was more than just a backdrop—it was a living, breathing aspect of our relationship that demanded both attention and respect.

Ethan had invited me to a family gathering, an event that promised to immerse me in the vibrant tapestry of his Mexican heritage. He spoke of it with such warmth and pride, his eyes lighting up as he described the traditional foods, the lively music, and the tight-knit community that defined his family's gatherings. I was eager to embrace this part of his life, but I couldn't shake the nerves that fluttered in my stomach.

The day of the gathering arrived, and Ethan's family home was alive with the buzz of preparation. The scent of spices and cooking wafted through the air as I walked through the door, and I was immediately enveloped by a sense of bustling energy and celebration. His family welcomed me with open arms, their smiles and warm hugs putting me at ease, though I was acutely aware of being an outsider in this rich cultural landscape.

The house was adorned with colorful decorations, a vibrant mix of reds, greens, and golds that spoke of festive traditions. A mariachi band played in the background, their music a lively soundtrack to the laughter and conversations that filled the space. I marveled at the way the room seemed to pulse with life, each corner brimming with the essence of Ethan's heritage.

As we mingled, Ethan introduced me to his relatives, each name and face blending into a chorus of warm greetings and curious glances. I tried to absorb as much as I could, noting the differences in customs and traditions from my own Southern upbringing. There was a fluidity to their interactions, a comfort in the way they moved between conversations and activities that felt both foreign and fascinating.

Dinner was a feast of traditional Mexican dishes—tender carnitas, rich mole, and homemade tortillas that were the epitome of culinary craftsmanship. I was eager to try everything, each bite a new experience that broadened my understanding of Ethan's background. The flavors were bold and complex, each dish telling a story of its own.

Throughout the meal, I felt the weight of my own cultural background pressing against me. My Southern roots had their own set of traditions, values, and expectations, which seemed so different from the lively, communal atmosphere I was now immersed in. It was a stark reminder of the differences that existed between us, but it also highlighted the beauty of our shared experience.

As the evening progressed, Ethan's family invited me to join in a traditional dance. The music was infectious, and though I hesitated at first, Ethan's encouraging smile gave me the courage to step onto the makeshift dance floor. The steps were unfamiliar, but with Ethan guiding me and his family cheering us on, I began to find my rhythm. The experience was exhilarating, a dance of integration and acceptance that symbolized our attempt to bridge our disparate worlds.

The night was filled with laughter and shared stories, and though there were moments of awkwardness and uncertainty, I felt a growing sense of belonging. Ethan's family was gracious and understanding, their efforts to make me feel welcome evident in every interaction. I saw the pride Ethan had in his heritage reflected in their eyes, and it made me appreciate even more the cultural richness he brought into my life.

When the evening drew to a close, and the guests began to say their goodbyes, I found myself reflecting on the experience. It had been both exhilarating and challenging, a glimpse into the heart of Ethan's world that was as enlightening as it was humbling. I understood now that the cultural challenges we faced were not obstacles but opportunities—opportunities to grow, to learn, and to weave our own unique story together.

Ethan and I walked back to his car, the night air cool against our skin. He took my hand in his, giving it a reassuring squeeze. "How did you find it?" he asked, his voice laced with both curiosity and concern.

I looked up at him, my heart full of mixed emotions. "It was incredible," I admitted. "I felt so welcomed and included, but I also realized how much we have to learn from each other. There's so much to navigate, but I'm excited to do it with you."

Ethan smiled, his eyes reflecting a deep sense of understanding. "I'm glad you enjoyed it. And I feel the same way. We have a lot to figure out, but I believe we can find a balance that honors both of our backgrounds."

As we drove away from the gathering, the city lights of Charleston beginning to blur in the distance, I felt a renewed sense of hope. Our relationship was being tested in ways I hadn't anticipated, but the challenges were shaping us, revealing the strength and resilience we had within. And as we faced these cultural crossroads together, I knew that our love was growing in depth and complexity, forging a path that was uniquely ours.

Stepping into Ethan's world felt like entering a vibrant, swirling tapestry where every thread was woven with love, history, and tradition. The family gathering was a celebration of this rich heritage, a world that was as unfamiliar to me as it was enthralling. As the evening progressed, I found myself both captivated and slightly overwhelmed by the intricacies of his background.

The warmth and vibrancy of Ethan's family contrasted starkly with my own Southern roots. My upbringing had been steeped in a quieter kind of tradition—one that revolved around slow Sunday dinners, genteel manners, and an understated, yet deeply felt sense of community. The Mexican traditions I was now part of were lively, passionate, and exuberant. Every interaction was charged with energy, every gesture seemed to carry weight and meaning.

Ethan's abuela, a petite woman with eyes as sharp as they were kind, took me under her wing. She had an air of quiet authority, but her smile was as welcoming as a warm embrace. She guided me through the culinary treasures of the evening, explaining each dish with a kind of reverence that spoke volumes about its importance. I watched as she prepared tamales with practiced ease, her hands working quickly and skillfully, a dance of tradition and love.

At one point, she invited me to help her in the kitchen. Despite my initial hesitation, I eagerly accepted, hoping to gain a deeper understanding of this aspect of Ethan's life. The kitchen was a bustling hive of activity, and as I worked alongside her, I could feel the generational bond that tied her to her family. The conversation was in rapid Spanish, and though I didn't catch every word, the warmth in her voice was unmistakable. She spoke of family, of shared experiences, and of the importance of carrying on these traditions.

I made an effort to join in the lively conversations, though I found myself stumbling over unfamiliar phrases and cultural references. Ethan was always close by, offering gentle corrections and explanations. His patience was remarkable, and his encouragement made me feel like I was making progress, even when I felt lost in translation.

As the night went on, we gathered around a long table laden with food. Ethan's family engaged in animated conversations, their voices rising and falling in a symphony of laughter and debate. The atmosphere was electric, a stark contrast to the more subdued gatherings I was used to. I found myself caught between admiration for the lively traditions and the subtle pressure of wanting to fit in seamlessly.

One of Ethan's cousins, Diego, playfully challenged me to a dance-off. The music was a blend of traditional Mexican rhythms and modern beats, a fusion that had everyone on their feet. I hesitated at first, feeling a wave of self-consciousness, but Ethan's encouraging nod gave me the boost I needed. I joined in, my steps awkward at first, but gradually finding a rhythm in the infectious energy of the dance. The experience was liberating, a beautiful, chaotic blend of culture and laughter that left me breathless.

Despite the fun and warmth, there was a moment of quiet reflection. I caught Ethan watching me, his expression a mix of pride and concern. It was as if he was gauging how well I was adapting, how comfortable I felt within this new facet of his life. It struck me how much we were both navigating uncharted waters. This celebration was not just a glimpse into Ethan's past but a test of how we could blend our worlds, each bringing our unique traditions and expectations to the table.

As the evening drew to a close, I found a quiet moment to speak with Ethan outside on the porch. The cool night air was a welcome respite from the vibrant chaos inside. He stood close, his hand finding mine, offering a silent support that spoke louder than words.

"I hope tonight wasn't too overwhelming," he said, his voice soft but earnest.

I looked at him, my heart full of mixed emotions. "It was a lot to take in, but it was also amazing. I felt so welcomed, and I'm grateful for that. But I also realize how much I need to learn and adapt."

Ethan squeezed my hand, his gaze steady. "You did great. It's a lot to process, and it takes time. But we'll figure it out together. Our backgrounds might be different, but I believe we can create something beautiful by embracing both."

The sincerity in his voice was comforting. I knew that the journey ahead would be filled with challenges as we continued to blend our different worlds. But in that moment, standing together under the starlit sky, I felt a renewed sense of hope and commitment. We were building a bridge between our cultures, one that was rich with potential and promise.

As we rejoined the festivities, the night's energy felt more familiar, less intimidating. I had taken my first steps into Ethan's world, and though it was a journey still in its early stages, it was one I was eager to continue. With every shared tradition and each new experience, we were writing a story that was uniquely our own, filled with the beauty of both our heritages and the love that bound us together.

The warmth of Ethan's family lingered long after the party ended, leaving me with a mixture of exhilaration and introspection. The next morning, as I walked through the quiet streets of Charleston, the contrast between my own world and Ethan's felt more pronounced. The city, with its old-world charm and Southern grace, seemed to echo with a rhythm that was comforting yet distant from the lively energy I had experienced the night before.

Ethan had insisted on driving me to a quaint little café for brunch, a place that had become one of our favorite spots. It was a charming blend of Southern hospitality and low-key elegance, and it offered a quiet refuge where we could talk about the evening without the interference of bustling family gatherings or cultural expectations.

As we settled into our booth, Ethan's eyes held a trace of concern. He studied me over his coffee cup, and I could sense the unspoken questions. I appreciated his patience and the way he gave me space to process everything without pressing for immediate responses.

"I've been thinking about last night," I began, taking a sip of my latte to steady my nerves. "It was... a lot, but it was also incredible.

I'm just trying to figure out how to balance my own traditions with what I've experienced."

Ethan nodded, his gaze thoughtful. "It's not easy, finding that balance. My family's traditions are such an integral part of who I am, and I know they can seem overwhelming, especially when they're new to someone. I'm glad you came, though. It means a lot to me."

There was a tenderness in his voice, and I felt a rush of gratitude for his understanding. I reached across the table, resting my hand on his. "I'm glad I came too. It was eye-opening, and I want to understand more, even if it feels like a lot to take in."

Ethan's fingers gently squeezed mine, and for a moment, it felt like we were the only two people in the world. "We can take it slow," he suggested. "There's no rush. And you don't have to embrace everything all at once. I appreciate your effort and willingness more than anything."

Our conversation shifted to lighter topics, but the undercurrent of our earlier discussion lingered. I couldn't shake the feeling that navigating these cultural differences was just one part of a larger journey we were embarking on together. Each new experience seemed to draw us closer, but it also highlighted the ways in which our paths had diverged over the years.

As we finished our brunch, Ethan suggested a walk through the nearby park, a serene spot that offered a respite from the city's hustle and bustle. The gentle autumn breeze rustled the leaves, and the golden light filtering through the trees created a picturesque backdrop for our continued conversation.

We strolled side by side, the silence between us filled with a comfortable familiarity. The park was a sanctuary, its tranquil beauty offering a stark contrast to the vibrant chaos of the previous night. It was a moment of peace, a chance to reflect and appreciate the journey we were on.

"I've been thinking about what you said last night," Ethan began, breaking the silence. "About how our backgrounds are so different. It's made me realize that we have more to learn about each other's worlds than I initially thought."

I nodded, feeling a sense of solidarity in his words. "Yes, it's not just about blending traditions but also about understanding and respecting each other's experiences. I think that's what makes our relationship unique."

Ethan stopped and turned to face me, his expression serious but soft. "I know it hasn't been easy, and there are still challenges ahead. But I believe in us. I believe that we can create something beautiful from this mix of cultures and backgrounds."

His words were a balm to my soul, and I felt a renewed sense of hope. We had faced so many hurdles already, and yet, here we were, standing together with a shared commitment to making our relationship work. The journey wouldn't always be smooth, but it was one we were determined to navigate together.

As we continued our walk, the conversation flowed naturally, the earlier tension giving way to a deeper understanding. We talked about our dreams, our fears, and the ways we hoped to grow together. The park, with its serene beauty and quiet ambiance, became a symbol of the space we were carving out for ourselves amidst the complexities of our lives.

By the time we reached the end of the path, the sun was beginning to set, casting a warm glow over the park. We paused for a moment, taking in the view of the city skyline in the distance. The sight was a reminder of the world beyond our personal struggles, a world full of possibilities and opportunities.

Ethan took my hand once more, his touch reassuring. "We've come a long way," he said softly. "And we have so much more to discover and experience. But I'm grateful to have you by my side through it all."

I looked up at him, my heart full of emotion. "I'm grateful too. For everything we've shared and everything that's yet to come."

As we walked back to the car, the night air was cool and invigorating, carrying with it the promise of new beginnings and continued growth. We had faced cultural challenges and personal hurdles, but through it all, we were finding our way—together.

# Chapter 8: Building Trust

The gentle hum of the coffee shop provided a cocoon of calm as Ethan and I settled into our corner booth, the soft clinking of cups and murmur of conversations weaving a comforting backdrop. I sipped my latte, feeling the warmth seep through the ceramic mug and into my hands, a small, soothing reminder of the peace I sought in this chapter of our lives.

Ethan's eyes, focused intently on me, spoke volumes more than his words ever could. His effort to rebuild trust was apparent in every gesture, every shared moment. He had begun to text me good morning every day, a simple but meaningful gesture that felt like a lifeline amid the turbulence of our renewed relationship. Yet, despite these efforts, old insecurities lingered like shadows, sometimes creeping into the spaces we were trying so hard to fill with new memories.

We had decided to spend our weekends together, engaging in activities that would not only help us rediscover each other but also reaffirm the connection we were working so hard to rebuild. Today, we were attending a local art fair, a blend of vibrant colors and creative energy that mirrored the changes we were trying to embrace in our relationship.

As we wandered through the rows of stalls, I noticed Ethan's occasional glances in my direction, a silent check-in to see how I was faring amidst the crowd. His attentiveness was reassuring, but it also reminded me of the fragility of our situation. It wasn't that I doubted his sincerity; rather, it was the echo of past hurts that made me hesitant to fully let go.

We paused in front of a booth showcasing handcrafted jewelry. Ethan's fingers lightly grazed a delicate silver bracelet, and he turned to me with a soft smile. "What do you think of this one?" he asked, holding it up for me to see.

I studied the piece, its intricate design catching the light. "It's beautiful," I said, my voice carrying a hint of appreciation. "Do you think it would suit someone special?"

Ethan's smile widened, a mixture of playfulness and earnestness. "I think it might be perfect for someone who's been very patient with me lately."

The comment was lighthearted, but beneath the surface, it was a reminder of the effort he was putting into our relationship. It was a reminder of the trust he was trying to rebuild, piece by piece.

As we continued exploring the fair, our conversations shifted from casual chatter to more profound reflections on our past and our future. Ethan was open about his own struggles, revealing vulnerabilities that I had not expected. He spoke of moments when he had felt unsure of himself, of decisions he regretted. It was a raw honesty that was both refreshing and intimidating.

We stopped for a moment in front of a street artist painting a mural. The artist's strokes were bold and deliberate, creating a vivid depiction of a cityscape. Ethan watched with interest, and I could sense his thoughts drifting, perhaps reflecting on the way he was working to paint a new picture of our relationship.

"This mural is incredible," Ethan said, his voice thoughtful. "It's like every color and brushstroke tells a story. I think we're doing something similar, you know? Each moment we share is like adding a new layer to our own canvas."

I turned to him, the metaphor striking a chord. "Yes, it's true. And sometimes, it feels like we're still figuring out the right colors and techniques. It's a work in progress."

His eyes met mine, and there was a depth to his gaze that spoke of shared understanding. "I know it's not always easy, and I know I haven't always been the best at showing it, but I want you to know that I'm committed to this. To us."

There was sincerity in his voice that tugged at my heart. I wanted to believe him, wanted to believe that the cracks in our foundation could be mended and that the trust we were working to rebuild could be more than just an aspiration. I wanted to believe that we could create something beautiful from the remnants of our past.

As the afternoon waned and the sky began to darken, we made our way back to the car, the fair's vibrant energy now replaced by a quiet sense of contentment. We had navigated the art fair, talked openly about our fears and hopes, and in doing so, had taken another step forward in our journey together.

Sitting in the car, Ethan reached over and took my hand in his, his touch warm and reassuring. "Thank you for today," he said softly. "For being open to this. For giving us another chance."

I squeezed his hand, feeling a glimmer of hope amidst the lingering doubts. "Thank you for being patient with me. For showing me that you're willing to work through this."

As we drove home, the city lights glimmering in the distance, I reflected on the progress we were making. It wasn't always smooth, and there were still moments of uncertainty, but there was also a growing sense of hope. Trust was a fragile thing, but with each shared moment, each honest conversation, it was becoming a little stronger. And for now, that was enough.

We found ourselves spending more weekends together, each outing a carefully planned attempt to weave new memories over the frayed threads of our past. Our time was filled with new experiences, from trying out eclectic restaurants to exploring hidden trails in the nearby parks. Yet, amid these efforts, the task of rebuilding trust was ever-present, a gentle, persistent hum beneath the surface of our interactions.

One Saturday afternoon, we decided to visit a local farmer's market. The sun was bright, and the air was filled with the tantalizing aroma of fresh produce and baked goods. Ethan's excitement was palpable as he eagerly pointed out different stalls, each offering a unique array of items. He was so animated, it was impossible not to feel drawn into his enthusiasm.

We wandered through the market, stopping to sample homemade jams and fresh bread. Ethan's casual chatter about the vendors and their stories was accompanied by the occasional sideways glance, as though he was trying to gauge my reactions. I appreciated his effort, even if it made me feel slightly self-conscious.

"Have you ever tried homemade peach preserves?" he asked, holding up a jar with a hopeful expression.

I shook my head, a smile forming on my lips. "I haven't. Let's give it a shot."

He handed me the jar, his fingers brushing mine in a fleeting but meaningful touch. We sampled the preserves with a piece of bread, and I couldn't help but be struck by the way his eyes lit up with simple joys. It was a side of Ethan I had missed—his capacity to find pleasure in the little things, his ability to share that joy with me.

As we continued to explore the market, our conversation drifted to more personal topics. Ethan spoke about his recent project at work, detailing the challenges and triumphs with a passion that was contagious. I listened intently, genuinely interested in the intricacies of his life that he was now sharing so openly.

In return, I opened up about my latest book, sharing the struggles and triumphs of my writing process. The exchange was refreshing, a reminder of the connection we had once shared and were now rekindling.

But even in these moments of camaraderie, the old insecurities sometimes surfaced, like unwelcome guests at a well-anticipated reunion. I noticed the way my pulse quickened when Ethan mentioned a new colleague, a woman he had been working closely with. It was a subtle reminder of the trust we had yet to rebuild fully.

In the midst of this, Ethan seemed to sense my discomfort. He paused, turning to face me with a serious expression. "I want you to know that I'm committed to this," he said quietly. "I know it's not easy, and I know I've given you reasons to doubt me before, but I'm here now, and I want to prove that I'm worthy of your trust."

His words, sincere and direct, cut through the cloud of my doubts. I could see the earnestness in his eyes, the desire to make things right. But despite this, the remnants of past betrayals made it hard to fully release my guard. Trust wasn't something that could be reassembled overnight; it was a painstaking process, marked by moments of vulnerability and courage.

As the day wore on, we continued to navigate the market, our conversations flowing more easily as we focused on the present. We stopped by a flower stall, where Ethan picked out a bouquet of sunflowers and handed them to me with a grin.

"For you," he said, his eyes warm.

The gesture was sweet and unexpected. I took the flowers, feeling their vibrant energy contrast with the tumultuous emotions I had been grappling with. It was a small but significant reminder of the affection we were working to restore.

We decided to cap off the day with a leisurely dinner at a quaint bistro we had passed by earlier. As we sat across from each other, the soft candlelight casting a gentle glow, I felt a sense of tentative peace. The meal was delicious, and the atmosphere was relaxed, a stark contrast to the anxiety I often felt when we discussed our past.

We talked about our plans for the future, our aspirations and dreams. Ethan spoke about his hopes for expanding his architectural firm and the desire to explore new projects. I shared my excitement about a new book idea I was working on, one that felt deeply personal and fulfilling.

As the evening drew to a close, we walked back to the car, the night air crisp and refreshing. Ethan took my hand in his, and for a moment, the world outside seemed to fade away. We had navigated another day together, facing the challenges and joys with a renewed sense of understanding.

The journey of rebuilding trust was far from complete, but each shared experience, each honest conversation, was a step forward. The path ahead was uncertain, but with each passing day, the foundation of our relationship grew a little stronger. For now, that was enough.

The following week, we took a small but significant step in our journey by attending a couples' workshop focused on improving communication. The workshop was held in a cozy, rustic community center on the outskirts of Charleston, a place that seemed to embrace both warmth and openness. We walked in together, Ethan's hand brushing against mine, a reassuring gesture that reminded me of how far we'd come.

Inside, the room was filled with other couples, each with their own stories and struggles. We took our seats at a round table, our fingers still linked, and I couldn't help but feel a mix of hope and trepidation. The facilitator, a gentle woman with a calming presence, introduced the session with a series of exercises designed to foster deeper understanding and connection.

One of the first exercises involved sharing personal stories—moments that had shaped who we were. Ethan went first, his voice steady as he spoke about his childhood memories and the influences that had molded his approach to relationships. He talked about his family's values, the importance of resilience, and the sacrifices his parents had made for his future.

Listening to him, I felt a pang of realization about how much I had missed these intimate glimpses into his life. His words were a reminder of the person he had been and still was underneath the layers of time and distance. It was both comforting and challenging to witness his vulnerability, knowing that my own insecurities and fears had been part of the distance between us.

When it was my turn, I shared stories of my upbringing in Charleston, the small-town values that had shaped me, and the way my career had become a refuge during our time apart. As I spoke, I saw Ethan's attentive gaze, a reminder that despite our struggles, he was still very much present and invested in understanding me.

The exercise allowed us to revisit the core of who we were, and it highlighted both our commonalities and differences. Afterward, we worked on a communication exercise where we were asked to express our feelings and listen without interruption. Ethan spoke about his frustrations and regrets, his voice tinged with the rawness of past hurts.

"I wish I could change the way things ended between us," he admitted, his eyes searching mine for understanding. "I know I can't undo the past, but I want you to know that I've learned from it."

I took a deep breath, feeling the weight of his words. "I appreciate that," I said softly. "It's not about changing the past. It's about learning from it and making sure we're honest with each other."

As the workshop continued, we practiced techniques for active listening and empathy. It was a process that required patience and openness, but it was also incredibly enlightening. Each exercise seemed to peel away a layer of misunderstanding, allowing us to see each other with clearer eyes.

One of the most poignant moments came when we were asked to write down our fears and hopes for the future. Ethan and I exchanged our papers, and as I read his heartfelt words, I was struck by the depth of his commitment to our relationship. He wrote about his desire for us to build a life together, one rooted in mutual respect and understanding.

In return, I shared my own fears—concerns about repeating past mistakes and the challenge of blending our lives. But I also wrote about my hopes for a future where we could rebuild and grow, a future that embraced the lessons of our past while moving forward with renewed purpose.

By the end of the workshop, there was a sense of cautious optimism between us. We had navigated a significant emotional terrain, and while the road ahead was still uncertain, there was a newfound clarity in our conversations. The exercises had not only helped us communicate better but had also reinforced the foundation of honesty and transparency that was vital to our relationship.

As we left the community center, Ethan took my hand again, his touch firm and reassuring. We walked to the car in comfortable silence, the weight of the day settling around us. The sun was setting, casting a golden hue over the city, and for the first time in a while, I felt a sense of peace.

We drove home with a quiet understanding that while rebuilding trust was an ongoing journey, we were taking it together, step by step. The workshop had provided us with tools to navigate our challenges, but it was the commitment to each other and to our shared future that would ultimately define our path.

In the weeks that followed, we continued to apply the lessons from the workshop to our daily lives. We made a conscious effort to communicate openly and address concerns as they arose. Each day brought new opportunities to reinforce the trust we were building, and while there were moments of doubt and vulnerability, there was also a deepening sense of connection.

The process of rebuilding trust was far from perfect, but it was real and tangible. It was a journey marked by both challenges and triumphs, each moment contributing to the strengthening of our relationship. As we faced the future together, it was with a renewed sense of hope and determination, knowing that the trust we were building was not just about overcoming past mistakes but about embracing the possibilities of a shared future.

# Chapter 9: Unexpected Obstacles

The phone call came on a crisp autumn morning, the kind where the chill in the air hints at the coming winter. I was sitting at my kitchen table, the sunlight filtering through the sheer curtains, casting a warm glow over the room. The phone's sudden ring jolted me from my thoughts, and I saw Ethan's name on the screen. I answered with a cheerful tone, hoping to lift the mood of our usual conversations.

"Hey, Ethan, what's up?" I asked, trying to sound casual.

"Mia, I need to talk to you about something important," Ethan's voice came through the line, serious and measured.

My heart skipped a beat. It wasn't like Ethan to sound so solemn, and the gravity in his voice instantly set my nerves on edge. "Sure, what's going on?"

There was a brief pause, and I could almost picture him gathering his thoughts. "I've been offered a major project at work, something I've been working towards for a long time. It's a fantastic opportunity, but it requires me to relocate temporarily—probably for about six months."

The words hung in the air like an unwelcome chill. Six months. The number seemed to echo in my mind, each repetition magnifying the weight of the news. "Relocate? As in, leave Charleston?"

"Yeah," Ethan confirmed. "The project is in New York. It's a big step for my career, but it means I'd be away from you for a while."

I swallowed hard, trying to process the implications. The thought of Ethan being so far away was a stark contrast to the intimacy we'd been nurturing. It felt like a cruel twist of fate, a test we hadn't anticipated. "Have you made up your mind?"

"I haven't decided yet," Ethan said. "I wanted to talk to you first. I know this changes everything for us, and I need to know how you feel about it."

I took a deep breath, trying to steady my racing thoughts. "Ethan, this is huge. I'm happy for you, truly, but I can't pretend this won't be incredibly difficult for us."

"I know," he said softly. "That's why I'm struggling with the decision. I don't want to jeopardize what we've worked so hard to rebuild. But this opportunity is a big deal for me, and I need to consider it."

The conversation stretched on, filled with pauses and hesitant words. We discussed the logistics, the emotional toll, and the impact on our relationship. The distance seemed insurmountable, a looming obstacle that threatened to pull us apart just as we were finding our footing again.

As we ended the call, I felt a mix of sadness and frustration. Ethan's career was important, but so was the fragile relationship we were trying to nurture. The choice he faced was not just a career decision but a potential turning point in our lives.

Over the next few days, the weight of the decision hung over me like a persistent cloud. I tried to stay focused on my work, but the constant worry about Ethan's absence gnawed at me. We continued to talk about the situation, our conversations increasingly strained as we grappled with the uncertainty.

One evening, after a particularly difficult day, Ethan and I met at a small café we frequented. The cozy atmosphere was a stark contrast to the tension between us. We sat across from each other, the dim light casting shadows over our faces, and I could see the exhaustion in Ethan's eyes.

"I've been thinking," he began, his voice low. "Maybe we should take a step back and reevaluate everything. This isn't just about me taking a job; it's about our future. We need to figure out what we want."

I nodded, feeling a lump form in my throat. "I agree. We need to be realistic about what this means for us. It's not just about the time apart but also about the strain it will put on our relationship."

Ethan reached across the table, his hand covering mine. "I don't want to lose what we've rediscovered. But I also don't want to hold you back from something you might want."

His words stung, but they also spoke to the core of our dilemma. The balancing act between personal aspirations and a shared future was more complex than either of us had anticipated.

We spent the evening talking through our fears, hopes, and the potential impact of Ethan's decision. It was a raw, honest conversation, one that brought us closer to understanding the gravity of the situation. We didn't have all the answers, but we were committed to facing the uncertainty together.

As the night drew to a close, we walked out of the café, the crisp autumn air a welcome change from the emotional intensity of our discussion. We embraced in the parking lot, the warmth of his hug offering a temporary solace from the cold reality we faced.

"We'll figure this out," Ethan said softly, his breath mingling with mine in the chilly night air. "No matter what happens, we'll get through it."

I nodded, holding on to his words like a lifeline. The road ahead was fraught with challenges, but I knew that facing them together was the only way forward. The unexpected obstacles had tested our resolve, but they had also illuminated the strength of our connection.

As we parted ways that night, I was filled with a mixture of hope and trepidation. The future was uncertain, but our willingness to confront these obstacles head-on was a testament to the depth of our commitment.

The days following Ethan's news were a turbulent mix of hope and apprehension. Our discussions about his job opportunity took on a weightier tone, each conversation more intense than the last. I found myself constantly replaying our talks, analyzing every nuance of his voice and the pauses between his words. It was as if I were trying to decode a message written in invisible ink, desperate to understand the true extent of his feelings.

The evenings grew quieter as I wrestled with the distance that seemed to stretch between us, not just physically but emotionally as well. I would lie awake at night, staring at the ceiling, feeling the ghost of our past arguments and the anxiety of our present dilemma weaving through my thoughts. The usual comfort of my bed felt like a cage, trapping me with my restless mind.

One Friday evening, after yet another tense conversation with Ethan, I decided to take a walk along the river. The city lights glistened on the water, creating a shimmering dance that did little to soothe the turmoil inside me. The familiarity of the river's path, once a place of peace and reflection, now felt like a reminder of what was slipping away.

As I walked, my phone buzzed with a message from Ethan. He wanted to meet at a park near my apartment, a place we had often visited during our early days together. I agreed, hoping that a change of scenery might help us navigate this stormy patch with more clarity.

When I arrived, Ethan was already there, sitting on a bench overlooking the lake. The park was bathed in the soft glow of streetlights, and the leaves rustling in the gentle breeze created a tranquil backdrop. Ethan stood up as I approached, his face a mixture of resolve and weariness. He pulled me into a tight embrace, his touch both comforting and bittersweet.

"I didn't know if I'd see you tonight," he said, his voice muffled against my hair. "I've been thinking a lot about everything we've talked about."

I nodded, pulling back slightly to look at him. "Me too. It's hard to imagine what the future holds with everything we're dealing with right now."

Ethan sighed, taking a seat on the bench and patting the space beside him. "I've been offered a chance to meet with some of the project's key players next week. It would be an opportunity to get a better sense of what the job entails and what my role would be. I want to understand if this is something I can commit to without losing sight of us."

I sat down beside him, my heart aching at the thought of him being so far away. "I appreciate that, Ethan. But we both know it's not just about the job. It's about us—how we fit into each other's lives now and what we want for the future."

He reached for my hand, his fingers intertwining with mine. "I'm torn, Mia. This job could be a turning point for my career, but I can't ignore how much I want to be with you. I need to figure out if there's a way to balance both or if I have to choose."

We sat in silence, letting the gravity of our situation sink in. The park was quiet, save for the occasional splash of water and the distant sound of laughter from a nearby playground. It was a serene setting for such a tumultuous conversation, but it also felt like the perfect place to confront our uncertainties.

"I've been thinking," I finally said, breaking the silence, "that maybe we need to consider what's truly important to us. Not just in terms of career or location, but in terms of our relationship and what we need from each other."

Ethan looked at me, his expression thoughtful. "What do you mean?"

"I mean," I began carefully, "that we need to think about whether we're ready to face the challenges this opportunity might bring. Are we both willing to invest in this relationship, despite the obstacles? Or are we setting ourselves up for more heartache?"

His eyes met mine, and I could see the struggle within them. "I want to believe that we can make this work. But I also don't want to make promises I can't keep."

We continued to talk, exploring every facet of our situation with an honesty that was both painful and liberating. It became clear that while we both wanted to fight for our relationship, we also needed to be realistic about the sacrifices we might have to make.

As we wrapped up our conversation, the weight of our decisions seemed to hang in the air like the autumn mist around us. We had come to a tentative understanding, a commitment to work through our issues with patience and empathy. It wasn't a resolution, but it was a start—a promise to keep communicating and to face our challenges together, no matter how daunting they seemed.

When we finally stood up to leave, Ethan's hand lingered in mine, his touch a reassuring reminder of the connection we shared. The path ahead was uncertain, but for now, we had decided to move forward with hope and determination.

As I watched him walk away, the cold night air biting at my cheeks, I felt a mixture of sadness and resolve. We were on the brink of a significant decision, one that would shape the future of our relationship. But despite the obstacles, I held on to the belief that our love was worth fighting for.

Days turned into weeks, and the reality of Ethan's impending relocation began to settle like an unwelcome shadow over our days together. We both tried to maintain a sense of normalcy, but the weight of his departure loomed ever larger, like a storm cloud waiting to burst. Our conversations, once filled with shared laughter and future dreams, now often circled back to the logistics of his move and the uncertainty it brought.

One rainy afternoon, as the city streets glistened under a heavy downpour, I found myself sitting alone at a café, the scent of freshly brewed coffee mingling with the sound of raindrops tapping against the window. The warmth inside was a stark contrast to the cold unease I felt. I flipped through a book I had been reading, but my mind was too restless to focus. Each page felt like a reminder of the time slipping away, each turn a silent echo of the conversations Ethan and I had shared about our future.

Ethan had been busy preparing for his relocation, his days filled with meetings and packing. It was a whirlwind that left little room for us to sit down and truly address the emotional distance growing between us. When he had a free moment, he would call or text, but the brief exchanges often felt like band-aids over a wound that needed more attention.

I couldn't help but feel that we were drifting apart, even as we tried to stay connected. It was as if the distance was pulling us in opposite directions, testing the strength of our rekindled relationship. I missed the ease of our earlier conversations, the spontaneity and warmth that once defined our time together. Now, every discussion felt like a negotiation, a balancing act between hope and reality.

One evening, after a particularly strained conversation, Ethan suggested we meet at a local park, hoping that the change in environment might help us reconnect. I agreed, though I was apprehensive, unsure of what to expect or whether we could bridge the emotional gap that had widened between us.

The park was quiet, bathed in the soft glow of the setting sun. We walked along the familiar path, the crunch of leaves underfoot a soothing backdrop to our uneasy silence. Ethan reached for my hand, and I hesitated for a moment before intertwining my fingers with his. It felt comforting, yet surreal, given the heaviness of our situation.

"I've been thinking a lot about us," Ethan began, his voice breaking the silence. "About what we want and what we're willing to sacrifice."

I nodded, squeezing his hand gently. "Me too. I think about it all the time. I just don't know how we're supposed to handle everything."

He stopped walking and turned to face me, his expression earnest. "I know this isn't easy. And I know I've been so focused on this opportunity that I haven't fully grasped how hard this is for you. I want us to make it through this, but I also need to understand what you need from me."

My heart ached at his words, and I took a deep breath before speaking. "I need you to be present, even if you're physically far away. I need to feel like we're working through this together, not just navigating it on our own."

Ethan's eyes softened, and he pulled me into a hug. "I'm sorry, Mia. I've been so caught up in the logistics and the excitement of the opportunity that I haven't paid enough attention to what we're going through."

We stood there for a moment, wrapped in each other's arms, finding solace in the embrace. The tension between us seemed to ease, if only temporarily, as we shared this quiet, intimate space. It was a reminder of the connection we still had, even amidst the chaos and uncertainty.

As we walked back to the car, the weight of our conversation lingered, but there was a renewed sense of understanding. We knew that we had to confront the challenges ahead with honesty and commitment. Our relationship, though tested by unexpected obstacles, was still worth fighting for.

We made a pact to communicate more openly, to support each other through the difficulties, and to find ways to bridge the physical distance with emotional closeness. It wasn't a perfect solution, but it was a step toward navigating the complexities of our situation.

In the weeks that followed, we did our best to honor our promise. Ethan's calls became more frequent, and we made a point to share our daily experiences and support each other's goals. The distance remained a challenge, but we found solace in the small moments of connection, the shared laughter, and the understanding that we were both working towards a future together.

The road ahead was still uncertain, but we faced it with a renewed sense of hope and determination. Our love, though tested by unexpected obstacles, continued to grow stronger as we navigated the complexities of our renewed relationship.

The days stretched out like a canvas, each one painted with the vibrant hues of our hopes and fears. The distance between Ethan and me, though daunting, was now marked by a new rhythm—a series of late-night calls and heartfelt messages that bridged the gap left by his relocation. The quiet of my apartment became the backdrop to our nightly rituals, where our voices became a lifeline, each conversation a thread weaving us closer despite the miles that lay between us.

Our phone calls often started with mundane updates, small snippets of daily life that were shared like treasures. Ethan would describe the architecture of his temporary city, his words painting pictures of streets and buildings that I would never see. I'd recount the rhythm of my days, the small triumphs and the quiet moments of solitude. It was in these exchanges, where the ordinary became extraordinary, that I found comfort. Each shared story, each laugh over a forgotten detail, built a bridge that spanned the physical divide between us.

But as the weeks wore on, the challenges of separation began to test our resolve. Ethan faced demanding projects and long hours, while I wrestled with the weight of our situation and the longing for his presence. Our conversations sometimes drifted into the realm of frustration, a natural byproduct of missing each other's company. Yet, even in these moments of tension, there was an underlying current of support and understanding.

One particular evening stands out in my memory. I had spent the day grappling with a new chapter in my book, struggling to capture the emotions I felt so deeply but found hard to articulate. I was on the brink of frustration when Ethan's call came through, his voice a soothing balm to my weary spirit.

"Hey, how's the writing going?" he asked, his tone gentle, aware of the struggles I had shared with him.

I sighed, a mix of exhaustion and relief escaping me. "It's been a rough day. I can't seem to find the right words. It's like I'm trying to catch smoke with my bare hands."

There was a pause on the other end, and then Ethan spoke, his voice filled with empathy. "I know how that feels. It's like being stuck in a fog, trying to navigate through it. But remember, you've faced these challenges before, and you've always found a way through. I believe in you."

His words were a small beacon of light in my darkened creative space. We talked about the story I was working on, and he offered encouragement and perspective that I hadn't been able to see on my own. Our conversation shifted from my writing struggles to his own experiences, and the exchange of support was reciprocal, each of us bolstering the other through our respective challenges.

The power of these late-night talks lay not only in the advice or the comfort they provided but also in the mere act of being present for each other. Even from afar, we managed to create a space where we could share our burdens and our triumphs, a virtual sanctuary where our love and support remained unwavering.

Yet, as our separation stretched into months, we faced new hurdles. The physical absence began to manifest in ways we hadn't anticipated. The longing for shared experiences—the simple joys of a morning coffee together or the comfort of a familiar embrace—became more pronounced. We navigated these emotions with a mix of determination and vulnerability, knowing that our commitment to each other was being tested in ways we had never imagined.

There were nights when the loneliness felt overwhelming, and days when the distance seemed almost unbearable. During these moments, we leaned on our established routines—our nightly calls, our shared playlists, and the heartfelt messages that bridged the gap between us. We learned to find solace in these rituals, drawing strength from the consistency they provided in our otherwise turbulent lives.

Despite the challenges, there was a profound realization that began to take root within us: our love had evolved, and so had our understanding of what it meant to be truly supportive. We discovered that support wasn't just about being there in the moments of joy but also about standing strong through the trials and uncertainties. Our love had to be resilient, adaptable, and patient, qualities that would sustain us through the inevitable hurdles of life.

In this new chapter of our relationship, the power of support became a cornerstone. It was in the quiet understanding, the shared laughter, and the unwavering faith in each other's dreams that we found the strength to endure. We learned that even in the face of separation, our bond could withstand the pressures and trials. And as we continued to navigate this phase of our relationship, we did so with a renewed appreciation for the depth of our connection and the strength that came from supporting each other, no matter the distance.

The echoes of our conversations became a constant presence in my life. Late into the night, the sound of Ethan's voice would wrap around me like a warm blanket, soothing the loneliness that crept into my quiet apartment. His words, both encouraging and tender, reminded me of the strength we drew from each other. Each call was a lifeline, a thread pulling us closer despite the miles that stretched between us.

One particularly poignant evening stands out vividly. I had just finished a grueling day at work, my mind weighed down by the demands of a project that seemed never-ending. I was tangled in a web of stress and exhaustion when Ethan's call came through. His voice, always a balm for my weary soul, was infused with a gentle concern that softened my defenses.

"How was your day?" he asked, his tone light but carrying an undercurrent of genuine interest.

I leaned back against the cushions of my couch, allowing myself a rare moment of vulnerability. "It was overwhelming," I admitted, my voice tinged with fatigue. "I'm juggling so many things right now, and it feels like I'm drowning."

There was a brief silence on the other end, and then Ethan's voice came through, steady and reassuring. "I'm sorry you're going through this. But remember, you've faced tough times before and come out stronger. I know you can handle this too."

His words were a soothing balm to my frayed nerves. We spoke at length about my frustrations and the intricacies of my workload. Ethan listened with a patience that felt almost like a physical embrace, his presence palpable even through the miles. In the midst of our conversation, he shared stories of his own challenges, his honesty about the difficulties he faced offering me a glimpse into his world. It was in these exchanges that our connection deepened, as we found solace in each other's struggles.

The separation, though painful, became a crucible for our relationship. We were tested not just by the physical distance but by the emotional and psychological toll it took on us. Our commitment was repeatedly examined by the pressures of our individual lives. Yet, through it all, we discovered a new depth to our bond.

One evening, as we exchanged our daily updates, Ethan's voice held a note of excitement. "I've been working on this new project," he began, his enthusiasm evident. "It's been challenging but rewarding. I'm really proud of how it's coming along."

His pride was infectious, and I felt a surge of happiness for him, tempered by the ache of missing him. "That sounds amazing," I replied, trying to picture his world through the snippets he shared. "I wish I could be there to see it in person."

We continued to talk about his project, and I found myself swept up in his excitement. It was these moments of shared joy, even from afar, that reminded us of why we had embarked on this journey together. Our conversations became a dance of mutual support, a testament to the strength of our connection.

As the weeks passed, our relationship evolved. The physical distance became less of an obstacle and more of a testament to our resilience. We learned to navigate the complexities of our individual lives while maintaining a sense of unity. The late-night calls became a cherished ritual, a reminder of the love that continued to thrive despite the challenges.

Yet, the strain of separation was not without its toll. There were nights when the ache of missing Ethan was almost unbearable, and moments when the reality of our situation felt overwhelming. We faced these feelings with a blend of honesty and determination, knowing that our love had to be strong enough to weather these storms.

Our support for each other was not just a series of comforting words but a tangible presence that gave us strength. We became adept at finding solace in each other's successes and providing comfort during times of struggle. Our commitment to making the relationship work became a shared mission, a testament to the love that had endured so much.

Through it all, we discovered that the true power of support lay in the everyday acts of understanding and encouragement. It was in the late-night conversations that bridged the gap, the shared moments of vulnerability, and the unwavering faith we had in each other. Our love was not just a feeling but a constant, evolving presence that carried us through the challenges of life.

In the end, the physical distance, though challenging, became a testament to the strength of our bond. We realized that our love could withstand the hurdles life threw at us, and our commitment to each other remained steadfast. The power of support became a cornerstone of our relationship, a reminder that even in the face of adversity, our love had the strength to endure and flourish.

The power of support is often revealed in the quiet moments, the ones that might seem mundane but are steeped in meaning. As the days turned into weeks, Ethan and I found ourselves navigating this long-distance chapter with a blend of resilience and affection that surprised even us. Each call, each message, became a testament to the strength of our bond.

One evening, as the golden light of sunset faded into the twilight of my room, I found myself sinking into an armchair with a sigh. My day had been exhausting, filled with an unrelenting string of deadlines and meetings that seemed to stretch into infinity. I clutched my phone in my hand, feeling the comforting weight of its familiarity. When Ethan's name flashed on the screen, a rush of warmth spread through me.

"Hey," I said, my voice carrying the fatigue of the day. "How's everything over there?"

His laughter came through, light and easy, as though no distance could ever dampen his spirit. "It's been a rollercoaster, but I'm hanging in there. I just got done with a presentation that went surprisingly well. How about you?"

I let out a small, relieved chuckle. "I'm surviving. Work is just... a lot right now. But hearing your voice makes it all a bit better."

We talked about everything and nothing, the conversation meandering through the details of our lives as if to stitch together the fragments of our shared experiences. There was something profoundly comforting about these calls—an unspoken agreement that no matter what happened in our separate worlds, this connection remained a constant.

Ethan's support extended beyond the confines of our conversations. He would send little reminders of his affection—a playlist of songs that reminded him of us, or a photograph of a sunset he thought I'd enjoy. These small gestures were like breadcrumbs leading me back to the warmth of our shared moments. They became a way of reminding each other that no matter how far apart we were, our hearts remained intertwined.

There were nights when the silence felt overwhelmingly heavy, a stark contrast to the vibrant conversations we'd had earlier. During these times, I would open up the messages Ethan had sent me, reading and re-reading them like cherished letters. Each word was a balm for my loneliness, a reminder that we were still very much a part of each other's lives.

One night, after a particularly tough day, I found myself staring at the ceiling, unable to shake off the weight of my worries. Ethan called, his voice breaking through the fog of my thoughts. "I'm here," he said simply. "I know it's late, but I just wanted to check in. How are you really holding up?"

His sincerity cut through the layers of my emotional armor. I told him about the stress I was under, the doubts that had crept into my mind. And as I spoke, I could hear the quiet intensity in his voice, the way he absorbed my concerns and responded with unwavering support.

"I wish I could be there with you," he said. "But even from here, I want you to know that I believe in you. You're stronger than you think, and I'm so proud of everything you're doing."

In those moments, the distance felt a little less daunting. Ethan's words became a lifeline, a reassurance that no matter how challenging things seemed, we were in this together. His ability to offer comfort and encouragement, even from afar, underscored the depth of our commitment to each other.

Our relationship was tested by the physical separation, but it also revealed the depth of our emotional connection. We learned to navigate the complexities of our individual challenges while holding on to the shared dreams and aspirations that had once united us. The late-night phone calls, the heartfelt messages—they were more than just ways to stay in touch. They were a testament to the strength of our bond, a reminder that even in the face of adversity, love could be a source of incredible resilience.

As the weeks continued, we grew more adept at balancing the demands of our separate lives with the need to nurture our relationship. We celebrated each other's successes and supported each other through difficulties, finding solace in the knowledge that our love could endure the trials of distance.

The separation, while challenging, became a testament to our dedication and the power of our support for one another. We faced each obstacle with a sense of unity, knowing that our love was strong enough to withstand the hurdles that life presented. In the end, it was not just about surviving the distance but thriving in the knowledge that our love was a source of unwavering strength and support.

# Chapter 10: A Family Reunion

When Ethan's plane touched down, a rush of anticipation mingled with a swirl of nerves. The few weeks apart had been a test of our resolve, but the promise of this reunion, of seeing him again after such a stretch of separation, felt like a balm for both our hearts. The family event—a wedding, vibrant and alive with tradition—was the perfect setting for us to reconnect, yet it was also fraught with the complexities of familial expectations and long-standing dynamics.

The day before the wedding, I found myself pacing in the soft light of my living room, the echoes of Ethan's last voicemail still fresh in my mind. He had sounded excited, his voice tinged with a mixture of eagerness and trepidation, as he prepared to immerse himself in a whirlwind of family activities. As much as I looked forward to our reunion, I knew that this gathering would be a delicate balancing act.

When Ethan finally walked through the door, the world seemed to momentarily pause. His smile was familiar, but it had a new, softer edge that spoke of our time apart and the journey we had shared. As he took me into his arms, I felt the weight of the last few weeks lift, replaced by the warmth of his embrace. It was as if we were rewriting the script of our reunion with every touch, every glance, reclaiming the intimacy that had been put on hold.

The family event was a kaleidoscope of colors and sounds, a whirlwind of bustling relatives, shared laughter, and clinking glasses. Ethan's family welcomed me with open arms, their hospitality a testament to their warmth and inclusiveness. Yet, beneath the surface of the joyful chaos, there was an undercurrent of scrutiny, a subtle pressure to fit seamlessly into the intricate web of their lives.

As the wedding progressed, I found myself drawn into conversations with Ethan's relatives, their questions and comments weaving through the night like threads in a tapestry. Each interaction was a delicate dance, a way of bridging the gap between my Southern upbringing and Ethan's Mexican heritage. I listened intently, absorbing the stories and traditions that formed the backbone of Ethan's world. In return, I shared snippets of my own life, striving to present a version of myself that harmonized with the vibrant mosaic around me.

Ethan was by my side, offering support with a reassuring smile and a gentle hand on my back. His presence was a constant source of comfort, a reminder that despite the differences in our backgrounds, we were united by something deeper. We navigated the evening together, our conversations flowing between the old and the new, between shared memories and the excitement of what lay ahead.

The true test came during the reception, when a particularly probing question from a distant relative sparked an unexpected moment of tension. "So, how long have you two been together?" she asked, her eyes narrowing as she scrutinized us. "I've heard so much about you, but it's nice to finally put a face to the name."

Ethan's hand tightened around mine, a silent reassurance that we were in this together. I met her gaze with a composed smile, aware of the undercurrent of curiosity that accompanied her question. "We've been working on reconnecting," I replied, choosing my words with care. "It's been a journey, but it's been worth every step."

The conversation shifted, but the moment lingered in the air, a reminder of the scrutiny we faced as we redefined our relationship in the context of family expectations. Despite the occasional awkward encounter, the evening proved to be a testament to our resilience. We danced, laughed, and enjoyed the celebration, finding solace in the fact that we were facing these challenges together.

As the night drew to a close, Ethan and I found a quiet corner away from the din of the party. The soft glow of the moonlight cast a serene light on our faces, and for a moment, it felt as though the world had narrowed down to just the two of us. We spoke softly, sharing our thoughts about the evening and the way we had navigated the complexities of family dynamics.

"I think we did well," Ethan said, his voice filled with a mixture of relief and contentment. "It wasn't easy, but we made it through."

I nodded, my heart full as I looked at him. "We did. And it's moments like these that remind me why we're doing this. It's not just about us; it's about creating something lasting and meaningful."

The reunion had been a mix of joy and challenge, a blend of old traditions and new beginnings. It reinforced our feelings for each other and offered a glimpse into what our future could hold. As we walked hand in hand, the weight of the evening's complexities seemed to lift, replaced by a renewed sense of hope and connection.

The family reunion had been a crucible, testing our ability to blend our lives, our cultures, and our dreams. Yet, it had also shown us the depth of our commitment and the strength of our love. Together, we faced the challenges of blending our worlds and emerged more united, more determined to build a future that honored both our pasts and our shared aspirations.

The morning of the family event dawned crisp and clear, with the kind of early sunlight that seemed to promise new beginnings. As I dressed for the occasion, my heart fluttered with a mix of excitement and apprehension. I wanted to make a good impression, to bridge the gap between my Southern roots and Ethan's vibrant Mexican heritage. Yet, there was an undeniable weight in knowing that today wasn't just about reuniting with Ethan; it was also about integrating into a world that had always felt just out of reach.

Ethan arrived early, his presence a comforting anchor amidst the whirlwind of preparations. His smile was a beacon of reassurance as we prepared to face the gathering. His family's home was alive with the scent of traditional dishes, the warm clamor of voices, and the hum of joyful chaos. It was a world both foreign and familiar, a beautiful tapestry of cultures woven together.

As the first guests trickled in, Ethan's family greeted me with open arms, their hospitality both gracious and overwhelming. I was introduced to a whirlwind of faces, each with its own unique story and flavor. It was a world of vibrant colors and spirited conversations, and while I tried to keep pace, I found myself occasionally retreating to the periphery, overwhelmed by the sheer volume of it all.

The wedding ceremony was a symphony of tradition, each moment steeped in meaning and cultural significance. The vows exchanged were not just promises but echoes of the values and beliefs that had shaped Ethan's family for generations. I watched, captivated, as the bride and groom sealed their commitment with rituals that spoke of love, respect, and unity.

Amidst the grandeur of the ceremony, Ethan remained by my side, offering quiet support with every step. His hand in mine was a constant reminder that we were navigating this together. Even as I marveled at the beauty of the event, I could feel the undercurrent of expectation, the subtle pressures that came with being the "outsider" in a tightly-knit family.

Dinner was a feast of sensory delights, with dishes that told stories of heritage and tradition. I found solace in the flavors, in the way food could bridge gaps between cultures. Yet, there were moments when I felt the weight of unspoken judgments, the curious glances that seemed to assess my place within this rich tapestry.

In the midst of this whirlwind, Ethan's family showed their warmth and genuine interest. His mother's kindness was a balm for my nerves, her gentle questions and shared stories offering a glimpse into the heart of her family. As we conversed, I began to see the threads that connected us, the shared values that transcended our different backgrounds. It was in these quiet moments of connection that I felt a shift, a growing sense of belonging.

As the evening wore on, the celebrations continued with the energy and vibrancy characteristic of Ethan's family. Music filled the air, and the dance floor became a riot of movement and laughter. Ethan pulled me into the throng, guiding me through the steps of traditional dances. His laughter was infectious, his joy evident as he twirled me around the floor. I felt a surge of happiness, a fleeting sense of freedom amidst the whirl of cultural immersion.

Yet, the night wasn't without its challenges. Conversations with some family members became moments of quiet tension, as if I were a puzzle piece struggling to fit into a pre-existing framework. The weight of their expectations and the challenge of bridging our cultural differences felt tangible, a reminder of the complexities of our shared journey.

As the night drew to a close, Ethan and I slipped away to the quiet of the garden, away from the clamor of the festivities. The moonlight cast a soft glow on the surrounding flowers, and the serenity offered a moment of respite from the day's intensity. We sat together on a secluded bench, the cool night air a soothing contrast to the warmth of the evening.

"It was... a lot," I said, my voice tinged with exhaustion and reflection. "I felt like I was constantly trying to find my footing."

Ethan took my hand in his, his touch gentle and reassuring. "I know it wasn't easy. I'm proud of you for handling it with such grace. It's not always simple to navigate these worlds."

I looked at him, the depth of my feelings evident in the soft light of the moon. "I want to be a part of your world, Ethan. I want to understand and connect. But sometimes, it feels like I'm struggling to fit in."

Ethan's eyes were filled with understanding, his expression a mixture of empathy and resolve. "We'll get through this, together. It's not about fitting into a mold but about creating something new from the pieces we have. Our love is strong enough to bridge these gaps."

In that quiet, moonlit moment, the weight of the evening seemed to lift. Our conversation was a balm for the day's trials, a testament to the strength of our connection. We sat in silence, finding solace in each other's presence, our hearts aligned despite the challenges we faced.

The family reunion had been a blend of joy and tension, a reminder of the complexities that came with blending lives and cultures. Yet, as Ethan and I faced these challenges together, we found a renewed sense of commitment and understanding. The night had been a test of our resolve, but it had also offered a glimpse into the future we could build—a future where our love could overcome any obstacle, where we could create a shared life that honored both our pasts and our dreams.

The next morning, the world felt quieter, the echoes of the previous night's celebrations softened by the gentle hush of dawn. Ethan and I had spent the night reflecting on the event, our conversation flowing easily in the comfort of our shared space. Now, as the first light filtered through the curtains, we found ourselves enveloped in a new kind of anticipation.

Ethan's parents had invited us for breakfast, a gesture that carried its own weight of significance. The morning sun painted the kitchen in warm hues, and the aroma of freshly brewed coffee mingled with the scent of pastries and fruit. The atmosphere was relaxed, and there was a sense of calm that contrasted with the whirlwind of the previous day.

We settled around the table, and as we ate, Ethan's parents exchanged stories of their own experiences with blending cultures, their words laced with humor and warmth. It was clear that they had faced their own share of challenges and triumphs, and their openness made the morning feel like a bridge between our worlds. I listened intently, feeling a growing connection not just to Ethan but to the family that had welcomed me with such grace.

The conversation drifted from lighthearted anecdotes to deeper discussions about traditions and values. Ethan's father spoke of the importance of family gatherings, of how they served as a touchstone for their shared history and collective identity. His mother shared her love for cooking, explaining how each dish was a homage to their heritage, a way to pass down stories through recipes.

I found myself drawn into their world, feeling less like an outsider and more like a participant in something beautiful and profound. The morning felt like a turning point, a moment where the pieces of our lives began to align in a way that was both comforting and inspiring. As I engaged in conversation, I could see the pride in Ethan's eyes, the way he looked at his parents with admiration and love. It was a reminder of the values that had shaped him, and it made me appreciate the depth of the family bond even more.

After breakfast, Ethan and I took a walk through the garden, the soft morning light casting a gentle glow on the blooming flowers and lush greenery. We talked about the night before, reflecting on the highs and lows, and began to envision what our future together might look like. The serenity of the garden offered a stark contrast to the intensity of the family gathering, and it allowed us to dream without the weight of expectations.

"I feel like we've made progress," Ethan said, his voice filled with a hopeful undertone. "Last night was challenging, but it also showed us how much we can grow together."

I nodded, feeling a sense of contentment. "It was a lot to take in, but I think we're stronger for it. There's something really special about the way we're blending our worlds."

Ethan took my hand, his touch a reassuring promise. "We're building something beautiful, and every step we take brings us closer to something amazing."

As we continued our walk, I felt a renewed sense of purpose. The challenges we faced were real, but so was the strength of our commitment to each other. The family reunion had been a test, but it was also an opportunity to see the depth of our love and the potential for a future where our lives and cultures could intertwine in harmony.

The day unfolded with a blend of relaxation and reflection. We spent time exploring the local area, sharing stories and experiences, and enjoying the simple pleasure of each other's company. The quiet moments we shared allowed us to connect on a deeper level, to appreciate the journey we had been on and the path that lay ahead.

As the day drew to a close, Ethan and I found ourselves back in the garden, the setting sun casting a warm glow over the landscape. We sat together, the tranquility of the evening offering a moment of peace and introspection.

"This weekend has been a whirlwind," I said softly, leaning into Ethan's embrace. "But it's also been a reminder of why we're doing this. Why we're fighting for us."

Ethan's arms tightened around me, his presence a steady anchor. "It's been a beautiful, challenging journey, and I wouldn't want to go through it with anyone else. We're making something incredible together."

In the quiet of the evening, as the stars began to appear in the sky, I felt a profound sense of gratitude. The family reunion had tested us, but it had also strengthened our bond, offering a glimpse into the future we could build. It was a reminder that love, while sometimes complicated, was always worth fighting for. And as we faced the challenges of blending our lives, I knew that our love was resilient enough to withstand anything that came our way.

The night ended with a sense of accomplishment and hope, the promise of a future filled with possibilities. Ethan and I had faced the trials of the family reunion, and in doing so, we had discovered a deeper understanding of each other and our shared dreams. The journey ahead was still uncertain, but the strength of our connection and the support of our families gave us the confidence to embrace whatever came next.

# Chapter 11: Taking a Leap

The crisp evening air wrapped around us as we sat on the balcony, the city lights below shimmering like stars fallen to earth. Ethan and I had spent the day in thoughtful silence, our conversations filtered through layers of meaning, yet unspoken. Now, as we looked out over the horizon, the weight of our decision hung heavily between us.

Our relationship, once rekindled, had navigated its share of trials. The blend of joy and tension from the family reunion had underscored the complexity of our situation. Each challenge seemed to draw us closer, yet also reveal the fragile threads upon which our love rested. We had come so far, but now faced the ultimate question: Was this love worth the leap?

Ethan's voice broke the stillness, a soft murmur against the backdrop of the bustling city below. "Do you ever wonder if we're chasing something impossible?" His question was tinged with vulnerability, a stark contrast to his usually confident demeanor.

I turned to face him, the moonlight casting a gentle glow on his features. "All the time," I admitted, my voice trembling slightly. "It's hard not to, when every decision feels like it could make or break us."

His hand reached for mine, our fingers intertwining with a familiarity that spoke of both comfort and concern. "We've been through so much, and every step forward feels like a risk. But is it worth taking if it means we could truly have a future together?"

The question lingered, echoing the internal struggle that had been building within me. Our journey had been one of rediscovery, of navigating the intricacies of our past and present. Yet, as we faced the future, the uncertainty loomed large. Could we commit to each other fully, despite the challenges that lay ahead?

I looked at Ethan, seeing the reflection of my own doubts and hopes in his eyes. "I think about the risks every day," I said softly. "But

I also think about how we've grown. We've learned so much about ourselves and each other. Maybe it's not just about whether we take a leap, but about whether we can trust ourselves to land safely."

Ethan's expression softened, and he leaned closer, his forehead resting gently against mine. "We've been through the fire, and we've come out stronger. I believe in us, but I also know that believing isn't always enough. We have to decide if we're willing to put everything on the line for this."

In the quiet of the evening, I could feel the gravity of our decision pressing against my chest. The idea of taking a leap was both exhilarating and terrifying. It meant embracing the unknown, committing to a future that was still shrouded in uncertainty. But it also meant acknowledging the depth of our feelings and the strength of our bond.

We had faced so many obstacles—family dynamics, cultural differences, career challenges—and each had tested us in its own way. Yet, here we were, standing on the brink of something profound, ready to decide if we were willing to risk it all for a chance at something truly meaningful.

As the night deepened, the city lights below seemed to pulse with a rhythm that mirrored our own hearts. I took a deep breath, summoning the courage to voice the thoughts that had been swirling in my mind.

"I want to take the leap," I said, my voice steady despite the tremor in my heart. "I want to believe in us, in what we have, and in what we can build together. I know it's risky, but I can't imagine facing the future without you."

Ethan's eyes met mine, a mix of relief and determination shining through. "I want that too," he said softly. "I'm willing to take the risk if it means we can create something beautiful out of this. We've come so far, and I believe we can face whatever comes next."

As we held each other close, the weight of our decision felt lighter, the path forward illuminated by the strength of our commitment. The leap we were about to take was not just about our relationship; it was about embracing the possibility of a future where our love could flourish.

In the stillness of the night, as the city below continued its relentless pulse, Ethan and I found solace in the certainty of our choice. We were ready to embrace the uncertainties, to face the challenges with open hearts and unwavering resolve. The leap we were taking was not just a risk; it was a testament to our belief in each other and in the future we could create together.

The decision was made, and with it came a renewed sense of hope and purpose. We were ready to face whatever lay ahead, knowing that the strength of our love would guide us through the uncertainties. As we looked out over the horizon, we knew that our journey was just beginning, and we were ready to take the leap, hand in hand, into the future we had always dreamed of.

The days following our balcony conversation were filled with a mixture of anticipation and anxiety. Every moment seemed to echo the gravity of our decision. Ethan and I navigated our daily lives with a newfound sense of purpose, but the looming question of our future loomed larger with each passing day. It was as though we were suspended in a moment of waiting, caught between what was and what could be.

The weight of our decision was never far from our minds, and it cast a shadow over the moments that were meant to be light and carefree. We spent evenings walking through the city, sharing quiet conversations that drifted from mundane to meaningful. Each touch, each glance held more significance as we wrestled with the choice before us. The playful banter we once shared seemed to have given way to a more somber, reflective dialogue, as if we were trying to unearth the truth beneath the surface.

One particularly crisp autumn afternoon, we found ourselves in a cozy café that seemed to embrace us with its warmth. The gentle hum of conversations and the scent of freshly brewed coffee created a soothing backdrop as we sat across from each other, our hands entwined on the table. We had decided to take a break from the weighty discussions and simply enjoy each other's company, but the conversation inevitably turned back to the future.

"What if we're making a mistake?" Ethan's voice was tinged with uncertainty, a stark contrast to the usual confidence he exuded. His gaze was fixed on the steaming cup of coffee, as if the answer might appear within its depths.

I reached across the table, gently squeezing his hand. "Sometimes, it's hard to know if we're making the right choice. But I think what matters most is that we're making it together. We've faced so much already, and I believe that's what has brought us to this point."

His eyes met mine, a flicker of hope amidst the doubt. "I want this, I want us. But the fear of the unknown is paralyzing. What if we can't handle it? What if we end up hurting each other more than we already have?"

I took a deep breath, choosing my words carefully. "Every relationship has its challenges, and we've learned that love isn't always easy. But we've also learned that facing those challenges together makes us stronger. We've grown so much since we first began this journey. Maybe the leap isn't about knowing everything will be perfect; maybe it's about trusting that we can handle whatever comes our way."

Ethan's gaze softened, and a small, contemplative smile curved his lips. "You're right. We've been through so much, and we've managed to come out stronger. Maybe the leap of faith is less about knowing what will happen and more about believing in ourselves and in each other."

The conversation lingered in the air as we finished our coffee, the decision hanging between us like a fragile thread. We both knew that taking this leap was more than a mere decision—it was an act of trust, a commitment to face the unknown with the assurance that we were not alone.

As the days turned into weeks, the decision to take the leap began to take shape. Our discussions became less about what-ifs and more about how we could build a future together. We talked about our dreams, our fears, and the steps we needed to take to make our relationship work. The process was both exhilarating and exhausting, as we grappled with the reality of our commitment.

We began to envision a future where our love could thrive despite the uncertainties. We made plans, discussed potential challenges, and worked on strengthening the foundation of our relationship. Every step we took felt like a testament to our dedication, a promise that we were ready to face whatever came our way.

One evening, as we walked through the park, the crisp air and the soft glow of the streetlights creating a serene atmosphere, I looked at Ethan and felt a deep sense of clarity. "I'm ready to take this leap with you," I said softly. "I believe in us, and I believe that we can build something beautiful together."

Ethan's eyes were filled with a mix of relief and resolve. "I'm ready too," he replied, his voice steady. "We've come so far, and I believe that we can create a future that's worth every leap we take."

As we held hands and walked through the park, the decision felt like a shared journey, a commitment to facing the future with courage and hope. The leap we were about to take was not just a risk; it was a celebration of our love and our belief in each other. And as we moved forward, we did so with the assurance that we were ready to embrace the uncertainties and create a future filled with promise and possibility.

Our decision to embrace the leap of faith was not immediate; it was a culmination of whispered promises, late-night confessions, and moments of profound clarity. It came during a quiet evening at home, when the weight of our conversations settled into a comfortable silence. We had spent the day sorting through the reality of our choices, discussing every possible outcome and exploring our deepest fears. The complexity of our situation had never felt so real, yet it also felt more manageable in the calm of that moment.

Ethan stood by the window, the soft light casting a warm glow across his face. The city lights below twinkled like distant stars, a reflection of the countless dreams we had shared. I watched him, the reflection of our relationship mingling with the view outside. The room seemed to hum with the quiet intensity of our decision.

"You know," Ethan began, his voice breaking the silence, "sometimes I wonder if we're making the right choice. I look at everything we've been through and think, are we really prepared for this?"

I walked over to him, resting my hand gently on his arm. "It's natural to have doubts. Every leap comes with uncertainty. But I think we've reached a point where our love and our commitment are stronger than the fear of the unknown."

He turned to face me, his eyes searching mine for reassurance. "I keep thinking about what we'll be leaving behind and what we'll be moving towards. It's a big step."

"It is," I agreed, my heart swelling with affection. "But isn't that what makes it worth taking? We've built so much together, and I believe that this leap is just another step in our journey. We've faced so much already, and I trust that we can handle whatever comes next."

Ethan's expression softened, and he took a deep breath, as though releasing the last of his apprehensions. "You're right. We've already proven that we can overcome challenges. Maybe this leap isn't about having all the answers. Maybe it's about trusting ourselves and each other enough to take the plunge."

In that moment, the tension that had been building between us seemed to dissolve. We stood together, united in our resolve. The decision had been made not out of certainty, but out of a shared belief in our potential. We had reached a point where the risk of parting ways seemed less daunting than the possibility of not trying at all.

Our commitment to each other was not a grand gesture but a quiet understanding, a promise made in the stillness of the night. It was about acknowledging the risks and embracing the rewards, about accepting that love, in its truest form, requires faith and courage. As we prepared to take this leap, we were not simply moving towards an unknown future but stepping into a space where we could fully embrace our second chance at love.

The days that followed were filled with a renewed sense of purpose. We began to make plans with a clarity that came from our decision. There were still moments of doubt, but they were overshadowed by the strength of our commitment. Our conversations became less about what-ifs and more about how we could make our dreams a reality. We focused on the steps we needed to take to build our future, and every small achievement felt like a victory.

We faced the practicalities of our decision with a mixture of excitement and trepidation. There were discussions about moving, adjustments to our daily routines, and the inevitable challenges that came with change. Yet, despite the hurdles, there was an underlying sense of optimism that carried us through. We found joy in the process of planning and preparing, knowing that each step brought us closer to the life we envisioned together.

Our leap of faith was not just a test of our relationship but a testament to the strength of our bond. It was a celebration of our love and a recognition of the growth we had experienced. The journey ahead was still uncertain, but we faced it with the confidence that came from our shared commitment.

As we stood on the threshold of our new chapter, the future stretched out before us like an open road. It was a path we were ready to walk together, hand in hand, facing whatever lay ahead with hope and determination. The leap we had taken was more than just a decision; it was a declaration of our love and our belief in each other.

In the end, the leap was not just about the destination but about the journey we had shared and the commitment we had made. It was about embracing the unknown with a heart full of hope and a spirit ready to face the challenges. And as we moved forward, we did so with the confidence that our love was strong enough to overcome any obstacle, and that our second chance at love was worth every leap we took.

# Chapter 12: New Beginnings

As we stand on the brink of this new chapter, the world around us seems to hold its breath, waiting to see if we will truly make this leap of faith. The decision to fully commit to each other is exhilarating and terrifying in equal measure. The anticipation of blending our lives into a shared existence pulses with both hope and anxiety. We have chosen to embrace the future together, and now, every step we take is both a discovery and a challenge.

The first few months of our renewed relationship are a whirlwind of emotion and adjustment. We dive headfirst into the everyday intricacies of our lives, eager to build a new foundation while navigating the complexities of our different backgrounds. There is a sense of exhilaration in the air, a feeling that we are forging something entirely our own. Yet, beneath the surface, there is an undercurrent of nervousness. Each decision, each shared moment, feels weighted with the gravity of our choice.

We find ourselves caught between the thrill of new beginnings and the reality of the adjustments required to make this work. Ethan's career demands and my own commitments create a tapestry of schedules and compromises that we must navigate with care. Our days are filled with a blend of laughter and logistical challenges as we learn to balance our individual needs with the demands of our shared life.

Evenings are often spent unpacking boxes or reorganizing furniture, a tangible manifestation of our desire to create a home together. Each piece of furniture, each photograph hung on the wall, is a symbol of our commitment. The physical act of merging our spaces feels emblematic of the emotional merging of our lives. In these moments, we find joy in the small victories and solace in the simple routines we establish together.

One of the most striking aspects of our new life is the way our different backgrounds interweave into a vibrant tapestry of experiences. Ethan's Mexican heritage adds a rich layer of tradition and celebration to our daily life, while my Southern upbringing brings its own unique flavor to our routines. The blending of these two worlds is a continuous adventure. We celebrate with impromptu salsa dancing in the kitchen and enjoy Southern-style barbecues with friends. Each experience is an opportunity to learn from each other, to appreciate the beauty in our differences, and to build new traditions that are uniquely ours.

Despite the excitement of our new beginnings, there are moments of doubt and tension. The challenges we face are not always easily resolved. We grapple with the nuances of our cultural differences, and the pressures of everyday life sometimes feel overwhelming. The commitment we have made requires patience and understanding, and there are days when we question if we are truly equipped to handle the complexities of our blended lives.

Yet, in these moments of uncertainty, we find strength in each other. Our conversations become a refuge where we can voice our fears and dreams. We talk late into the night, our words a balm for the anxieties that arise. These conversations are not just about addressing immediate concerns but about reaffirming our dedication to each other. They remind us of why we took this leap in the first place and why it is worth fighting for.

Our love grows stronger with each passing day, and it is in the small, everyday moments that we find the true essence of our commitment. We discover new facets of each other's personalities and learn to navigate the ebb and flow of our emotions. The process of building our life together is not always smooth, but it is marked by a deepening understanding and an unwavering support for one another.

The joy we find in these new beginnings is palpable. There are moments of pure bliss when everything seems to fall into place, when laughter fills our home, and when we feel truly at peace in each other's presence. These moments are a testament to the strength of our love and the resilience we have cultivated.

As we continue to navigate our renewed relationship, we remain aware of the uncertainties that lie ahead. The journey is ongoing, and there are still obstacles to overcome. However, we face these challenges with a renewed sense of purpose and a shared commitment to making our relationship work. Each day is a step forward, a chance to build upon the foundation we have laid and to embrace the future with open hearts.

In the end, our new beginnings are a celebration of our love and our willingness to embrace the unknown. The leap of faith we took has led us to a place of profound connection and growth. As we move forward, we do so with a sense of excitement and anticipation, ready to face whatever the future holds together.

The morning sunlight filters through the sheer curtains, casting a warm glow over the room where Ethan and I lie tangled in the soft sheets. It's one of those rare, peaceful mornings when the world outside seems to pause, giving us a moment to simply exist together. I turn to him, my heart swelling with a mixture of love and uncertainty. Our new life together, while thrilling, is a constant dance between the joy of discovery and the reality of compromise.

The days blend into a mosaic of moments that are both ordinary and extraordinary. We wake up to the sound of the coffee maker brewing, its rich aroma filling the kitchen. Ethan, still bleary-eyed, stumbles into the kitchen with a smile that lights up his face. I watch him from the table, my heart warmed by the sight of his unfiltered, morning self. Our conversations over breakfast are easy, punctuated by laughter and the occasional comfortable silence.

Yet, beneath these everyday routines lies the delicate work of weaving our lives together. Our evenings are spent arranging furniture and unpacking boxes, each new addition to our home symbolizing another piece of the puzzle we're putting together. We debate over where to place the bookshelf, each decision a minor negotiation, each compromise a step towards understanding one another better.

Our cultural differences often emerge in the most unexpected ways. Ethan's family traditions—vibrant, passionate, and filled with rich customs—clash with my own. I find myself fascinated by his stories about the lively festivals and the elaborate meals his family prepares. At the same time, I'm learning to blend these traditions with my own quieter, more reserved Southern ways. One evening, as Ethan prepares a traditional Mexican dish, the kitchen fills with the tantalizing scent of spices. I watch him, captivated by the way he moves with confidence and ease. I offer my own Southern touch—sweet cornbread, a dish that reminds me of home. Together, our meals become a fusion of cultures, a testament to the beauty of our blended lives.

Despite the growing comfort in our shared spaces, there are moments of tension that remind us of the challenges we face. Our different backgrounds, once a source of excitement, now sometimes feel like barriers. We find ourselves caught in small misunderstandings that echo the deeper, unspoken fears we have about our future. Ethan's occasional frustration when I struggle with a new recipe or my own worries about fitting into his family's social circles reveal the cracks in our seemingly perfect picture.

But it's in these moments of friction that we find the true strength of our commitment. Our late-night conversations, where we lay bare our insecurities and dreams, become a sanctuary. We talk about everything—the future, the past, the fears that keep us awake at night. Ethan's voice, always steady and reassuring, helps to calm the storm inside me. We discuss the challenges of blending our traditions and the pressures of our individual careers. Each conversation, though sometimes difficult, reinforces our bond and our resolve to make this work.

The weekends are our sanctuary, a time when we can escape from the demands of daily life and reconnect with each other. We explore new neighborhoods, take long walks in the park, and visit local markets. These outings become our mini-adventures, a way to rediscover the city we now call home together. As we walk hand in hand through the bustling streets, our laughter mingles with the hum of city life, a testament to the joy we find in each other's company.

Even in the midst of our new routines, there are moments of profound connection that remind us why we chose to take this leap of faith. One evening, as we sit on the couch, wrapped in a blanket and watching a movie, Ethan's hand finds mine. The simple gesture, so ordinary yet so meaningful, fills me with a deep sense of contentment. It's in these quiet, intimate moments that I realize how far we've come and how much we've grown.

Our journey is still unfolding, and there are days when the weight of our decisions feels heavy. We face the uncertainty of our future with a mixture of hope and trepidation. The challenges we encounter—whether they are related to our careers, our family dynamics, or the ongoing adjustments to our life together—test our resolve and our patience. But each hurdle we overcome brings us closer, strengthening the foundation of our relationship.

The excitement of our new beginnings is tempered by the knowledge that we are building something lasting. We are creating a life together that reflects both our individual selves and our shared dreams. The road ahead is filled with both promise and uncertainty, but we face it with a renewed sense of commitment and a deepening love.

As we navigate this chapter of our lives, I am filled with gratitude for the chance to embark on this journey with Ethan. Our love, tested by time and distance, has emerged stronger and more resilient. Each day is a step towards building a future that we can both cherish and be proud of. And as we continue to weave our lives together, I am reminded that the beauty of our relationship lies not in its perfection, but in its ability to grow and evolve with each passing day.

The days stretch into weeks, and the weeks into months, as Ethan and I navigate the intricate dance of building a life together. Each morning, the world feels like a blank canvas, ready for us to paint our shared dreams upon. The early days of our renewed relationship are marked by a kind of exhilarating vulnerability, a blend of hope and apprehension as we take each step forward.

Our routines have settled into a rhythm that feels both familiar and brand new. We fall into the comforting pattern of shared meals and evenings spent in each other's company. The laughter that fills our home is a balm, soothing the occasional tension that bubbles up when our differences come into focus. Ethan's habit of leaving his shoes in the hallway meets my own need for order, a minor clash of habits that we tackle with patience and humor. It's these small, everyday moments that test our ability to adapt and compromise.

Our weekends become our sanctuary, a time when we can escape the pressures of our daily lives and reconnect. We explore new places together—charming bookstores, cozy cafes, and hidden parks that become our little havens. The city is our playground, a backdrop to our burgeoning love story. We relish these moments, finding joy in the simplicity of our shared adventures. A spontaneous road trip to a nearby town, an impromptu picnic in the park—each experience adds a layer of depth to our relationship.

Yet, beneath the surface of our new beginning lies the ongoing work of blending our lives. Ethan's family, vibrant and full of life, continues to be a source of both warmth and challenge. Their traditions are rich and lively, a stark contrast to my own more reserved Southern upbringing. The family gatherings are a tapestry of colors and sounds, a celebration of culture that can be overwhelming yet profoundly beautiful. I find myself drawn to their energy, eager to understand and embrace their ways, even as I grapple with feeling like an outsider.

The holidays become a poignant reminder of our divergent backgrounds. We spend Thanksgiving with Ethan's family, surrounded by a feast that is as much a feast for the senses as it is for the soul. The smells of traditional Mexican dishes fill the air, mingling with the aroma of turkey and stuffing. It's a beautiful chaos, a celebration of both our cultures coming together. I feel a sense of belonging, but also an undercurrent of unease as I try to navigate the complexities of fitting into a new family dynamic.

In contrast, Christmas is spent in the more subdued comfort of my own family's traditions. The familiar routines—decorating the tree, baking cookies, and exchanging gifts—offer a sense of solace. Ethan, ever the supportive partner, immerses himself in these customs, his presence a testament to his commitment to our shared life. The blending of our traditions creates a mosaic of celebrations that are uniquely ours, a testament to the strength of our love.

The emotional journey of our new beginning is not without its challenges. There are nights when doubt creeps in, whispering questions about the future and the feasibility of our dreams. We talk through these doubts with open hearts, sharing our fears and hopes. Ethan's unwavering support and understanding become the bedrock upon which we build our future. We learn to lean on each other, finding solace in the strength of our partnership.

As we move forward, the excitement of our new life is tempered by the reality of its demands. The challenge of balancing careers, personal goals, and our relationship requires constant effort and communication. We establish new routines that honor both our individual aspirations and our shared dreams. Each compromise, each adjustment, is a testament to our commitment to making this work.

There are moments of profound connection that remind us of the beauty of our journey. Sitting together on a quiet evening, sharing our thoughts and dreams, we find a deep sense of intimacy. These moments are a balm to the stresses of daily life, reinforcing the love that binds us together. It's in these quiet times that I am reminded of why we took this leap of faith, why we chose to commit to each other despite the uncertainties.

Our love story, rich with the complexities of blending lives and cultures, continues to unfold. The excitement of new beginnings is matched by the depth of our growing bond. Each day brings new challenges, but also new opportunities for connection and understanding. As we build our future together, we do so with the knowledge that our love is resilient and capable of overcoming the obstacles that come our way.

The journey of blending our lives is ongoing, but each step we take strengthens the foundation of our relationship. The love that brought us together remains a guiding light, illuminating the path as we navigate this new chapter. Our commitment to each other, tested and strengthened by time and experience, is a testament to the power of love and the promise of new beginnings.

The holidays are on the horizon, casting a festive glow over the city. The air is crisp with a touch of winter, and lights twinkle in every window, reflecting the spirit of the season. This year, for the first time, I am invited to Ethan's family's annual celebration—a gathering steeped in tradition and bursting with the vibrancy of Mexican culture. It's a chance for me to immerse myself in his world, to experience firsthand the festivities that are such a vital part of his life.

As I prepare for the event, a mix of excitement and anxiety churns within me. I've heard so much about the lively celebrations and the rich traditions, and I want to honor and embrace them fully. Yet, beneath my anticipation lies a thread of apprehension, the kind that comes from stepping into a world that is both familiar and foreign. Ethan has been my rock through this journey, and now it's my turn to show him that I can be a part of his world in ways that truly matter.

The day of the celebration arrives with a flurry of activity. The aroma of tamales and pozole fills the air as I walk into Ethan's family's home. The kitchen is a whirlwind of activity, with his mother and aunts moving gracefully between counters laden with delicious dishes. The scent is intoxicating, a promise of the feast to come. I am greeted with warm hugs and kisses on the cheek, a genuine welcome that helps to ease my nerves. Despite my initial feelings of being an outsider, the family's embrace is reassuring.

As I join in the preparations, I'm struck by the beauty of the traditions that unfold around me. The vibrant colors of the decorations are a feast for the eyes—red and green streamers, glittering ornaments, and a towering nativity scene that captures the essence of the season. Music plays softly in the background, a blend of traditional Mexican carols and modern tunes that set the mood for the evening. The rhythm of the music is infectious, and I find myself tapping my feet along with the beat, feeling the pull of the celebration's energy.

Ethan's family is a lively group, their laughter and conversation filling the room with an infectious joy. The holiday traditions they uphold are a testament to their cultural heritage, and I am honored to be a part of it. The meal is a celebration in itself, with a spread of dishes that reflect the depth and variety of Mexican cuisine. Each bite is a new experience, from the rich, spicy flavors of the tamales to the savory warmth of the pozole. I savor each taste, grateful for the opportunity to share in this feast.

The evening progresses with a blend of traditional festivities and modern celebrations. As the night deepens, the music grows louder and more spirited. The living room transforms into a dance floor, and I watch in awe as Ethan's family moves with a grace and confidence that is captivating. The dance is a reflection of their culture—a joyful, rhythmic celebration of life and togetherness. I am invited to join in, and though I feel hesitant, Ethan's encouraging smile gives me the courage to step into the circle.

The dance floor is alive with energy, the movements a beautiful expression of the joy and unity that define the evening. I stumble at first, my steps awkward and uncertain, but Ethan is by my side, guiding me with a patience and kindness that makes me feel less like an outsider and more like a participant in this beautiful tradition. As I find my rhythm, the initial discomfort fades, replaced by a sense of belonging and connection.

Throughout the evening, the bond between Ethan and me strengthens. His family's warm acceptance and the joy of shared traditions create a deeper understanding between us. I see Ethan through a new lens, witnessing the ways in which his cultural heritage has shaped him and the values he holds dear. The celebration is not just a festive event; it's a glimpse into the heart of who he is and what he values.

By the end of the night, as the final notes of the music fade and the last remnants of the feast are cleared away, I am filled with a sense of gratitude and fulfillment. The experience has been both humbling and enriching, a testament to the power of embracing each other's worlds. The laughter and warmth of Ethan's family, the richness of their traditions, and the shared moments of joy have deepened our connection and solidified our bond.

As we say our goodbyes and prepare to leave, Ethan's hand in mine feels like a promise—a commitment to continue exploring and embracing the worlds that shape us. The evening has been a celebration of more than just the holidays; it has been a celebration of our journey together and the love that guides us through every step. The memory of this night will linger with me, a reminder of the beauty of blending lives and the strength of a love that grows with each shared experience.

The energy in Ethan's family home is contagious, a whirlwind of color and sound that draws me in completely. The laughter of children playing in the background, the clinking of glasses, and the rich aroma of traditional Mexican dishes create a sensory tapestry that's both exhilarating and overwhelming. It feels like stepping into a world that's both foreign and intimately familiar, the kind of place where the heart learns to embrace new traditions and forge deeper connections.

Ethan, ever the attentive guide, stays close by as we navigate the festivities. His presence is a comforting anchor amidst the sea of faces and unfamiliar customs. He introduces me to his relatives with an easy grace, his pride in his family evident in the way he speaks about them. Each introduction feels like a small step towards belonging, a bridge between my world and his. I can't help but notice how seamlessly he moves between the two, a testament to the deep-rooted connection he has with his heritage.

As the night progresses, I find myself drawn to the kitchen, where the magic of the evening's feast is unfolding. Ethan's mother, a radiant woman with warm eyes and a gentle smile, takes me under her wing. She shows me how to prepare tamales, her hands deftly working the masa with a skill that comes from years of tradition. Her patience is boundless, and her instructions are accompanied by stories of past holidays, each tale adding layers of meaning to the dishes we're preparing. The tamales we create together are more than just food; they're a tangible connection to Ethan's past, a way for me to share in the essence of his family's celebrations.

Despite my initial trepidation, I'm slowly drawn into the rhythm of the evening. The music, vibrant and rhythmic, fills the air, and I find myself moving to the beat with a newfound confidence. The lively melodies are infectious, and I can't help but smile as I attempt to keep up with the steps. Ethan's encouragement is a constant, his presence a reassuring comfort as I stumble through the dance. The joy on his face as he watches me try my hand at his family's traditional dances is a testament to the love and acceptance that surrounds us.

As the evening wears on, I take a moment to step outside for some fresh air. The night sky is clear, and the stars twinkle like the lights that adorn the house. The quiet of the backyard provides a stark contrast to the lively scene inside, and I find solace in this brief solitude. It's a moment of reflection, a chance to appreciate how far Ethan and I have come. The challenges we've faced, the differences we've navigated, all seem to dissolve under the vast, starry sky. It's clear that the love we share has the strength to transcend boundaries and adapt to new experiences.

Returning inside, I'm greeted by a scene of celebration and togetherness. The family has gathered around the table, their faces illuminated by the soft glow of candlelight. The warmth of their camaraderie is palpable, a living testament to the strength of their familial bonds. As I join them, I feel a sense of inclusion that goes beyond mere acceptance. It's as though I'm being woven into the fabric of their lives, each shared moment adding to the tapestry of our relationship.

The evening culminates in a heartfelt toast, a moment where Ethan's father stands to address the room. His words are filled with warmth and gratitude, a reflection of the love and support that surrounds us. He speaks of family, tradition, and the importance of embracing the new while honoring the old. His speech resonates deeply with me, a poignant reminder of the significance of our shared journey. As Ethan and I exchange glances, I can see the unspoken understanding between us, a mutual recognition of the commitment we've made to each other and to blending our lives together.

As the night draws to a close, and the last of the guests begin to depart, I find myself reflecting on the significance of this celebration. It's more than just a holiday gathering; it's a symbol of our relationship's evolution. The acceptance I've felt from Ethan's family, the joy of participating in their traditions, and the love that permeates the evening are all integral parts of our shared story. This night has been a testament to our ability to overcome obstacles and embrace each other's worlds, a reminder that the journey of love is one of continuous discovery and growth.

Walking out into the cool night air, hand in hand with Ethan, I feel a deep sense of contentment. The path we've chosen is paved with both challenges and triumphs, but moments like these—filled with love, laughter, and shared experiences—make every step worthwhile. As we drive away from the festivities, the glow of the holiday lights fading in the rearview mirror, I know that this celebration will be a cherished memory, a milestone in our journey together.

As the night deepens and the festivities continue, I find myself caught between the exhilaration of the celebration and a quiet introspection. The house, filled with the sounds of laughter and music, feels like a living, breathing entity, pulsating with the energy of the people within it. Ethan's family, with their warm smiles and open arms, have made me feel like a part of something larger than myself. Yet, amid the vibrant colors and joyful chaos, I can't shake the feeling of being an outsider trying to find her place.

The dance floor is alive with movement, and despite my initial awkwardness, I find myself slowly adapting to the rhythm. Ethan's family dances with a natural grace that's both enchanting and intimidating. I'm hesitant at first, stumbling over my feet, but Ethan's encouraging glances and gentle guidance make all the difference. His laughter, light and carefree, becomes a balm to my nerves, and I begin to lose myself in the music.

The traditional Mexican songs play, their melodies both foreign and familiar, weaving through the air like a gentle promise of connection. I watch as Ethan dances with his mother, his movements fluid and effortless, a testament to the years of shared memories and joy. Seeing them together, I can't help but feel a pang of longing for that same sense of belonging within this world. Yet, as I join in, I'm met with smiles and applause from Ethan's family, their acceptance easing the discomfort I initially felt.

The highlight of the evening is the moment when Ethan's father steps forward to lead a toast. The room quiets, the anticipation palpable. He raises his glass, and the room echoes with the clinking of glasses as everyone joins in. His words, spoken with heartfelt sincerity, reflect on the importance of family, the strength found in unity, and the joy of embracing new beginnings. He looks directly at me as he speaks, his gaze warm and welcoming. It's a gesture that speaks volumes, a silent acknowledgment of my place within this family.

Ethan's hand finds mine, and I squeeze it, drawing strength from his presence. His fingers intertwine with mine, a silent promise that we are navigating this together. As his father continues, I listen intently, feeling the weight of his words and the significance of the moment. The toast is a celebration of family, of the bonds that hold us together, and of the new chapters we write in each other's lives.

The evening's activities continue, with more dancing, laughter, and heartfelt conversations. I find myself engaged in animated discussions with Ethan's relatives, learning about their lives, their dreams, and the traditions that have shaped their lives. Each story, each shared memory, adds a layer of depth to my understanding of Ethan's world. The more I learn, the more I appreciate the richness of his heritage and the warmth of his family.

As the night winds down, and the last of the guests begin to depart, I feel a profound sense of gratitude. The celebration has been a whirlwind of sensory experiences, emotions, and revelations. Ethan's family has welcomed me with open arms, and their acceptance has made this evening not just a celebration of the holidays, but a testament to the strength of our relationship. The experience has deepened my appreciation for Ethan's culture and has brought us closer together.

Walking out of the house, the cool night air wraps around us like a comforting embrace. Ethan and I stand together under the stars, the twinkling lights of the celebration fading in the distance. The silence is a stark contrast to the lively atmosphere inside, but it's a peaceful silence, filled with the promise of the future. We share a quiet moment, reflecting on the night's events and the journey we've embarked upon together.

As we drive away from the festivities, I look over at Ethan, seeing him in a new light. The way he navigated the evening, balancing his heritage with his love for me, fills me with admiration. His ability to bridge our worlds, to honor his past while building a future with me, is a testament to the strength of our bond.

The holiday lights that line the streets twinkle in the night, a fitting end to an evening that has been both a celebration of family and a reflection of our love. The journey we've shared has been one of growth, acceptance, and discovery. As we move forward, I know that the experiences we've shared and the connections we've made will continue to shape our relationship.

In the quiet of the car, with Ethan's hand still holding mine, I feel a deep sense of contentment. The holidays have brought us closer, and the celebration has strengthened our bond. We've faced challenges and embraced new experiences, and through it all, our love has grown. As we continue on our journey together, I'm filled with a renewed sense of hope and excitement for the future.

# Chapter 13: Bridging the Gap

Hosting a gathering to introduce Ethan to my Southern roots was both exhilarating and nerve-wracking. I meticulously planned every detail, from the menu to the guest list, hoping that the fusion of our worlds would feel seamless, rather than jarring. As the day approached, I found myself caught between excitement and anxiety, eager to share my world with Ethan but unsure how he would navigate the quirks and customs of my Southern upbringing.

The house, adorned with a mix of seasonal decorations and personal touches, was ready to welcome our guests. The aroma of collard greens and cornbread filled the air, mingling with the scent of blooming magnolias from the garden. I had chosen a date that would allow my family and closest friends to gather, hoping that their warmth and hospitality would create a bridge between our two worlds.

When Ethan arrived, his expression was a mix of curiosity and determination. He had taken special care with his attire, donning a button-up shirt that was both casual and polished, a nod to the Southern casual elegance he was about to encounter. He looked around with an open gaze, taking in the homey décor and the vibrant energy of the gathering. His presence alone seemed to calm my nerves, and I took a deep breath, reminding myself that this was the beginning of a beautiful blending of traditions.

As guests arrived, I introduced Ethan with a blend of pride and nervousness. My family, with their genuine smiles and warm greetings, embraced him immediately, but I noticed subtle glances exchanged among them, as if trying to measure up this new addition to our circle. Ethan, ever the diplomat, greeted everyone with charm and genuine interest. His ability to engage in conversation with both my grandparents and my childhood friends showcased his remarkable adaptability.

The evening unfolded with a relaxed Southern ease. We gathered around the dinner table, which was laden with a feast that spoke to my heritage—roasted chicken, creamy mac and cheese, and my grandmother's famous pecan pie. Ethan's genuine appreciation for the food was evident; he asked questions about each dish and praised the flavors with an enthusiasm that did not go unnoticed. His eagerness to understand and respect the traditions that shaped my upbringing spoke volumes, and I watched as my family began to warm to him.

The highlight of the evening was a lively game of charades, a tradition that had become a staple at our family gatherings. As we played, Ethan's willingness to dive into the fun, despite being new to the game, was endearing. His animated gestures and infectious laughter created a bridge of shared joy and lightheartedness. I could see my family's apprehensions melting away, replaced by the genuine pleasure of seeing Ethan as part of our world.

Conversations flowed effortlessly as the night went on, with stories and laughter punctuating the air. Ethan took the opportunity to share some anecdotes about his experiences, weaving in bits of his own culture with the ease of someone who genuinely wanted to connect. My family responded in kind, sharing their own stories and making Ethan feel more like one of us with every passing minute.

In quieter moments, as we retreated to the porch to catch our breath and enjoy the evening's gentle breeze, I found myself reflecting on the significance of the day. The contrast between Ethan's Mexican heritage and my Southern upbringing had been stark, but the way we were able to blend our worlds felt like a testament to our love and commitment. The evening was not just about introducing Ethan to my family but about weaving our lives together into a tapestry of shared experiences and mutual respect.

As the night drew to a close and the last of our guests departed, Ethan and I stood together on the porch, looking out at the flickering lights of the garden. There was a sense of accomplishment in the air, a quiet acknowledgment that we had taken a significant step forward. The blending of our worlds had not been without its challenges, but the evening had proven that our love was strong enough to bridge any gaps that existed between us.

Ethan's hand found mine, and I felt a surge of gratitude and affection. His willingness to embrace my Southern roots, to immerse himself in the traditions and customs that defined my upbringing, was a testament to his dedication and love. We stood there in the cool night air, the sound of crickets and distant laughter mingling with our own contented silence. The journey of blending our lives had only just begun, but this evening had laid a foundation of understanding and acceptance that would support us as we continued to build our future together.

The evening had settled into a comfortable rhythm by the time we reached dessert. I watched from the sidelines, my heart swelling with a mix of pride and relief as Ethan engaged effortlessly with everyone around him. There was a genuine ease in his manner that seemed to disarm any lingering skepticism from my family. I saw my mother, usually reserved and careful in her judgments, leaning in with genuine interest as Ethan recounted a humorous story about his childhood. Her laughter, light and melodic, filled the room, bridging the gap between the unfamiliar and the cherished.

The Southern charm of our home was something Ethan had stepped into with an open heart, and now, it seemed to embrace him in return. The evening's conversations had revealed his warmth and adaptability, qualities that reson with my family. As the night wore on, I noticed that the initial reservations my relatives had harbored were gradually replaced by a genuine curiosity and fondness for Ethan. The way he listened, his eyes bright and attentive, his genuine compliments about the food and the atmosphere, all contributed to creating a sense of belonging that transcended our cultural differences.

After the main course, as the table was cleared and everyone settled into comfortable chairs with glasses of sweet tea or coffee, Ethan and I took a moment to step outside onto the porch. The night air was cool and crisp, and the stars were beginning to peek through the veil of the dusk. We leaned against the railing, the gentle hum of conversation and occasional bursts of laughter drifting out from inside. I turned to Ethan, taking in the contentment that radiated from him.

"This has been wonderful," he said, his voice filled with sincerity. "I feel like I'm starting to understand more about where you come from, and it means a lot to me."

I smiled, feeling a rush of warmth at his words. "I'm glad. It's important to me that you feel a part of this world, just as I've felt welcomed into yours."

We stood there in companionable silence for a few moments, the quiet of the night wrapping around us like a comforting blanket. It was in these small, shared moments that I felt the most connected to Ethan, the weight of our commitment feeling lighter and more certain. The challenges of blending our lives seemed less daunting when I looked at him, knowing that he was as invested in making this work as I was.

When we re-entered the house, the atmosphere had shifted slightly. There was a new ease in the interactions, a sense of camaraderie that hadn't been there before. The conversations were livelier, the laughter more frequent. My father, usually reserved, was animatedly discussing his favorite sports teams with Ethan, their shared enthusiasm for the subject bridging another gap between them. It was heartening to see my family, who had been so crucial in shaping my life, accepting Ethan with such openness.

The final touch to the evening was a lively round of music and dancing. My family's tradition of breaking into impromptu dance routines had always been a highlight of our gatherings, and tonight was no exception. Ethan hesitated for only a moment before joining in, his movements a bit tentative but filled with genuine effort. The sight of him, trying to follow along with the Southern two-step, brought peals of laughter from everyone. It was a joyous, unfiltered display of acceptance, and I could see that Ethan was not just participating but genuinely enjoying the experience.

As the night drew to a close and the guests began to say their goodbyes, the sense of accomplishment was palpable. The evening had been more than just an introduction; it had been a celebration of our combined cultures and a testament to our willingness to embrace each other's worlds. My family, having seen Ethan's sincere efforts and his respect for our traditions, had begun to genuinely appreciate him.

When the last guest had left and the house was finally quiet, Ethan and I took a moment to reflect on the evening. We sat together on the couch, the remnants of dessert still on the table and the soft glow of the lamp casting a warm light over the room. I looked at Ethan, my heart full as I saw the satisfaction and relief in his eyes.

"Thank you for being so open tonight," I said softly. "It means more to me than I can express."

He took my hand in his, his touch reassuring and tender. "Thank you for sharing this part of your life with me. I know it was important to you, and it was important to me, too. I feel like I've gained a deeper understanding of where you come from, and that makes me even more certain about where we're headed."

As we sat there, wrapped in the quiet comfort of our shared space, I felt a profound sense of connection. The evening had not only bridged the gap between our worlds but had also deepened our bond, reinforcing the foundation of our relationship. The blending of our families and traditions was not without its challenges, but seeing Ethan and my family come together in such harmony made me believe in the strength of our love and the promise of our future.

As the evening wore on, the warmth of the house seemed to seep into every corner, knitting together the diverse threads of our lives. The clinking of glasses and the gentle murmur of conversation provided a comforting backdrop to the night. Ethan had become an integral part of the gathering, seamlessly fitting into the rhythm of our family's traditions. His genuine curiosity and willingness to immerse himself in our customs had not gone unnoticed.

The backyard, once a canvas of twinkling fairy lights and the soft rustling of the wind through the trees, now echoed with the sound of laughter and animated chatter. Ethan's presence had a way of drawing people in, and it was heartening to see my friends and family embrace him with open arms. My best friend, Lily, who had always been a tough critic when it came to my romantic choices, was now engaged in a spirited conversation with Ethan about her latest project. The ease with which they connected was a testament to Ethan's ability to navigate different social landscapes with grace.

My uncle George, known for his penchant for storytelling, took Ethan under his wing, regaling him with tales of our family's quirks and legends. Ethan listened with rapt attention, his occasional chuckle mingling with the collective laughter of the group. The way he engaged with everyone, without pretense, spoke volumes about his character. He was genuinely interested in learning about our world, and it was clear that his interest was sincere.

As the night progressed, the focus shifted to the traditional Southern dessert table. Ethan, with his ever-present curiosity, took the time to sample each treat with the same enthusiasm he had shown throughout the evening. I watched as he hesitated over a particularly rich pecan pie, then took a bite and savored it with a contented sigh. It was a small but significant gesture, one that reflected his willingness to embrace every aspect of my heritage, no matter how foreign it initially seemed.

The atmosphere was infused with a sense of accomplishment and joy. My parents, who had initially been cautious, now displayed a visible sense of approval and warmth towards Ethan. The evening had unfolded as a beautiful mosaic of shared experiences, where our different backgrounds had converged into something profoundly harmonious. Ethan's efforts to connect with my family had not gone unnoticed, and it was evident that the barriers that once stood between us were slowly but surely dissolving.

As the clock ticked towards midnight and the last of the guests began to drift away, Ethan and I found a quiet moment alone amidst the lingering echoes of the party. We stood on the porch, the cool night air a soothing balm after the warmth of the house. The stars were out in full force, casting their gentle glow over the world, and the tranquility of the moment felt like a perfect conclusion to an evening filled with meaningful connections.

Ethan turned to me, his expression soft and reflective. "Tonight was something special," he said, his voice low and sincere. "I feel like I've not only learned more about where you come from but also experienced a part of your world that I wouldn't have otherwise."

I smiled, feeling a swell of gratitude and affection for him. "I'm so glad you think so. It means a lot to me that you took the time to understand and appreciate my world. It's moments like these that make me realize just how lucky I am to have you in my life."

He reached out, taking my hand in his, and we stood there together, savoring the peaceful silence. It was in these quiet moments, away from the bustle of the evening, that I felt the depth of our connection most acutely. The barriers between our worlds had been gently but firmly bridged, and the path ahead seemed clearer and more promising than ever before.

As we re-entered the house to help with the final cleanup, the lingering warmth of the night wrapped around us like a comforting embrace. The success of the evening had been more than just a personal victory; it had been a collective triumph of understanding, acceptance, and love. The integration of our families and traditions, though still a work in progress, had taken a significant step forward.

The evening's experiences had forged a new bond, one that was built on mutual respect and genuine connection. The blend of our worlds, once marked by stark contrasts, now felt like a vibrant tapestry of shared values and traditions. Ethan and I stood at the threshold of our future, buoyed by the knowledge that we had successfully navigated one of the most significant challenges of our relationship. The journey ahead was still unknown, but the foundation we had laid together, grounded in love and understanding, promised a future rich with possibility.

# Chapter 14: Overcoming Cultural Barriers

Navigating the labyrinth of our merged lives, Ethan and I found ourselves at a crossroads marked by cultural differences that seemed both vast and intricate. The initial enchantment of our union, colored by shared moments and new experiences, was now tempered by the inevitable frictions of blending two distinct worlds. Each day brought its own set of challenges, but also opportunities for growth, understanding, and compromise.

The first hint of discord surfaced in the form of holiday traditions. Ethan's family had always celebrated the Day of the Dead with a reverent blend of festivity and remembrance. The holiday, deeply rooted in Mexican culture, was an occasion to honor lost loved ones with vibrant altars, marigolds, and heartfelt offerings. I had always admired this tradition from afar, fascinated by its beauty and depth. But when the time came to integrate this celebration into our shared life, I found myself struggling with the emotional and practical implications.

My own family had long held a tradition of Thanksgiving, a time steeped in Southern comfort foods and stories of family heritage. The thought of merging these two holidays, each rich with its own significance, felt like an overwhelming task. I worried about how to honor both traditions without losing the essence of either.

Ethan sensed my hesitation and approached the topic with a blend of patience and encouragement. "We don't have to choose one over the other," he suggested one evening as we sat on the porch, the twilight casting soft shadows around us. "Why not try to blend them? We could create a new tradition that honors both of our heritages."

The idea was as daunting as it was appealing. Blending our customs felt like trying to mix two powerful, distinct colors on a canvas, each with its own intensity and shade. Yet, Ethan's suggestion seemed to be the perfect metaphor for our relationship: a work in progress, evolving with every stroke of compromise and understanding.

We began to explore ways to integrate our traditions. The first attempt was to have a combined celebration where we set up a small altar for the Day of the Dead alongside the Thanksgiving feast. We included marigold decorations and candles, creating a space where we could remember and celebrate, while the table was laden with turkey, cornbread, and sweet potatoes. It was a delicate balance, but the result was a unique celebration that resonated with both of us.

The first year, however, was not without its difficulties. As we sat down to the blended feast, a sense of unease lingered. Ethan's family was gracious, yet I could sense their curiosity about how this integration of traditions was unfolding. My own family was supportive but struggled to grasp the full significance of the Day of the Dead, which made me wonder if we were truly honoring either tradition or merely creating a superficial blend.

The challenges didn't end there. Small disagreements cropped up, like which customs to prioritize or how to introduce new elements into our already established routines. It was clear that merging our worlds required more than just compromise; it demanded a deep, respectful understanding of each other's values and traditions.

We faced our first significant clash over wedding plans. Ethan wanted to incorporate traditional Mexican wedding customs, including a mariachi band and a ceremony steeped in his cultural heritage. I, on the other hand, envisioned a classic Southern wedding with a quaint, garden setting and old-fashioned charm. The contrast between our visions was stark, and as the planning progressed, tensions flared.

We decided to confront our differences head-on, setting aside an evening to discuss our preferences and find common ground. Sitting across from each other, surrounded by wedding magazines and notes, we expressed our concerns and desires with a raw honesty that we hadn't fully embraced before.

"Why is it so hard to find a middle ground?" I asked, frustration evident in my voice. "I love your culture and want to honor it, but I also have my own dreams for this day."

Ethan's eyes softened with empathy. "I understand. I guess I'm worried that we're not fully acknowledging my background, and I don't want that to be a source of resentment."

Our conversation was a turning point. We realized that our love for each other was more important than any single tradition or expectation. We began to explore ways to incorporate both of our visions into the wedding, finding creative solutions that paid homage to both cultures. In the end, our wedding became a celebration of our union, marked by the harmonious blend of Mexican and Southern elements that reflected who we were as a couple.

The process of overcoming these cultural barriers taught us valuable lessons about the nature of compromise and understanding. We learned that honoring each other's traditions didn't mean sacrificing our own but rather finding ways to embrace and integrate them into our shared life. The journey was not always smooth, and there were moments of frustration and doubt, but the love that bound us together provided a foundation strong enough to weather the storms.

Through these challenges, we discovered that our relationship was not just about finding common ground but about celebrating the richness that each of our backgrounds brought to our lives. It was a continuous dance of give-and-take, a testament to our commitment to one another and our willingness to build a future together, despite the complexities of blending two distinct worlds.

Our journey to blend our lives was not without its hurdles, and each cultural barrier we faced became a test of our resolve and affection. Ethan and I had spent so much time navigating the intricacies of each other's worlds that we'd come to appreciate the beauty in our differences. Yet, there were still moments when those differences felt like walls rather than bridges.

One particular challenge arose when we began planning for our first holiday season as a couple. Ethan was excited about celebrating Las Posadas, a traditional Mexican holiday that re-enacts Mary and Joseph's search for shelter before the birth of Jesus. It involved festive processions, singing, and a communal spirit that was new to me. On the other hand, my family's Christmas traditions revolved around a cozy, quieter gathering with homemade Southern dishes, a massive Christmas tree, and a sense of serenity that was both comforting and familiar.

The anticipation of blending these traditions was accompanied by a palpable tension. I had embraced many aspects of Ethan's culture, but Las Posadas was a step into unfamiliar territory that left me feeling both exhilarated and anxious. Ethan's excitement was infectious, yet I worried about how my family would react to this vibrant tradition that seemed so different from what they were used to.

We decided to host a joint celebration, where we would integrate elements from both of our traditions. The planning process became an emotional rollercoaster. Ethan was enthusiastic about setting up a piñata and preparing tamales, while I focused on organizing the Christmas decorations and preparing a feast that included both traditional Mexican dishes and Southern favorites. We found ourselves arguing over details as small as the placement of the nativity scene and as significant as the timing of the meal.

One evening, amidst the whirlwind of holiday preparations, we found ourselves sitting on opposite ends of the couch, both exhausted and frustrated. The glow of the Christmas lights did little to ease the tension that hung between us. I could see Ethan's disappointment mirrored in his eyes, and it was clear that our struggle was not just about holiday plans but about deeper issues of compromise and acceptance.

"Maybe this was a mistake," I said quietly, breaking the silence. "I wanted to make this work, but I feel like we're losing sight of what really matters."

Ethan's face softened as he looked at me. "It's not about the decorations or the food. It's about us finding a way to honor both of our traditions. I know this is important to you, and it's important to me too. We just need to find a way to make it work."

In that moment, the weight of our disagreements lifted slightly, replaced by a shared sense of purpose. We had always known that our relationship would involve compromise, but this was a reminder of how crucial it was to approach our challenges with empathy and understanding.

We took a step back and re-evaluated our approach. Instead of trying to merge everything into a single celebration, we decided to create distinct moments within our holiday season—one for Las Posadas, where we invited Ethan's family and friends to join us in the festivities, and another for Christmas, where my family could enjoy the traditions they cherished. By honoring both celebrations separately, we allowed each tradition its own space and significance.

The result was a holiday season that felt like a tapestry woven from the threads of our diverse cultures. Las Posadas became a vibrant, joyful event filled with singing and laughter, while our Christmas gathering was a serene, intimate affair marked by familiar Southern comforts. The separation of the celebrations allowed us to fully immerse ourselves in each experience without feeling as though we were compromising one tradition for another.

Our families responded positively to the approach. Ethan's family appreciated the effort to celebrate their traditions, while mine were grateful for the inclusion of their own customs. The contrast between the two celebrations became a testament to our willingness to blend our worlds in a way that honored and respected both.

In the weeks that followed, our relationship grew stronger as we learned to navigate these cultural barriers with a renewed sense of partnership. The holidays had tested our ability to compromise and adapt, but they also highlighted the depth of our commitment to each other. We realized that overcoming these barriers was not about finding a perfect solution but about embracing the imperfections and challenges that came with blending two rich, diverse cultures.

Our love was not just about the grand gestures or the perfectly executed celebrations. It was about the small moments of understanding and the willingness to see each other's worlds through compassionate eyes. As we continued to build our life together, we knew that our journey would involve more challenges and adjustments, but we faced them with the knowledge that our bond was resilient and capable of weathering any storm.

Through our shared experiences, we discovered that cultural barriers were not obstacles but opportunities for growth and connection. By facing these challenges together, we strengthened our relationship and deepened our appreciation for the unique blend of traditions that made our life together so richly rewarding.

Navigating our blended lives, we encountered moments that were as challenging as they were revealing. Every day seemed to present a new test of our ability to reconcile our differing customs and traditions. Yet, it was through these trials that we discovered not only the strength of our relationship but also the profound depth of our commitment to one another.

One of the most poignant challenges arose when we began planning our first vacation together—a trip to explore Ethan's childhood home and my own beloved southern town. What started as an exciting adventure quickly became a battleground of differing expectations. Ethan envisioned a trip filled with vibrant cultural experiences and social gatherings, while I longed for tranquil, cozy days surrounded by my favorite local haunts and familiar faces.

The discussions about our vacation plans became more than just disagreements over itineraries; they revealed the underlying fears and desires we each held. For Ethan, the trip was an opportunity to reconnect with his roots, to show me the world he had grown up in, and to share with me the experiences that had shaped him. For me, it was a chance to revisit the places that held sentimental value and to create new memories in a setting that felt deeply personal.

We found ourselves stuck in a cycle of compromise that felt both necessary and exhausting. I remember one evening, after a particularly heated discussion about our travel plans, sitting across from each other at the kitchen table, both of us exhausted and frustrated. The room was silent except for the ticking of the clock, each tick a reminder of the growing divide between us.

"Why is this so hard?" I asked quietly, my voice trembling with a mix of frustration and vulnerability. "I thought this was supposed to be a time of joy, not stress."

Ethan's eyes softened as he reached across the table to take my hand. "I know, and I'm sorry. I want us both to be happy. I guess I'm just struggling to balance showing you my world and honoring the things that are important to you."

His words, simple yet profound, cut through the fog of our argument. It wasn't about who was right or wrong; it was about finding a way to honor both of our worlds in a way that felt genuine and fulfilling.

We decided to approach the vacation with a new perspective. Instead of viewing it as a competition between our preferences, we framed it as an opportunity to create a shared experience that honored both of our backgrounds. We planned a trip that included days dedicated to exploring Ethan's cultural landmarks and other days spent in my favorite Southern locales. Each day was a carefully crafted balance between his vibrant heritage and my cherished traditions.

When we finally set out on our journey, the tension that had plagued our planning phase began to dissipate, replaced by the excitement of discovery and mutual appreciation. Visiting Ethan's hometown, I was welcomed into a world of lively festivals, delicious cuisine, and the warmth of his extended family. It was a vivid tapestry of colors, sounds, and smells that left me feeling both exhilarated and deeply connected to his past.

In return, Ethan embraced my Southern roots with open arms. He joined me in exploring the charming streets of my hometown, savoring the simple pleasures of cozy coffee shops and familiar local gatherings. He understood why these places held such significance for me and allowed himself to be enveloped in the comfort of my traditions.

Our vacation became a symbol of our ability to blend our lives in a way that respected and celebrated our differences. The challenges we faced in reconciling our customs became stepping stones to a deeper understanding of each other. We realized that the key to overcoming our cultural barriers was not about erasing the differences but about embracing them and finding harmony within the contrasts.

As we returned home, the experiences we shared during our trip became a cherished part of our story. We carried with us the lessons learned from our journey and the realization that our love was resilient enough to weather any storm. Our relationship grew stronger as we continued to navigate the complexities of blending our worlds, finding joy in the shared moments and appreciating the unique beauty that each of our cultures brought to our lives.

In the end, it was not just about overcoming cultural barriers but about discovering the richness that came from intertwining our lives. We learned that compromise was not about losing ourselves but about finding new ways to connect and grow together. Our love thrived on the foundation of mutual respect and understanding, proving that even the most challenging obstacles could become opportunities for deeper connection and lasting joy.

# Chapter 15: The Unexpected Surprise

There are moments in life that catch you completely off guard, the kind that leave you breathless and wide-eyed with a mix of wonder and disbelief. Ethan's surprise was exactly one of those moments. It began on an ordinary Tuesday morning, with the sun barely peeking over the horizon and the world still wrapped in the soft blanket of dawn. I had barely stirred from sleep when Ethan's gentle touch woke me, his lips pressing a soft kiss to my forehead.

"Wake up, sleepyhead," he murmured, his voice carrying a hint of mischief that immediately piqued my curiosity. "I've got a surprise for you."

My heart fluttered, as it always did when Ethan had a secret up his sleeve. I sat up in bed, my mind racing through the possibilities of what this surprise could be. Was it a special dinner? A new piece of jewelry? But nothing could have prepared me for the revelation that followed.

Ethan handed me a neatly folded piece of paper, its edges crisp and its surface adorned with a vibrant, artistic map. As I unfolded it, the map revealed the outline of a destination that held a special place in both of our hearts—a charming coastal town where we had once spent a weekend together, exploring its cobblestone streets and savoring its exquisite sunsets. The place had always felt like a hidden gem, a retreat from the hustle of everyday life, and the thought of returning there filled me with an inexplicable joy.

"You've been working so hard lately," Ethan said, his eyes sparkling with affection. "I thought we could use a little escape, just the two of us."

The sheer thoughtfulness of his gesture left me momentarily speechless. It wasn't just the destination that mattered, but the love and care behind the decision. The spontaneity of it all was intoxicating, a reminder of the playful and adventurous spirit that had first drawn us to each other.

We spent the next few hours in a flurry of excitement, packing our bags with the essentials for a getaway. The anticipation was palpable, an electric current that buzzed through our conversations and lingered in our stolen glances. Ethan's enthusiasm was infectious, and I found myself swept up in the romance of the surprise, eager to experience every moment of this unexpected adventure.

As we drove toward our destination, the landscape shifted from the familiar confines of our city life to the open expanse of rolling hills and sparkling waters. With each mile that passed, I felt the weight of our daily routines lift off our shoulders, replaced by the promise of relaxation and reconnection.

The moment we arrived at the coastal town, I was enchanted by its timeless charm. The salty breeze kissed our faces, and the rhythmic sound of waves crashing against the shore created a soothing backdrop to our escape. Ethan had chosen a quaint little cottage nestled right by the beach, its windows offering an uninterrupted view of the horizon. It was the perfect sanctuary, a place where we could let go of everything and simply be together.

We spent our days exploring the picturesque surroundings, wandering hand-in-hand through the narrow streets lined with colorful boutiques and charming cafes. Each evening, as the sun dipped below the horizon, we watched the sky burst into hues of pink and gold, marveling at the beauty of nature and the serenity of our surroundings.

In the quiet moments, when we were alone together, the true magic of the trip unfolded. We shared long conversations under the starlit sky, our voices mingling with the distant sound of the ocean. We laughed, reminisced, and dreamed aloud about the future, our hearts intertwined with a renewed sense of purpose and hope.

It was in these intimate moments that we reaffirmed our commitment to each other. The simplicity of our surroundings, combined with the deep connection we shared, made it clear that our bond was stronger than ever. We talked about our hopes and aspirations, about the life we wanted to build together, and the journey we were willing to embark on.

The unexpected surprise had done more than just offer us a temporary escape; it had provided us with a space to rediscover the depth of our love and the strength of our partnership. As we stood on the beach, watching the first light of dawn paint the sky, I felt an overwhelming sense of gratitude for the man beside me and for the incredible journey we were on.

The getaway, with its breathtaking scenery and intimate moments, had become a testament to our love—a love that could weather any storm and flourish in the most unexpected places. Ethan's thoughtful surprise had given us a precious gift: the chance to reconnect, to dream, and to reaffirm our commitment to a future filled with love and endless possibilities.

The days we spent in that quaint coastal town felt like a dream wrapped in sunlight and sea breeze. Every morning, the ocean's lullaby gently coaxed us from our sleep, and every evening, the sunset offered a spectacular show that seemed just for us. The beauty of the place was matched only by the depth of our conversations and the simplicity of our shared experiences.

Our days were filled with exploration and discovery, both of the town and of each other. Ethan and I meandered through the local market, where the smell of freshly baked bread mingled with the tang of citrus. We sampled local delicacies, savoring each bite as if it were a piece of the town's soul. Each meal became an adventure, a culinary journey that mirrored the way we were rediscovering each other.

The mornings, however, were my favorite. We would stroll along the deserted beach, our feet sinking into the cool, damp sand. The early hours brought a serene quiet that allowed us to talk freely, without the usual interruptions of our busy lives. Ethan would share stories from his childhood, tales filled with laughter and a few mischievous exploits. I found myself falling in love with these stories as much as I was falling for him all over again. It was in these unguarded moments that I felt the weight of the world lift from our shoulders, leaving only us and the ocean.

One afternoon, Ethan suggested we take a boat out to explore a nearby island. The idea was spontaneous, a perfect reflection of the adventure we were embracing. We rented a small, charming boat, and as we navigated the waters, I was struck by the sheer beauty of our surroundings. The island was a small, untouched paradise, a perfect blend of rugged cliffs and golden sand. We anchored the boat and spent hours simply basking in the sun, our laughter mingling with the sound of waves gently lapping against the shore.

As the day wore on, we found a secluded spot where the ocean met the land in a serene embrace. Ethan pulled out a blanket and a picnic basket filled with delicious treats we had picked up earlier. We sat together, sharing the food and the moment, our conversations flowing as easily as the gentle sea breeze. I watched Ethan as he spoke, the way his eyes sparkled with enthusiasm, and I realized just how much this trip had renewed our connection. It was as if the world had narrowed down to this perfect moment, where nothing mattered but our shared joy and our love.

In the evening, we returned to our cozy cottage, the sky painted in shades of twilight. Ethan had planned a surprise dinner on the terrace overlooking the ocean. The table was set with candles flickering softly, casting a warm glow over our faces. The scent of grilled fish and fresh herbs filled the air, mingling with the salty sea breeze. We dined under the stars, our hearts full and our spirits lifted. Each bite was savored, each moment cherished, as we talked about our dreams and our plans for the future.

As the night deepened, we found ourselves dancing to the soft strains of a love song playing in the background. There was no need for grand gestures or elaborate declarations; the simplicity of the moment was enough. We held each other close, our bodies swaying in rhythm with the music, our hearts beating in sync. It was in these quiet, intimate moments that I felt the depth of our commitment to each other. The uncertainties and challenges we had faced seemed distant, overshadowed by the strength of our bond.

The trip, though spontaneous, had become more than just a getaway. It was a testament to our love, a reminder of the beauty in our shared experiences and the joy in our journey together. As we returned to our daily lives, the memories of that time lingered like a sweet fragrance, a constant reminder of the strength of our connection.

Ethan's surprise had given us the gift of a renewed perspective. We returned with a deeper appreciation for each other, for the life we were building together, and for the future that lay ahead. The trip had been a beautiful interlude, a moment of clarity amidst the chaos of life, and it had strengthened our resolve to face whatever challenges lay ahead, hand in hand.

In the end, it wasn't just the destination that had made the trip special—it was the love and thoughtfulness behind it. Ethan's spontaneous gesture had rekindled the spark in our relationship and reminded us of the joy in the simple moments we shared. As we stepped back into our routine, we carried with us the warmth of the sun, the sound of the waves, and the certainty of our unwavering commitment to each other.

As the days on our spontaneous getaway flowed seamlessly, the sense of freedom and intimacy we experienced began to redefine our understanding of our relationship. Each morning, the world seemed to awaken just for us, the golden rays of the sun casting a gentle glow over our shared moments. The little cottage we'd chosen was nestled on a hill overlooking the vast expanse of blue, its simple charm a perfect backdrop to the profound rediscovery of each other.

We spent one day hiking along a rugged coastal trail that wound through vibrant wildflowers and offered breathtaking vistas. Ethan's hand in mine, we ventured through the lush greenery, pausing occasionally to take in the panoramic views of the ocean crashing against the cliffs. The journey wasn't always easy; there were steep inclines and narrow paths that tested our stamina. Yet, it was in these challenging moments that we found an unexpected joy—supporting each other, cheering each other on, and sharing in the triumph of reaching each viewpoint. It was a metaphor for our relationship, illustrating how we could navigate life's ups and downs together.

The evenings were reserved for quiet moments under the stars. We'd often find ourselves lying on the soft sand of a secluded beach, the only sound the rhythmic lull of the waves. Wrapped in each other's arms, we would talk for hours, our conversations flowing freely between dreams and memories. Ethan would share stories of his childhood, anecdotes that painted vivid pictures of his past and brought me closer to understanding his essence. I would recount tales of my own upbringing, weaving together the threads of our lives in a tapestry that bridged our worlds.

One particularly memorable evening, we decided to have a candlelit dinner on the beach. Ethan had planned this surprise meticulously, setting up a beautiful table adorned with candles and flowers. As the sun dipped below the horizon, the sky transformed into a canvas of deep purples and fiery oranges. The scene was so perfect, it felt like something out of a fairytale. We dined on fresh seafood and local delicacies, the flavors enhanced by the romance of the setting. Between sips of wine and laughter, we spoke of our hopes and fears, our desires for the future, and the dreams we held dear.

The trip also provided a welcome escape from the everyday pressures that often weighed us down. The rhythm of our routine was replaced by the leisurely pace of vacation life. Without the usual distractions and obligations, we had the space to truly focus on each other. The experience reminded us of the importance of taking time for ourselves and for our relationship, and how these moments of respite were vital for maintaining the strength of our bond.

On our final night, as we stood on the terrace of our cottage, watching the stars glittering in the clear night sky, I felt a profound sense of contentment. The journey had been more than just a romantic getaway; it had been a journey into the heart of our relationship, revealing the depth of our connection and the strength of our commitment. Ethan had orchestrated this surprise with such thoughtfulness and love, and it had reawakened a sense of wonder and appreciation in me.

As we packed our bags and prepared to return to our everyday lives, I realized that the true gift of the trip wasn't just the stunning scenery or the luxurious moments, but the reaffirmation of our love and commitment. We had navigated this getaway with grace and joy, and it had given us a renewed sense of purpose and direction. We knew that the path ahead wouldn't always be smooth, but the experience had fortified our resolve to face whatever challenges came our way, knowing that we had each other's unwavering support.

Ethan's spontaneous trip had done more than just provide a beautiful escape; it had deepened our connection and clarified our vision for the future. The memories we created would serve as a reminder of our love's resilience and the power of taking time to nurture our relationship. As we returned to our daily routine, we carried with us not only the beautiful memories of our time away but also a renewed commitment to each other and to the life we were building together.

# Chapter 16: Facing the Past

The air was charged with an uneasy tension, an unexpected visitor stirring the calm surface of our lives. Ethan's ex-partner, someone I'd heard about but never met, arrived unannounced, her presence a jarring note in our otherwise harmonious symphony. The news of her visit had come like a sudden storm, unsettling and disruptive, throwing both of us into a whirlwind of emotions we thought we had long left behind.

The day she arrived, the sun seemed to hesitate before fully emerging from its morning haze, as if it too sensed the significance of the moment. Ethan and I were sitting in the living room, a cozy space that had recently become a sanctuary of our shared joys and quiet reflections. The tranquility we'd cultivated together was abruptly interrupted by the ring of the doorbell—a sound that suddenly felt heavy with foreboding.

When Ethan opened the door, I saw the briefest flicker of discomfort pass across his face before he masked it with a polite smile. The woman standing there, elegant yet distant, was undeniably familiar. She carried herself with an air of confidence that spoke of shared history, and it was clear from the outset that her presence was more than just a casual visit. My heart skipped a beat, a mixture of apprehension and curiosity flooding me.

Her name was Lila, and as she stepped into our home, the air seemed to thicken with unspoken words. We exchanged pleasantries, though the conversation was stilted, the familiarity between Ethan and Lila underscoring the awkwardness of the situation. They spoke in subdued tones, fragments of their past life together slipping into the conversation like shadows on the wall. I listened, my heart pounding, as old fears and insecurities began to resurface.

The initial meeting was a dance of superficial niceties, but as the hours passed, the underlying tension became palpable. Ethan and I retreated to the kitchen, away from Lila's prying eyes, and the discussion that followed was charged with a rawness I hadn't anticipated. Ethan's face was a mixture of guilt and frustration, his eyes betraying the weight of unresolved feelings he had hoped were buried.

"We need to talk," he said, his voice low but firm. The urgency in his tone made my stomach twist. We sat across from each other at the kitchen table, the space between us a chasm filled with uncertainty. "I didn't expect her to show up like this. I thought we'd moved past this."

I nodded, trying to steady my voice. "I know. It's just... I didn't think I'd feel this way. It's like all the old insecurities are bubbling up again."

Ethan reached across the table, taking my hand in his. His touch was warm and grounding, a reassurance I desperately needed. "I'm sorry. I never wanted to bring this kind of tension into our lives. But I want you to know that you're the one I'm committed to. My past with Lila... it's over. I'm here with you, and I want to work through this together."

The sincerity in his voice was both comforting and sobering. I could see the depth of his remorse and the struggle he faced in reconciling his past with his present. It was clear that our relationship was being tested in a way we hadn't anticipated. Yet, in this moment of vulnerability, there was a glimmer of hope—a chance for us to confront these hidden fears and reaffirm our bond.

Later that evening, after Lila had left, Ethan and I took a walk through the quiet streets of our neighborhood. The cool night air was a welcome relief from the intensity of the day, and we walked side by side, our steps echoing the rhythm of our unspoken thoughts.

As we strolled, Ethan spoke about his past with Lila, not as an attempt to justify or excuse, but to shed light on the reasons why this chapter was still lingering in our lives. "There's so much history there," he said, his voice tinged with regret. "But I need you to understand that it's just that—history. What we have now is different, and it's something I want to build on."

We stopped by a park, the silence around us punctuated only by the distant hum of traffic. I looked at Ethan, the sincerity in his eyes unmistakable. "I do understand. It's just hard not to feel overshadowed by the past sometimes."

Ethan pulled me close, his embrace a protective shield against the lingering shadows of insecurity. "We'll face it together. I promise we'll work through this, one step at a time. Your feelings are valid, and I want us to be honest with each other about everything."

The conversation that night was a turning point. We acknowledged the lingering echoes of Ethan's past and addressed the insecurities that had surfaced. It wasn't an easy process, but it was a necessary one. Through our heartfelt discussion, we managed to find a path forward, one that was paved with renewed trust and a deeper understanding of each other's fears.

As the days went by, the strain of Lila's visit began to ease. The initial discomfort gave way to a strengthened resolve to nurture our relationship, to move beyond the shadows of the past. We learned that facing these challenges head-on, with honesty and commitment, was the key to fortifying the bond we had so carefully built. The experience, though painful, had brought us closer, and the trust we reinforced became the cornerstone of our shared future.

The echoes of the day Lila arrived lingered, a muted but persistent reminder of the shadows we had to confront. Ethan and I spent the following days in a delicate dance, navigating our emotions and striving to reclaim the normalcy we had worked so hard to build. Each moment seemed to carry a weight that neither of us could entirely shake off. The air between us was thick with unspoken words and fragile hopes, but there was also a determination to mend the fissures that had formed.

One evening, as we settled into the comforting routine of our shared space, Ethan reached for my hand, his touch both reassuring and fraught with the burden of recent events. We had planned a quiet night, a much-needed reprieve from the turbulence of the past week. Yet, as we sat together on the couch, the silence between us was anything but peaceful. It was charged with the tension of unresolved feelings, the kind of quiet that precedes a storm.

"I've been thinking," Ethan began, his voice hesitant but earnest. "About everything that's happened. I don't want us to just gloss over it. We need to talk about it, really talk."

I met his gaze, my heart swelling with a mixture of relief and apprehension. "I agree. We need to face this head-on. Pretending it's not affecting us won't help."

We both knew that our feelings were raw and vulnerable, but acknowledging them was a crucial step in healing. Ethan's face was a canvas of conflicted emotions as he took a deep breath, the lines of worry etched deeply into his features. "I want you to know that my past with Lila doesn't diminish what we have. It's just... that part of my life is tangled with regrets and unresolved issues. I'm trying to sort through them, but I don't want them to overshadow what we're building together."

I nodded, feeling the sting of past insecurities rise to the surface. "I understand that. And I know it's not easy to navigate these feelings. But seeing her, hearing about the things you two shared—it brought back all the fears I thought I had overcome."

Ethan squeezed my hand gently, a gesture of solidarity and affection. "You don't have to go through this alone. I'm here, and I'm committed to making this work. We need to address these insecurities together. If there's anything you need to say or ask, I'm ready to listen."

The honesty in his words was a balm to my wounded heart. We spent the night unraveling the threads of our fears and doubts, each revelation a step towards understanding and healing. Ethan spoke about the complexities of his relationship with Lila, the emotions that had been stirred up, and the ways in which their past continued to ripple into his present. His willingness to be open about his vulnerabilities was both brave and reassuring.

"I guess I never fully realized how much of my past was still affecting me," he admitted, his voice tinged with regret. "I thought I had moved on, but seeing her again—being reminded of those old wounds—it's been harder than I expected."

I reached out to touch his face, feeling the weight of his struggle and the depth of his honesty. "It's okay to acknowledge that. We all have parts of our past that influence us, but it doesn't mean we can't work through them together. I want to understand what you're going through, and I want us to be stronger because of it."

The conversation was cathartic, a release of pent-up emotions and unspoken fears. We both confronted the ghosts of the past and reaffirmed our commitment to each other. It was not an easy process—there were tears and moments of silence, but there was also a renewed sense of intimacy and trust. We began to see that the challenges we faced were not obstacles but opportunities to deepen our connection and build a stronger foundation for our future.

As we lay in bed that night, the moon casting a soft glow over the room, I could feel the shift in our dynamic. The weight of unresolved feelings had lightened, replaced by a sense of mutual understanding and resolve. Ethan's arms around me were a comforting embrace, a silent promise that we would face whatever came our way together.

"I'm grateful for you," Ethan whispered, his voice a soothing murmur in the darkness. "For your patience, your willingness to work through this. It means more than I can express."

I snuggled closer, feeling the warmth of his body and the steady rhythm of his heartbeat. "And I'm grateful for you. For being open and honest. For reminding me that we're in this together, no matter what."

As we drifted off to sleep, the echoes of the past slowly receded, replaced by the hopeful anticipation of the future we were building. The road ahead was still uncertain, but we had faced the past with courage and commitment, emerging from the experience with a renewed sense of unity and strength. In the quiet of the night, we found solace in the knowledge that our love, tempered by honesty and understanding, was more resilient than any challenge that lay ahead.

As the days unfolded, the weight of the past settled into our lives with a subtle yet persistent pressure. The unexpected visit from Ethan's ex-partner, Lila, had stirred up a storm of unresolved feelings and insecurities that we had to face. What had started as an ordinary week quickly transformed into a journey of introspection and emotional confrontation.

Ethan and I had spent days trying to find our footing again. Every glance and every touch carried an undertone of the turbulence we had just endured. The days were spent in a haze of disjointed conversations and half-hearted smiles, while the nights were filled with the kind of silence that only deepens the distance between two people. It wasn't the kind of silence where words were unspoken; it was the kind where everything that needed to be said was too heavy to utter.

In the midst of this, we found ourselves having to navigate through a complex web of emotions and insecurities. I could see it in Ethan's eyes—he was wrestling with his own doubts and regrets, while I grappled with my own fears and uncertainties. We both wanted to reassure each other, to rebuild the fragile trust that had been momentarily shaken, but we weren't entirely sure how to begin.

One evening, as the sun dipped below the horizon, casting a warm glow over the living room, Ethan finally broached the subject we had been avoiding. He took a deep breath, his hand resting on the arm of the couch, a silent invitation for me to join him in this difficult conversation. I could see the struggle etched across his face, and my heart ached with the empathy of knowing how hard this was for him.

"I need to talk about something," Ethan began, his voice laced with vulnerability. "I've been thinking a lot about what happened with Lila and how it's affected us. I realize now that I didn't fully grasp how deeply it was affecting you, and for that, I'm sorry."

I settled beside him, the familiar warmth of his presence offering a small comfort amid the storm of emotions. "It's okay," I said softly. "We both have things to work through. I think what's been hardest for me is not just the encounter itself, but the feelings it stirred up—doubts and insecurities I thought I had put to rest."

He nodded, his eyes searching mine as if looking for a way to bridge the gap that had momentarily widened between us. "I want to understand what you're feeling. I want us to be able to talk about these things without any barriers. I'm committed to working through this with you, no matter how tough it gets."

The sincerity in his voice was a balm to my wounded heart. It was in these moments of raw honesty that I found the strength to confront my own insecurities. "I guess I just need to know that what we have is real and strong enough to withstand these kinds of challenges. Seeing Lila and dealing with the remnants of our past brought back a lot of old fears."

Ethan took my hand in his, his grip firm yet gentle. "I understand. I want to be transparent with you, to share everything that's on my mind. The truth is, seeing Lila again made me realize how far I've come since then and how much I value what we have. It also made me confront some of the mistakes I made in the past, but I want to assure you that my future is with you."

As we talked through the evening, the conversations were a mixture of introspection and reassurances. We shared our fears, our regrets, and our hopes for the future. There were moments when tears flowed freely, washing away some of the pain and uncertainty that had clouded our relationship. It wasn't just about addressing the past; it was about laying the groundwork for a stronger, more resilient future.

By the time the night drew to a close, the air between us felt lighter, as if we had cleared away some of the lingering fog. We had faced the past together, acknowledged the challenges it presented, and come out stronger on the other side. The commitment to each other, reinforced through these candid discussions, was a testament to the depth of our love and the strength of our bond.

In the quiet aftermath of our conversations, as we lay together in the soft glow of the bedroom light, there was a renewed sense of peace. The past, though it would always be a part of us, no longer held the power to define our relationship. We had faced it together, confronted our fears, and emerged more united than before.

Ethan wrapped his arms around me, his touch tender and reassuring. "Thank you for being so understanding and open," he whispered. "I know it hasn't been easy, but I'm grateful for your patience and love. We've faced something difficult, but we've done it together."

I nestled closer to him, feeling the steady rhythm of his heartbeat against my cheek. "And I'm grateful for you. For your honesty and commitment. We've turned a corner, and I believe we're stronger for it."

As we drifted into sleep, the comfort of each other's presence was a soothing balm to our troubled hearts. We had navigated the storm of unresolved issues and emerged on the other side with a renewed sense of purpose and unity. The future, once tinged with uncertainty, now seemed full of promise and possibility, illuminated by the strength of our shared commitment and the love that had carried us through.

# Chapter 17: Career Crossroads

The weight of uncertainty settled heavily over us as Ethan faced the major career decision that loomed on the horizon. It wasn't just a choice between job offers; it was a pivotal moment that could reshape the trajectory of our lives together. The opportunity was thrilling and daunting all at once, promising professional growth but also demanding a significant upheaval in our lives.

The days following the offer felt charged with a tense energy that was hard to ignore. Ethan's excitement was palpable, but so was his apprehension. He would have to relocate, leaving behind the life we had built together in our current city. It was more than just a move; it was a complete realignment of everything we had known. I watched as he poured over the details of the offer, his brow furrowed in concentration, his mind racing through every possible outcome.

I understood the gravity of the decision. This was a dream opportunity for Ethan, one he had worked tirelessly to reach. Yet, the thought of leaving behind the life we had painstakingly crafted together, the routines and friends we had made, was equally overwhelming. It was not merely a career crossroads; it was a relationship crossroads.

We spent countless evenings talking it through. Our conversations were a mixture of excitement and trepidation, with both of us grappling with the implications of each choice. The quiet hum of the city outside our window became the backdrop to our discussions, the stillness punctuated only by the murmurs of our deliberations.

"I never imagined it would come to this," Ethan admitted one night as we sat on the couch, the soft glow of the lamp casting shadows on his face. "It's everything I've ever wanted professionally, but it means leaving behind so much of what we have here."

I reached out, taking his hand in mine, the warmth of his skin a grounding force amidst the swirling chaos of our thoughts. "I know this is huge, Ethan. I want to support you, but it's not just about your career. It's about us. And I can't help but feel anxious about what this means for our future."

He nodded, his gaze distant as he contemplated the weight of my words. "I've been thinking about that too. I keep imagining what our life would look like if we made this move. And it's exciting but also terrifying. I want to make sure that whatever decision we make, it's the right one for both of us."

We explored every angle, from the logistics of the move to how it would impact our relationship. We talked about the new city, the opportunities it would present, and the sacrifices it would entail. Every discussion was punctuated with a mix of hope and apprehension, as we tried to envision a future that would be fulfilling and sustainable.

One evening, as we walked through the park, the cool air refreshing against our faces, Ethan took a deep breath, the weight of the decision apparent in his every step. "What if we made a pro and con list?" he suggested, trying to bring a semblance of order to the chaos in his mind.

I smiled, appreciating his attempt to bring some structure to our discussions. "I think that's a good idea. Let's lay everything out and see where we stand."

Back at home, we spread out a sheet of paper, each of us contributing our thoughts as we made the list. It was a cathartic exercise, helping to crystallize our thoughts and feelings. We listed the professional benefits, the personal sacrifices, the potential for growth, and the challenges we would face. As we wrote, it became clear that while the opportunity was indeed enticing, it also came with its share of trade-offs.

In the midst of our list-making, I could see Ethan grappling with his own internal struggle. The offer was more than just a job; it was a reflection of his ambitions and dreams. And yet, it was entwined with our shared life, making the decision all the more complex.

"I think we need to consider how this aligns with our long-term goals," I suggested, trying to steer our focus towards the bigger picture. "What are our dreams as a couple? How does this move fit into those dreams?"

Ethan paused, his pen hovering over the paper. "We've always talked about building a life together, one where we support each other's dreams. I want this job, but I also want us to be happy. I don't want to make a decision that jeopardizes what we have."

We spent hours discussing our future, mapping out our shared aspirations and how they could be affected by this decision. It was a process that required us to confront not only our individual desires but also our collective vision for the future.

In the end, our decision was not just about evaluating the pros and cons but about understanding how our choices aligned with our core values and dreams as a couple. It was about finding a balance between individual aspirations and our shared life, and coming to a decision that honored both.

As we sat together, the finality of our decision looming, I could see the resolve in Ethan's eyes. We had navigated this crossroads together, and while the path ahead was still uncertain, we knew that whatever choice we made, it would be one made with love and mutual respect. The journey ahead, with its challenges and opportunities, was one we would face hand in hand, fortified by the strength of our commitment and the depth of our shared dreams.

The weight of Ethan's career decision hung over us like a heavy mist, its presence undeniable in every conversation and quiet moment. We had spent weeks trying to weigh the impact of this pivotal choice, the uncertainty hanging between us like a tightrope we had to walk together. The decision was not just about a new job or a different city; it was about our shared future and the life we had envisioned for ourselves.

Ethan's enthusiasm for the opportunity was infectious. I could see the spark in his eyes whenever he spoke about the new role, the innovative projects, and the potential for growth. Yet, that spark was dimmed by the shadows of what we would be leaving behind. He was eager, but there was also a hesitance in his voice that spoke volumes about his inner conflict.

Our evenings were spent in quiet contemplation, the hum of our apartment a constant backdrop to our discussions. The offer was compelling, promising a significant leap in Ethan's career, but it was also a daunting change that required us to uproot our lives. We were facing a complex matrix of choices, each with its own set of ramifications.

One particularly crisp autumn evening, the air tinged with the scent of falling leaves, we decided to take a walk through the park. It was a familiar routine, one that often provided clarity amidst the confusion. The park, with its winding paths and dappled sunlight, had always been a place where we found solace and perspective.

As we strolled hand in hand, our steps synchronized, I could feel the tension in Ethan's grip. "I keep thinking about what we'd be leaving behind," he said, his voice tinged with frustration. "We've built so much here—our home, our friendships, everything."

I squeezed his hand reassuringly. "I know, Ethan. It's a lot to consider. But we have to think about what this move means for us in the long run. It's not just about what we're leaving; it's about what we're gaining and how it fits into our dreams."

He nodded, his eyes scanning the path ahead. "I've been thinking about that, too. This opportunity could be a game-changer for my career. But I don't want to make a decision that risks what we have. I keep wondering if it's worth the trade-off."

We paused by a large oak tree, its branches heavy with golden leaves. The tranquility of the park contrasted sharply with the turmoil inside us. I turned to Ethan, trying to capture the essence of our dilemma. "What if we made a list of what we would gain and lose from this move? It might help us see things more clearly."

Ethan agreed, and we spent the next few days meticulously outlining our pros and cons. The list was exhaustive, capturing every facet of the move—professional benefits, personal sacrifices, and the impact on our relationship. The process was both therapeutic and daunting, laying bare the complexities of our decision.

As we reviewed our lists, it became clear that while the professional opportunities were significant, they came with a series of compromises. We would be leaving behind the familiar comfort of our surroundings, the close-knit community we had built, and the rhythms of our daily life. The move would mean starting over in many ways, navigating a new city, and building new connections from scratch.

We also explored the emotional and relational aspects of the move. How would it affect our relationship? How would we adapt to the new environment and the challenges it would bring? The questions were numerous and complex, each demanding thoughtful consideration.

One night, after a particularly intense discussion, we sat together on the couch, the soft glow of the lamp casting a warm light around us. Ethan looked at me with a mixture of hope and apprehension. "What if we looked at this from a different angle? Instead of focusing on what we might lose, what if we focused on what we could gain?"

I tilted my head, considering his suggestion. "What do you mean?"

He took a deep breath, his gaze steady. "We've always dreamed of growing together, of supporting each other's ambitions. This opportunity could be a chance for us to do just that. It's not just about me; it's about us and how we can build our future together. Maybe it's about finding a balance between the professional and the personal, between our individual dreams and our shared goals."

His words resonated deeply with me. It was easy to get caught up in the fear of change and the comfort of the familiar, but it was also important to recognize the potential for growth and new experiences. We had always been partners in navigating life's challenges, and this was no different.

As we continued to explore our options, it became clear that the decision was not just about weighing pros and cons but about envisioning a future that aligned with our values and aspirations. We needed to find a way to balance our individual desires with our collective goals, to make a choice that honored both our personal dreams and our shared life.

In the end, our decision was less about the specifics of the move and more about our ability to navigate this crossroads together. It was about the strength of our commitment and the depth of our partnership. Whatever choice we made, we knew it would be one that we faced as a team, guided by our shared vision for the future and the unwavering support we had for each other.

In the weeks that followed, we found ourselves living in a liminal space, caught between the familiar comfort of our current life and the daunting promise of the unknown. Ethan and I spent hours talking, not just about the career move itself, but about the life we envisioned together—our hopes, fears, and what truly mattered to us.

One evening, as the golden light of the setting sun filtered through our living room window, Ethan and I settled into our favorite spots on the couch, a soft blanket draped over our laps. It was a quiet moment, one that had become a sanctuary from the whirlwind of decision-making.

"I keep thinking about how this move could change everything," Ethan said, his voice low and contemplative. "It's not just a job; it's a new chapter, a completely different setting for us to explore."

I nodded, trying to capture the essence of our conversation. "It's like standing on the edge of a cliff, isn't it? We can see the potential for something amazing, but there's this leap we have to take. And it's not just about whether we're ready to jump; it's about making sure we're jumping together."

Ethan's eyes met mine, and in that instant, I saw a flicker of the vulnerability that had been there throughout this process. "I've never doubted our relationship, but this decision feels like it could either propel us forward or pull us apart. I don't want to risk us for the sake of a career move."

There was a profound sincerity in his voice, and I could feel the weight of his words settle between us. "I don't want that either," I said softly. "But maybe we can look at it from a different angle. Instead of seeing it as a risk, what if we view it as an opportunity to grow? To build something new together?"

We spent the rest of the evening discussing our dreams, not just in terms of the career move but in the broader scope of our lives. We talked about the places we wanted to visit, the goals we wanted to achieve, and the kind of life we wanted to build. It was a conversation filled with excitement and trepidation, but it also reminded us of why we had chosen to be together in the first place.

One weekend, we took a short trip to a nearby town, seeking a change of scenery to help clear our minds. As we wandered through quaint streets and explored new cafes, the conversations about the career move took on a new tone. It wasn't just about the logistics anymore; it was about how this change could be a part of our journey together.

During a quiet moment in a cozy park, Ethan took my hand and led me to a bench overlooking a serene pond. The setting sun cast a warm glow across the water, creating a peaceful backdrop for our discussion.

"I've been thinking," he began, his voice steady, "about what we talked about the other night. I realize now that this move isn't just about the job; it's about the kind of life we want to create. And maybe the risk isn't in the move itself but in not taking it and wondering what might have been."

I squeezed his hand, feeling a surge of emotion. "I've been feeling the same way. This could be an opportunity for us to embrace change, to explore new possibilities together. And if we face challenges, we'll face them as a team."

As the days passed, we continued to weigh our options, not just from a practical standpoint but from an emotional and aspirational one. We made lists, had discussions, and sought advice from friends and family. Each conversation brought us closer to a decision that felt right for us.

The decision wasn't easy, and it wasn't clear-cut. It involved sacrifices and adjustments, but it also held the promise of new experiences and growth. We realized that the key to navigating this crossroads was not in avoiding the risks but in embracing the journey together.

One evening, as we sat in our living room, the final decision looming, Ethan turned to me with a sense of calm resolve. "I've thought about everything we've discussed, and I think we're ready to take this leap. We've always supported each other, and I believe this is another chance for us to grow together."

I smiled, feeling a deep sense of relief and anticipation. "I agree. It's not just about the move; it's about the future we're building together. Whatever comes next, we'll face it together, just like we always have."

In that moment, with the weight of the decision finally lifted, we felt a renewed sense of unity and purpose. The crossroads had brought us closer, reinforcing our commitment to each other and to the future we envisioned. As we prepared to embark on this new chapter, we did so with the confidence that our love and partnership would guide us through whatever lay ahead.

As the day of our move approached, the air was thick with anticipation and a touch of apprehension. The decision to embrace Ethan's new career opportunity had not been an easy one, but it was one we faced together with a shared sense of adventure. The packing boxes scattered around our apartment were more than just physical objects; they were symbolic of the life we were leaving behind and the new experiences awaiting us.

Ethan and I spent our evenings sorting through belongings, reminiscing about the memories each item held. The process was bittersweet, a mixture of excitement and nostalgia that made the impending change feel both exhilarating and daunting. Each box packed was a step further into this new chapter, each label a promise of the future we were about to build.

One particular evening, after a long day of packing and organizing, we sat on the floor amidst the sea of cardboard and bubble wrap. The living room, once vibrant with the colors of our shared life, was now reduced to a canvas of transitional chaos. Ethan reached over and took my hand, his gaze steady and warm.

"We're really doing this," he said softly, a smile playing on his lips. "I never imagined we'd be here, on the brink of such a big change."

I squeezed his hand, feeling a rush of emotions. "I know. It's a huge step, but it feels right. We've talked about it, weighed the pros and cons, and we've decided this is the path we want to take. And no matter what, we'll be navigating it together."

Our days leading up to the move were a flurry of final preparations and goodbyes. Friends and family came by to offer their support and share in the bittersweet farewell. Each goodbye was a reminder of the life we were leaving behind but also of the new beginnings that lay ahead.

On moving day, we stood together in the empty apartment, taking one last look at the space that had been our home. The echoes of our laughter and the memories of our shared moments seemed to linger in the air, a testament to the life we had built together. Ethan wrapped his arm around me, pulling me close.

"Are you ready?" he asked, his voice filled with a mixture of excitement and nervousness.

I looked up at him, feeling a sense of calm settle over me. "I am. Let's embrace this change and see where it takes us."

The drive to our new city was filled with a sense of adventure. We talked about our hopes and dreams for this new chapter, envisioning the life we would build together. The road stretched out before us, a metaphor for the journey we were embarking on, full of possibilities and new experiences.

Arriving in our new home was both exhilarating and overwhelming. The unfamiliarity of the surroundings was a stark contrast to the comfort of our previous life, but it was also filled with potential. We spent the first few days unpacking and setting up our new space, turning the house into a home with our personal touches and shared memories.

The transition was not without its challenges. Navigating a new city, finding our favorite spots, and adjusting to a new routine tested our patience and adaptability. Yet, through it all, Ethan and I found solace in each other's company. The moments of frustration were tempered by our mutual support and the understanding that this change was an integral part of our journey together.

In the quiet moments of our new life, whether it was exploring a new neighborhood or enjoying a simple meal at home, we found comfort in the knowledge that we had made this decision together.

The challenges of relocation were tempered by the joy of discovering new aspects of our relationship and our shared life.

As the weeks went by, our new city began to feel like home. We created new routines, made new friends, and embraced the opportunities that came our way. The initial feelings of uncertainty and displacement gradually gave way to a sense of belonging and contentment.

Ethan's career move had not only introduced us to a new environment but had also brought us closer together. The experience of facing this change united us in ways we had not anticipated. We learned to navigate the uncertainties of our new life with optimism and resilience, drawing strength from our commitment to each other.

In the end, the journey of embracing change proved to be a transformative experience for both of us. It reinforced the depth of our bond and our ability to face challenges together. As we settled into our new life, we did so with the confidence that our love and partnership would guide us through whatever lay ahead.

The move was more than just a change in geography; it was a reaffirmation of our shared dreams and the strength of our relationship. We had faced the uncertainties of relocation with courage and optimism, and in doing so, we had strengthened our commitment to each other. The new chapter of our lives was just beginning, and we embraced it with open hearts and unwavering support for one another.

Settling into our new surroundings was both a challenge and a discovery. Each day brought with it a new facet of the city that we had yet to explore. From the bustling markets to the tranquil parks, every corner held the promise of new experiences and memories. Yet, amidst the excitement, there were moments when the unfamiliarity of it all felt overwhelming.

Our new apartment, though charming, seemed vast and empty in those early days. The once vibrant walls of our previous home had been replaced by a blank canvas, waiting for us to imprint our essence upon it. It was in these quiet moments of transition that we both felt the weight of our decision—how it had changed not just our location but the rhythm of our lives.

One evening, as we sat on the floor surrounded by unpacked boxes and half-assembled furniture, Ethan looked at me with a mixture of exhaustion and excitement. He reached over, his fingers brushing against mine in a gesture of reassurance.

"How are you holding up?" he asked, his voice soft but filled with concern.

I looked around at the scattered remnants of our move, the echoes of our old life mingling with the fresh start we were trying to create. "It's a lot to take in, but I'm okay. I'm actually excited about it all. It just feels... different."

Ethan nodded, understanding the complexity of our emotions. "Yeah, it feels different for me too. It's like we're on the edge of something new and unknown, but it's also thrilling. We've done this together so far, and we'll get through this too."

His words were a balm to my uncertainties, reminding me of the strength we had found in each other. Our shared journey had always been marked by these moments of uncertainty, but our ability to face them together had been our greatest strength.

As we continued to unpack and settle in, we discovered the small joys of our new environment. We found a cozy café down the street that quickly became our favorite spot for weekend brunches. The barista, with her warm smile and familiarity, became a small anchor in the sea of change.

Our weekends were filled with exploring our new city. We wandered through local markets, sampled cuisine from different cultures, and attended neighborhood events. Each adventure brought us closer, not just to the city but to each other. The shared experiences were like small threads weaving a new tapestry of our lives.

Yet, not every day was filled with discovery and delight. There were moments of frustration—misplaced items, confusing directions, and the occasional pang of homesickness. During these times, we clung to each other, finding solace in our shared resolve. Our conversations often turned to our plans and dreams, a way to remind ourselves why we had embarked on this journey.

One particularly challenging day, as we struggled with the logistics of setting up our new home, Ethan looked at me with a tired smile. "Remember when we first started dating and we talked about all the dreams we had for the future? I think we're living them, one step at a time."

I took a deep breath, letting his words wash over me. "I do remember. It feels like we're still in the middle of that dream, working through the hurdles to get to the next chapter. But with you by my side, it feels like we can handle anything."

Our ability to find joy amidst the struggle was a testament to our resilience. The challenges of relocating were significant, but they were also opportunities for growth. Each obstacle we overcame together strengthened our bond and deepened our understanding of one another.

In the quiet moments of our new life, whether it was a late-night conversation or a shared laugh over a homemade dinner, we found comfort in our unity. The unfamiliarity of our surroundings became less daunting as we navigated it hand in hand. The transition was a test of our commitment, but it was also a chance to reaffirm our love and partnership.

As the weeks turned into months, our new city began to feel like home. The once-foreign streets became familiar paths, and the new experiences we had sought became part of our daily routine. We had faced the uncertainties of change with courage and optimism, and in doing so, had woven a new chapter into the tapestry of our lives.

The journey of embracing change had not been easy, but it had been transformative. It had reinforced our commitment to each other and our ability to navigate life's challenges together. The new chapter we had embarked upon was filled with possibilities, and as we looked ahead, we did so with the confidence that our love and resilience would guide us through whatever lay ahead.

Navigating through the sea of boxes and the disarray of our new apartment, there was a palpable sense of anticipation in the air. Each day felt like a new beginning, full of promise and potential. We tackled our unpacking with a mix of determination and humor, finding joy in the mundane tasks that came with making a new place our own.

One evening, after a particularly grueling day of sorting through piles of clothes and kitchenware, we decided to take a break. We found ourselves on the small balcony of our apartment, watching the sunset paint the sky in hues of pink and orange. It was a rare moment of tranquility amid the chaos.

Ethan pulled me close, his arms wrapping around me in a comforting embrace. The warmth of his body against mine was a reminder of the strength we drew from each other. We stood there in silence, the city lights beginning to twinkle below, sharing a quiet reflection on our journey.

"This view is incredible," Ethan said softly, breaking the silence. "It's hard to believe we're actually here."

I sighed contentedly, leaning my head against his shoulder. "It really is. It's like we've stepped into a new chapter of our lives, and it feels both exhilarating and a little overwhelming."

He kissed the top of my head, his touch gentle and reassuring. "We've faced so many changes together, and each time, we've come out stronger. I know this is a big transition, but I believe we can handle it just like we've handled everything else."

His confidence was a balm to my anxieties. The transition had indeed been challenging, but in those quiet moments, I found clarity and strength. Our love and commitment were our anchors, keeping us grounded even as we faced the waves of change.

As the days turned into weeks, we began to find our rhythm in the new city. We established routines that blended our old habits with new discoveries. Morning jogs in the nearby park, weekend visits to local markets, and evenings spent exploring hidden gems of the city became part of our new normal.

One weekend, as we wandered through a bustling street fair, we stumbled upon a small bookstore with a cozy café tucked inside. The smell of freshly brewed coffee and the sight of rows of bookshelves filled with literary treasures immediately drew us in. It became our new favorite spot—a haven where we could escape the whirlwind of relocation and immerse ourselves in our shared love for stories and quiet moments together.

Amidst the excitement of exploring our new surroundings, there were still moments of doubt and homesickness. The familiarity of our old home and the comfort of our previous routines were missed. Yet, each time we encountered a challenge, we faced it with a renewed sense of partnership and determination.

One evening, after a particularly tough day at work, Ethan came home looking exhausted. I met him at the door with a smile, a simple gesture that spoke volumes about our unwavering support for one another. We spent the evening talking about our day, sharing our frustrations and victories, and finding solace in each other's company.

"It's been a long day," Ethan said, sinking onto the couch. "But I'm so grateful for you. Your support means everything to me."

I joined him on the couch, resting my head on his shoulder. "And I'm grateful for you too. We're building something incredible here, and even though it's tough, I wouldn't want to do it with anyone else."

His arms tightened around me, and for a moment, the weight of the move and the uncertainty of our new chapter seemed to lift. We were in this together, facing each challenge as a team, and that was what made the journey worthwhile.

As the months passed, the city began to feel more like home. We developed friendships, found favorite spots, and made countless memories in our new environment. The initial discomfort and disorientation gave way to a sense of belonging and contentment.

Our commitment to each other had been tested, but it had emerged stronger. The relocation, while daunting, had reinforced our bond and deepened our appreciation for the life we were building together. Each day, we faced the challenges with optimism and resilience, knowing that our love was the foundation upon which we built our future.

In the end, embracing change had been a transformative experience for us. It had tested our strength, but it had also brought us closer, reaffirming our commitment to each other. As we looked ahead, we did so with confidence, knowing that whatever challenges lay ahead, we would face them together, united by our love and shared dreams.

# Chapter 18: Building a Home

The first rays of morning light filtered through the gauzy curtains, casting a soft glow over the empty space that would soon become our home. Boxes were strewn about, their contents still packed away in neat layers of bubble wrap and cardboard. The apartment, though bare, held the promise of transformation, a blank canvas waiting for the imprint of our shared dreams.

Ethan and I stood together in the middle of the living room, a shared smile passing between us. We had spent countless hours discussing how we envisioned our space, blending our individual tastes into a harmonious whole. It was more than just decorating; it was about creating a sanctuary where we could nurture our relationship and our future.

Our first task was to tackle the living room. The walls, painted a neutral beige, were the backdrop for a vibrant tapestry of memories we intended to weave. Ethan's love for bold colors and rich textures was evident as he eagerly picked out a deep, royal blue sofa that stood in striking contrast to the light walls. It was a choice that spoke to his heritage, a nod to the lively culture he brought into our lives.

I, on the other hand, had always been drawn to softer hues and cozy, inviting fabrics. My touch was evident in the selection of throw pillows in muted pastels and a plush area rug that promised warmth underfoot. We debated over patterns and textures, each decision a delicate dance of compromise and collaboration. Our differing tastes were a reflection of our unique backgrounds, and the process of merging them into one cohesive design felt like a metaphor for our relationship.

As we carefully arranged the furniture and placed each decorative item in its spot, our home began to take shape. Each piece we chose held significance: the hand-painted Mexican ceramic vases Ethan picked up during his travels, the vintage Southern prints I had collected over the years. They were more than just decor; they were pieces of our stories, symbols of where we came from and where we were headed.

In the kitchen, where we spent many of our evenings cooking together, the blending of our cultural influences was particularly evident. I had always adored the charm of a well-stocked kitchen, complete with classic Southern cookware and cheerful, patterned dishware. Ethan's touch added a layer of vibrancy with colorful ceramic bowls and traditional Mexican utensils. Together, we created a space that was not only functional but a true reflection of our shared love for food and family.

One afternoon, as we were placing the final touches on the bedroom, Ethan looked around and said, "I never realized how much of ourselves we put into our space. It's like we've built a little piece of our lives here."

I nodded, admiring the way the room had come together—a perfect blend of my affinity for delicate, vintage-inspired furnishings and Ethan's bold, modern accents. "It feels like home, doesn't it? Like a place where all our pieces fit perfectly."

As we hung the final picture on the wall—a photograph of a sunset we had watched together on one of our trips—the room seemed to come alive with our shared history. It was in those small, intimate details that our love story was woven into the fabric of our home.

The process of decorating had not always been easy. There were moments of disagreement and compromise, late-night debates over design choices, and a few small arguments about which shade of paint would work best. But through it all, we learned to navigate our differences with patience and understanding. Each decision made was a testament to our commitment to one another and to the life we were building together.

The final result was more than just a well-decorated apartment; it was a tangible representation of our journey. Our home was a reflection of both our personalities and our shared experiences—a place where our cultures met, mingled, and created something uniquely our own.

As we stood together in the middle of our newly furnished living room, holding hands and taking in the fruits of our labor, I felt an overwhelming sense of contentment. The space around us was no longer just four walls; it was a haven where we could build our future and cherish our past. It was a place where our love could grow, nurtured by the warmth of our shared experiences and the dreams we held for the years to come.

In that moment, surrounded by the pieces of our lives and the marks of our shared efforts, I realized that home wasn't just about a physical space. It was about the love and commitment we poured into it, the way we navigated our differences, and the joy we found in creating something together. Our home was a living testament to our journey, a beautiful, ever-evolving reflection of the life we were building side by side.

The sun had begun to dip below the horizon, casting a warm, golden hue across our newly furnished living room. The gentle hum of the city outside was a distant murmur, softened by the cocoon of our home. We had spent the entire day unpacking, arranging, and debating over the perfect placement of our belongings. Each item, whether it was a piece of art or a simple vase, felt like a fragment of our journey—a story waiting to be told in the way it was displayed.

The living room was now alive with color and texture. Ethan's choice of a vibrant blue couch seemed to anchor the space, its boldness softened by the array of throw pillows that had found their place like puzzle pieces on the cushions. I had insisted on a collection of pastels and florals, a nod to my Southern upbringing, and seeing them nestled against the deep blue made me smile. The contrast was striking, yet it worked in a way that felt both refreshing and familiar.

As we took a moment to step back and admire our work, Ethan's gaze lingered on a piece of art that had become a centerpiece of the room—a Mexican folk art painting we had chosen together. It was vibrant, filled with life and color, a stark yet beautiful contrast to the more subdued Southern prints that adorned the walls. It was a symbol of our shared journey, a blending of cultures that spoke to our commitment to creating something uniquely ours.

"You know," Ethan said, running a hand through his hair, "I was a bit worried about how this would all come together. Our tastes are so different, but it seems like we've found a balance."

I laughed softly, leaning against the arm of the couch. "I think that's what makes it work. It's not about one style overpowering the other. It's about finding harmony in our differences."

He nodded, reaching out to tuck a stray strand of hair behind my ear. "It's like a dance. We each have our own steps, but together, we create something beautiful."

The bedroom had been a project of its own. We had spent hours deliberating over the right bedding, the perfect arrangement of furniture, and how to incorporate elements from both our lives. Ethan's choice of a modern, sleek bed frame contrasted with my preference for soft, vintage-inspired linens. But in the end, the combination felt like a perfect reflection of us—modern and classic, bold and gentle.

On the dresser, we had placed a series of framed photographs, each capturing a moment from our time together. From our first trip to the mountains to the quiet evenings spent cooking in our old apartment, each photo was a reminder of the life we had built. Surrounding them were small trinkets we had collected over the years—a mix of Mexican ceramics and Southern antiques. They seemed to tell our story in a way that words alone could not.

As we arranged the last few items, the scent of dinner began to waft through the apartment. Ethan had taken on the task of cooking, a role he embraced with enthusiasm. He was in the kitchen, his laughter and the clinking of pots creating a comforting backdrop to our work. I joined him, my fingers brushing against his as I helped with the final touches. The kitchen, like the rest of our home, was a blend of our influences—bright Mexican tiles alongside classic Southern cookware.

Dinner was a simple affair, but the meal itself was a celebration. We sat down at the table we had carefully chosen—a wooden piece that felt sturdy and timeless, much like our relationship. As we shared our meal, the conversation flowed easily, punctuated by laughter and the occasional clink of glasses. The food was delicious, a mix of traditional Mexican dishes and Southern comfort foods, a culinary representation of our blended lives.

After dinner, we sat on the couch, the room now illuminated by the soft glow of table lamps and the gentle flicker of candles. The space felt like a warm embrace, each corner reflecting our personalities and our shared experiences. We talked about our future plans, the dreams we had for our home and our lives together. There was a sense of peace in the way we spoke about what lay ahead—an understanding that, no matter what challenges we might face, we were in this together.

As the night wore on and the city outside grew quieter, we took a moment to simply enjoy the stillness. Our home, still fresh with the scent of new beginnings, felt like a sanctuary—a place where we could be ourselves, build our dreams, and nurture our relationship.

In that quiet, intimate moment, I realized that our home was more than just a place. It was a symbol of our journey, a testament to our love and commitment. It was a reflection of who we were as individuals and as a couple, a space where we could grow, thrive, and build the future we had always envisioned.

As the days turned into weeks, our home gradually transformed from a blank canvas into a vibrant tapestry of our shared life. The process, though sometimes fraught with decisions and compromises, felt exhilarating. Every choice we made—whether it was the placement of a piece of artwork or the selection of a new throw blanket—became a testament to our journey together, each detail meticulously chosen to represent our collective story.

The kitchen, once a neutral space, now sang with color and life. Ethan's insistence on a bold Mexican tile backsplash had initially clashed with my more subdued Southern sensibilities. Yet, as the tiles were installed, their intricate patterns blended seamlessly with the warmth of our wooden cabinets and the classic charm of my grandmother's old ceramic dishes. It was a marriage of styles, as effortless as the way we navigated our differing tastes. The result was a kitchen that felt lively and welcoming, a perfect setting for the countless meals and memories yet to come.

The living room had become a cozy retreat, its walls adorned with a carefully curated mix of our favorite pieces. The large bookshelf we had found at a vintage market now held not just books but also souvenirs from our travels—trinkets and mementos that told the story of us. Each item was strategically placed to catch the eye and spark a conversation, from the small, colorful Mexican figurines to the framed Southern folk art prints. It was a room that invited relaxation and conversation, a place where we could truly be ourselves.

One of our favorite parts of the house was the small garden we had begun to cultivate. What started as a patch of bare earth behind our new home had gradually taken shape as a vibrant garden, filled with both Mexican and Southern flora. We planted sunflowers alongside marigolds, their bright colors and cheerful faces a daily reminder of the merging of our lives. The garden became a shared project, a place where we could escape the hustle and bustle of everyday life and connect with nature and each other.

On weekends, we would spend hours out there, hands dirty and hearts light. We'd laugh as we attempted to identify which plants needed more sun or less water, often with mixed results. The garden, much like our home, was a work in progress. But with each new bloom and every fresh sprout, it became a more beautiful reflection of our shared commitment.

Evenings often found us curled up on the couch, surrounded by the soft glow of string lights and the gentle hum of our carefully curated playlist. The atmosphere was intimate, each corner of the room whispering tales of our past and dreams for the future. We would talk late into the night, discussing everything from our plans for the next vacation to the small, everyday things that made us laugh.

It wasn't always easy—there were moments of frustration, decisions that felt overwhelmingly complex, and times when the blend of our different backgrounds seemed like a challenge rather than a joy. Yet, in those moments of tension, we would pause and remind ourselves of the bigger picture. Each challenge was an opportunity to grow, to deepen our understanding of one another, and to solidify our bond.

One rainy afternoon, as we sat together in the living room, Ethan pulled out a small box from beneath the coffee table. Inside was a collection of notes and sketches we had made over the months, ideas for future improvements and dreams for our home. It was a scrapbook of sorts, capturing the evolution of our space and the plans we had for it. As we looked through it together, there was a profound sense of accomplishment and contentment. We had created a home that was not just a place to live but a living testament to our shared journey and growth.

By the time the final touches were added, our home had become a sanctuary, a space filled with warmth, love, and a deep sense of belonging. It was a place where we could escape the outside world and find solace in each other's company. Each room was a chapter in our story, a reflection of who we were and who we hoped to become.

The process of building this home had been a journey of discovery and connection. It had tested our patience and our creativity, but it had also brought us closer together. In every choice we made and every detail we added, we found new ways to understand and appreciate each other. Our home was more than just a physical space; it was a manifestation of our love and our commitment to building a future together.

As we stood in the doorway, looking out at the garden we had nurtured together, we knew that this home was just the beginning. It was a place where we could build our dreams, create new memories, and continue to grow as a couple. And as we faced the future, we did so with a sense of excitement and optimism, knowing that no matter what came our way, we had already created something truly special.

# Chapter 19: Navigating New Challenges

Settling into a new city is like being handed a blank canvas and a palette of colors you've never quite used before. The city's rhythm is a tune we don't yet know by heart, and every street, every corner, every turn is a note in a melody that feels both thrilling and overwhelming. The unfamiliarity of it all can be daunting, but with Ethan by my side, the uncertainties seem more like opportunities than obstacles.

Our apartment, once a cozy sanctuary, now feels like a small boat drifting on a vast sea of new experiences. The city's pulse is constant, its energy vibrant and relentless. We find ourselves caught between the excitement of discovery and the quiet frustration of feeling like outsiders in our own lives. The pace here is different—faster, perhaps more urgent—and adapting to it requires more than just physical relocation; it demands a shift in mindset, a new way of engaging with the world around us.

Mornings are a whirlwind of activity. We're both trying to find our footing in our new jobs, which come with their own set of challenges and adjustments. Ethan's work, though fulfilling, is demanding, and the hours are long. I watch him navigate his new role with a blend of determination and fatigue, and I am reminded of the sacrifices he's made for this opportunity. His resilience inspires me, but it also highlights the need for us to find our rhythm together amidst these new demands.

Evenings are a different story. Our attempts to recreate the comforting rituals of home—cooking dinner together, watching our favorite shows—become more like cherished islands of calm in an otherwise tumultuous sea. We're learning to navigate this new normal, finding solace in the small moments of connection that anchor us amidst the whirlwind of change.

The social landscape here is unfamiliar, and forging new friendships feels like stepping into a new world of etiquette and expectations. I remember our first few outings, where every conversation felt like a dance of polite gestures and tentative smiles. Ethan, ever the extrovert, seems to thrive in these social settings, effortlessly engaging with colleagues and neighbors. I, on the other hand, find myself grappling with the nuances of small talk, feeling like a puzzle piece that doesn't quite fit.

Yet, through these social forays, I begin to appreciate the beauty of the new city's diversity. Each new person we meet adds a different shade to our experience, and slowly, the city's unfamiliarity begins to feel less like an imposition and more like a canvas we're learning to paint on. We find ourselves drawn to the city's eclectic mix of culture, food, and experiences, and our adventures together become a source of bonding and discovery.

Professionally, the adjustment is equally challenging. Ethan's career demands more of him than we anticipated, and the balance between his professional aspirations and our personal life requires constant negotiation. The pressure of success, while invigorating, also brings a weight that sometimes feels heavy. We have to find ways to support each other through these demands, knowing that our relationship is as much a priority as our individual goals.

For me, navigating my own career in this new environment has its own hurdles. The sense of starting from scratch, of needing to prove myself all over again, is both daunting and invigorating. I find solace in the routine of my work but struggle with the pangs of homesickness that creep in when the days feel long and the connections feel thin.

Despite these challenges, the process of navigating them together strengthens our bond. We become each other's support system, the steady presence in the storm of change. There are moments of tension, of frustration, and of longing for the familiar. But through each challenge, we discover new facets of our relationship, new ways of understanding and supporting one another.

The city, with its relentless pace and constant change, becomes a backdrop to our journey of adaptation and growth. We find ourselves facing challenges that test our patience, our resilience, and our love. But with each passing day, we also discover new strengths within ourselves and each other. The hurdles we face are not just obstacles but opportunities for us to deepen our connection and solidify our commitment to building a life together.

In this new chapter of our lives, the city's rhythm becomes our own. We learn to dance to its beat, finding moments of joy and comfort in the midst of the chaos. The challenges, though daunting, become the threads that weave our story together, creating a tapestry of shared experiences and triumphs. And as we continue to navigate this new terrain, we do so with the knowledge that, no matter how daunting the challenges may be, we face them together, and together, we are stronger.

Every morning, the city greets us with its cacophony of sounds—honking horns, distant chatter, and the steady hum of activity that never seems to pause. Ethan and I have begun to adapt to this new rhythm, finding our way through the maze of unfamiliar streets and faces. We've become adept at navigating the subway system, though every journey still feels like an adventure in its own right.

Our weekends have become a refuge, a time to escape the demands of our new routines and reconnect with each other. We explore neighborhoods we haven't yet discovered, finding hidden cafes and parks that slowly make this sprawling metropolis feel like home. These outings are a balm to our often-overwhelmed spirits, a chance to breathe and remind ourselves of why we took this leap of faith.

As we establish our lives here, it's clear that the city has its own tempo, one that often clashes with our own. The fast-paced nature of our workweeks leaves us feeling drained, and the balancing act of maintaining a healthy relationship amidst the hustle and bustle is no small feat. Ethan, with his ambitious goals and demanding job, often finds himself absorbed in work long after the office hours have ended. I, too, feel the strain of my new professional responsibilities, the pressure of proving myself in an environment where I'm still finding my footing.

Despite the challenges, our evenings together offer a sanctuary. We cook dinner side by side, our conversations punctuated by the clinking of utensils and the aroma of our favorite dishes. These moments, though simple, become anchors in the sea of change, reminding us of our shared history and the comfort of our familiar routines. It's in these quiet times that we reaffirm our commitment to one another, finding solace in the mundane and joy in our togetherness.

Navigating social circles in a new city has been another test of our resilience. The friends we've made so far are a mix of friendly faces and fleeting acquaintances. I often find myself longing for the depth of connections I left behind, the easy camaraderie of old friends. Yet, as Ethan thrives in social settings and effortlessly mingles with colleagues and new acquaintances, I'm learning to find my own way. The social fabric of the city is rich and varied, and while building new friendships is a slow process, each interaction adds a new layer to our experience here.

Ethan's work demands also bring their own set of challenges. His career, while exciting and full of potential, often requires long hours and frequent travel. The strain of maintaining our relationship while he's away can be tough. We make a point to stay connected through calls and messages, but it's not always easy. The distance, both physical and emotional, sometimes creates a void that we struggle to fill. Yet, each time he returns home, the reunion is a sweet reminder of the strength of our bond and the importance of our time together.

The city's pace often feels like a race we're trying to keep up with. The whirlwind of activity can be overwhelming, leaving little room for the quiet moments that we cherish. We find ourselves craving the simple pleasures—a lazy Sunday morning, a quiet walk in the park, a heartfelt conversation over a shared meal. These moments, though fleeting, become treasures that sustain us amidst the busyness of our new life.

Through these trials, we're learning to lean on each other more than ever. Our communication, once perhaps more casual, has become a lifeline. We talk openly about our fears, our frustrations, and our dreams. The honesty between us deepens, allowing us to navigate the complexities of our new life with a sense of partnership and shared purpose. Every challenge we face together strengthens the foundation of our relationship, reminding us of the love and commitment that brought us here.

As we continue to settle into this new chapter, it becomes clear that the city, with all its vibrancy and chaos, is shaping our journey in ways we hadn't anticipated. The adjustment is a process of discovery, of finding balance in the midst of change. We're learning to embrace the unpredictability of our new life, finding joy in the small victories and comfort in our shared experiences.

Together, Ethan and I are carving out a space for ourselves in this bustling metropolis, creating a life that reflects both our dreams and our realities. The challenges we face are shaping us, but they are also bringing us closer. Each day, as we navigate the twists and turns of our new life, we do so with the knowledge that, no matter how daunting the journey may seem, we are in it together, and together, we are building something truly special.

The days continue to blend into each other, each one presenting its own set of hurdles and triumphs. Ethan and I navigate our new routines with a mix of determination and patience. The city, once an intimidating expanse of concrete and steel, has begun to reveal its nuances. We've discovered our favorite spots—little cafes with the best coffee, parks where the sunlight filters through the trees just right, and quirky bookstores that seem to have a soul of their own. These places are becoming landmarks in our shared adventure, a way to ground ourselves amidst the whirlwind of change.

Amidst the excitement of exploration, we also face the inevitable setbacks. There are days when the weight of the new city's demands feels overwhelming, and we find ourselves exhausted by the constant push and pull of adapting. Ethan's long hours at work sometimes stretch into the evenings, and I, too, struggle to keep up with the fast-paced rhythm of my job. We miss the luxury of time, the slow, leisurely weekends we used to enjoy. The constant adjustment takes its toll, and the brief moments of frustration and fatigue occasionally cloud our interactions.

Yet, even on those tough days, we find solace in each other. Our evening routines become a sanctuary from the chaos. We cook together, the rhythmic chopping of vegetables and the comforting aroma of simmering sauces creating a cocoon of normalcy. During these moments, we're reminded of the simplicity and strength of our connection. There's a quiet understanding between us—a shared appreciation for the small joys and the unspoken bond that holds us together.

The process of making new friends and establishing ourselves professionally is both exhilarating and daunting. Ethan's charisma makes it easier for him to strike up conversations and network, while I'm slowly finding my footing. I attend social events and networking functions, often feeling like an outsider in a sea of familiar faces. Yet, every time I engage in conversation, I take a small step towards feeling more integrated. Ethan's encouragement and support during these times are invaluable, his belief in me helping to ease my apprehensions.

We often reflect on our journey together, recognizing how far we've come and the strength we've gained. The city's challenges have forced us to confront our vulnerabilities and to rely on each other in ways we hadn't anticipated. There are moments when we question our choices, wondering if we've bitten off more than we can chew. But as we face these doubts, we lean into our shared commitment, reminding ourselves of the reasons behind our decision to embark on this new chapter.

Each challenge we overcome becomes a testament to our resilience and adaptability. Whether it's adjusting to a new work environment or figuring out how to balance our personal time, we're learning to navigate these obstacles with grace and patience. Our relationship is tested, but it's also strengthened by the trials we face together. We're building a new life from the ground up, and each small victory—a successful presentation, a new friend, a quiet evening together—serves as a reminder of what we're capable of achieving.

The transition to our new life is a journey of continual growth and discovery. We're finding our rhythm in this vibrant, fast-paced city, learning to blend our personal and professional lives into a harmonious balance. The challenges, though demanding, are shaping us into a stronger, more unified team. Each day brings its own set of lessons, and as we navigate these new experiences, we do so with a deepening sense of purpose and connection.

Despite the inevitable struggles, we're learning to embrace the unpredictability of our new life. The city, with all its vibrancy and complexity, is becoming a part of our story. The trials we face are no longer just obstacles; they are opportunities for growth and understanding. Together, we're adapting to our new environment, carving out a space for ourselves amidst the chaos.

As we continue to explore and adapt, our love and commitment remain the constant anchors in our lives. We face each challenge with the knowledge that we're in it together, that our shared experiences are building a foundation for our future. The journey is far from easy, but it's ours, and with every step, we're writing a story that is uniquely our own.

# Chapter 20: A Milestone Celebration

The anniversary of our second chance at love arrived with the gentle grace of an autumn breeze, carrying with it the promise of reflection and celebration. It wasn't just another date on the calendar; it was a testament to the journey we'd navigated together, a milestone that marked the resilience and strength of our bond. As the day approached, Ethan and I found ourselves both excited and contemplative, savoring the significance of this moment in our lives.

In the weeks leading up to the anniversary, we poured our hearts into planning an event that would reflect the essence of our relationship. It wasn't about grandeur or extravagance; instead, we focused on the details that spoke to our shared experiences and the growth we had achieved together. We envisioned a celebration that would capture the spirit of our journey—a blend of intimacy and festivity, laughter and introspection.

The venue we chose was a quaint, rustic hall nestled on the outskirts of the city, a place that felt like an extension of our shared story. Its charm lay in its simplicity—a blank canvas that we could transform into a reflection of us. The space was adorned with soft, twinkling lights that cast a warm, golden hue over everything. Floral arrangements of deep burgundy and cream adorned the tables, and candles flickered gently, creating an ambiance of warmth and nostalgia.

As the evening unfolded, the hall filled with the people who had been integral to our journey. Friends and family gathered, their faces beaming with joy and love. Each person's presence was a reminder of the network of support and affection that had buoyed us through our ups and downs. Their smiles and heartfelt conversations served as a poignant reminder of how far we had come, and how deeply we had been loved and supported.

Ethan and I took a moment to step back and absorb the scene. The laughter, the clinking of glasses, the soft strains of music in the background—it all felt like a beautiful echo of our journey. We looked at each other with a mix of pride and tenderness, knowing that this celebration was more than just a party. It was a reflection of the love and commitment we had nurtured, a celebration of our shared resilience and growth.

The speeches began, and as friends and family took to the floor to share their thoughts, their words were a tapestry of memories and well-wishes. Each story and anecdote was a piece of the mosaic that represented our relationship. There were laughs and tears, heartfelt confessions, and affectionate jabs. The sincerity of their words touched us deeply, reminding us of the many layers of our journey together.

When it was our turn to speak, Ethan and I took the microphone together. Standing side by side, we looked out over the sea of familiar faces, feeling a profound sense of gratitude and connection. Ethan's voice trembled slightly as he spoke, his words laced with emotion. He talked about the unexpected twists and turns of our journey, the moments of doubt and hope, and how, through it all, our love had remained a constant, guiding light.

As he spoke, I couldn't help but reflect on our shared experiences—the challenges we had overcome, the dreams we had realized, and the many quiet moments of support and understanding that had defined our relationship. I added my own thoughts, expressing my appreciation for the strength of our bond and the beauty of the life we were building together. Our words were simple but sincere, a testament to the depth of our feelings and the significance of this milestone.

The evening continued with dancing and laughter, the joy in the room a testament to the happiness and contentment we had found in each other. Each dance, each shared glance, was a reaffirmation of our commitment and the strength of our bond. As the night wore on, Ethan and I took a quiet moment to step outside, the crisp night air a refreshing contrast to the warmth inside.

Underneath the vast, star-studded sky, we held each other close, feeling the gentle pulse of our shared heartbeat. We spoke softly, our words a mix of reflections and dreams for the future. The quiet of the night provided a perfect backdrop for our intimate conversation, and in that moment, we felt an overwhelming sense of contentment and love.

The milestone celebration wasn't just a reflection of the past; it was a reaffirmation of our commitment to each other. It was a reminder of the strength we had found in our love, and the joy we had discovered in building a future together. As we embraced beneath the stars, we knew that this celebration was more than just an anniversary—it was a promise of the continued journey ahead, filled with love, laughter, and unwavering support.

The evening unfolded with a warmth that seemed to embrace everyone present. The laughter and music intermingled, creating a soundtrack to our shared history. Each detail of the celebration, from the carefully chosen décor to the lovingly prepared menu, was a tribute to the love and effort we had invested in each other. Every corner of the venue seemed to whisper stories of our past and dreams for the future.

As guests mingled and enjoyed the festivities, Ethan and I took a moment to reflect on the significance of the night. The people around us were more than just guests; they were witnesses to our journey, supporters of our love, and participants in the chapter we were celebrating. Their presence was a reminder of the community that had surrounded us through our highs and lows, a tapestry of shared experiences that wove together our story.

The dinner was a blend of comfort and elegance, mirroring the balance we had found in our relationship. As we moved from one course to the next, the conversations flowed effortlessly, punctuated by moments of deep connection and light-hearted banter. It was a night where the small, meaningful conversations carried as much weight as the grand gestures.

When it came time for the toasts, the atmosphere was charged with anticipation. Each speaker took to the floor with a unique perspective on our relationship. Friends and family shared anecdotes that ranged from the humorous to the deeply poignant. Their words painted a vivid picture of our journey, from the early days of uncertainty to the present, where our love had grown into something beautiful and enduring.

The stories that resonated the most were the ones that highlighted the quiet, everyday moments of support and understanding that had defined our relationship. The times when Ethan had been my rock, and when I had been his safe haven, were the moments that seemed to echo through the room, reminding us of the foundation of our bond. It was these seemingly mundane but incredibly significant moments that had built the strong, resilient love we were celebrating.

As the evening wore on, Ethan and I took to the dance floor for our first dance. The music played softly, a song that held special meaning for us, and we moved together in a slow, intimate embrace. In that moment, it felt as though the world had faded away, leaving only the two of us and the rhythm of our hearts. The dance was more than just a physical movement; it was a reflection of the harmony we had found in each other.

The night was filled with moments of connection and joy, but it also carried an undercurrent of reflection. We had come so far, and the road ahead was still unfolding. As we mingled with our guests, we felt a renewed sense of commitment to each other. The celebration was not just about marking a milestone but about reinforcing the vows we had made to support, love, and cherish one another.

As the evening drew to a close, we found ourselves standing together at the edge of the dance floor, taking in the final moments of the celebration. The room was filled with the soft glow of candlelight, and the laughter of our friends and family lingered in the air. Ethan squeezed my hand gently, and we exchanged a look that spoke volumes. It was a look of gratitude, of love, and of anticipation for the future.

The milestone we were celebrating was a testament to our journey, but it was also a launchpad for the future. We had faced challenges, embraced changes, and celebrated victories together. Each step of our journey had brought us closer, and this celebration was a reflection of that growth and unity.

As the last of our guests departed, Ethan and I took a moment to ourselves, stepping outside to enjoy the cool night air. The stars above seemed to shine a little brighter, as if celebrating with us. We stood together in the quiet of the night, feeling a profound sense of peace and fulfillment.

In the silence, we spoke softly about the journey ahead, about the dreams we still wanted to chase and the goals we hoped to achieve. The night was a celebration of our past, but it was also a reminder of the many adventures yet to come. With hearts full of gratitude and hope, we embraced each other, knowing that whatever the future held, we would face it together, hand in hand.

The anniversary was more than just a celebration; it was a reaffirmation of our love and a promise of the continued journey we would share. As we looked out into the night sky, we felt ready for whatever came next, buoyed by the strength of our bond and the joy of the moment we had just shared.

As the night unfolded, the celebration took on a rhythm of its own, like a living testament to our love and the journey we had navigated together. The soft murmur of conversations blended with the mellow tunes playing in the background, creating an atmosphere that was both intimate and exhilarating. The evening's glow seemed to echo the warmth of our hearts, wrapping us in a cocoon of shared happiness.

We spent a quiet moment together, away from the festivities, on a balcony that overlooked the softly lit garden. The view was nothing short of magical—the twinkling lights mirrored the stars above, and the gentle hum of nature added a serene soundtrack to our conversation. We talked about the past, the present, and the future with a sense of clarity that only such moments of reflection could provide. There was a calmness in our voices, an unspoken understanding that this night was not just a celebration but a reaffirmation of our journey and our commitment to one another.

When we returned to the party, the energy had shifted to a more relaxed, yet still vibrant, mood. People were beginning to wind down, sharing their final thoughts and farewells. We made our rounds, expressing our gratitude and soaking in the last of the evening's joy. Each hug and smile was a reminder of the support system we had, the friends and family who had been with us through every twist and turn of our story.

The speeches had left us both emotional, but not in a way that was sad or overwhelming. Instead, they had given us a deeper appreciation for the people who had been part of our journey. Their words were like pieces of a mosaic, each one adding to the larger picture of our relationship—a picture that was rich in color and texture, full of life's complexities and simple joys.

As the last of the guests said their goodbyes, we took a moment to ourselves, standing together in the quiet of the night. The house was now a tranquil sanctuary, the remnants of the celebration scattered around like gentle reminders of the love and laughter that had filled the space. We looked around at the carefully chosen decorations, the photographs that told our story, and the subtle touches that made the evening uniquely ours.

We lingered on the balcony, wrapped in each other's arms, watching as the last of the stars began to fade. There was a profound sense of peace in the stillness, a feeling that we had reached a milestone not just in time but in our hearts. We had faced challenges, embraced new beginnings, and now we were celebrating the strength of what we had built together.

In the soft glow of the moonlight, we spoke about our hopes and dreams with a renewed sense of optimism. The future felt both thrilling and comforting, like a blank canvas waiting to be filled with our continued journey. We talked about the places we wanted to visit, the experiences we wanted to share, and the life we envisioned for ourselves. The conversation was filled with excitement, but also with a deep understanding of the commitment required to make those dreams a reality.

The celebration had been a beautiful tribute to our past, but it was also a promise to our future. It was a reminder of how far we had come, and a declaration of our intention to continue moving forward together, hand in hand. We knew that life would continue to bring its share of challenges, but we also knew that we had each other to lean on, to laugh with, and to love.

As we finally retreated from the balcony and into the quiet of our home, we felt a profound sense of gratitude. The evening had been a beautiful reflection of our journey—a testament to our love and resilience. It was a moment to cherish, not just for the memories we had created, but for the reassurance it gave us about our future.

In the solitude of the night, we embraced the sense of completion that the celebration had brought. It was a chapter closed, but not an ending. It was a beginning of sorts, a new phase in our journey together. We drifted into the night, carrying with us the echoes of laughter, the warmth of hugs, and the promise of many more milestones to come.

The celebration was more than just an anniversary; it was a celebration of us, of our love, and of the life we were building together. And as we settled into the quiet of the night, we felt ready to face whatever came next, buoyed by the strength of our bond and the joy of the journey we had shared.

# Chapter 21: The Future Unfolds

As the first light of dawn filtered through the curtains, Ethan and I found ourselves cocooned in the soft warmth of our bed, the world outside still shrouded in sleep. The night had been filled with whispered dreams and hopeful plans, and now, in the quiet of the morning, we allowed ourselves to dream even bigger.

We had always been drawn to each other by our shared passion for exploring new possibilities, and it was this very quality that had led us to this point in our lives. But now, as we lay side by side, it felt like the time had come to turn those dreams into tangible goals. The room was bathed in a golden glow, the sun's rays casting a serene light on our intertwined forms.

Ethan's hand rested gently on my stomach, a subtle gesture that spoke volumes about the dreams we were nurturing. We had talked about expanding our family in the past, but now, the conversation had taken on a new urgency. With each word, our visions began to align, revealing a shared understanding of the path we wanted to take. The idea of nurturing a new life was more than just a possibility; it was a deeply felt desire, one that had been building silently in the background of our lives.

Our discussions were never rushed or forced; they were conversations that flowed naturally, born out of the mutual respect and love that had grown between us. Ethan's eyes sparkled with excitement as he spoke about the future, his words weaving a tapestry of possibilities that we could hardly wait to explore. We imagined the laughter of children filling our home, the joy of watching them grow and learn, and the way our family would evolve as we navigated the challenges and triumphs of parenthood together.

Yet, as we spoke about our family, our conversations also naturally extended to other aspects of our lives. We talked about our career aspirations, the dreams we had for our professional growth, and how we could support each other in achieving those goals. Ethan had recently been offered a significant opportunity in his career, one that had the potential to redefine his professional trajectory. It was a move that could bring about profound changes, both exciting and daunting, and we both knew that navigating this path would require careful consideration.

As we discussed the potential implications of this new opportunity, I found myself reflecting on my own aspirations. My career had always been a source of pride and fulfillment, but it had also been a space where I had longed for new challenges and growth. The idea of pursuing further education, exploring new career paths, or even taking on more significant projects was something that I had quietly dreamed about. Ethan's unwavering support made these dreams feel more attainable, and together, we began to map out a plan that would allow us both to thrive professionally while maintaining the harmony we had cultivated in our personal lives.

We also talked about our personal growth, the ways in which we wanted to continue evolving as individuals and as a couple. We had learned so much from our journey together, and we were eager to keep growing, both together and apart. The idea of taking up new hobbies, traveling to new places, and deepening our understanding of ourselves and each other was a thrilling prospect. Each idea and aspiration was a thread in the rich tapestry of our future, one that we were excited to weave together.

As our conversations unfolded, there was a palpable sense of excitement in the air. The possibilities felt endless, and with each new idea, our sense of partnership grew stronger. We were no longer just two individuals making decisions; we were a team, united in our vision for the future. The love that had brought us together was now guiding us forward, giving us the strength and courage to embrace the unknown.

By the time the sun was fully risen, casting its golden light over our room, we had mapped out a vision for our future that was as clear as it was thrilling. Our plans were not just about the milestones we wanted to achieve but about the journey we would undertake to reach them. We were committed to supporting each other's dreams, to growing together and individually, and to embracing every opportunity that came our way.

As we lay there, the morning light bathing us in its warmth, I felt a profound sense of gratitude for the life we were building. The future was bright with promise, and our hearts were full of hope and excitement. The love that had brought us together was now the foundation on which we were building our dreams. We knew that there would be challenges ahead, but with each other by our side, we were ready to face whatever came our way.

With a final, shared glance, we knew that the future was unfolding exactly as it was meant to, filled with love, adventure, and the promise of a lifetime together.

The gentle hum of the city outside our new apartment window was a steady reminder of the life we were building together. As the weeks passed, Ethan and I found ourselves increasingly immersed in the rhythm of our new surroundings, and the conversation naturally turned to what lay ahead. We were on the cusp of crafting our future, a prospect both exhilarating and daunting.

Sitting together on the couch one evening, our legs intertwined under a shared blanket, we began to outline our dreams for the future. The flickering light of a nearby lamp cast a soft glow over the room, making the space feel both intimate and expansive. With a comfortable silence between us, I could sense the gravity of the discussion we were about to have. It wasn't just about planning; it was about weaving our individual aspirations into a collective tapestry.

Ethan was the first to break the silence, his voice filled with a mix of enthusiasm and contemplation. "I've been thinking a lot about the possibilities that lie ahead for us," he began, his gaze fixed on a spot on the floor as if trying to map out the future in his mind. "There's this new project at work that could be a game-changer for my career. It's a big step, but it's also an opportunity to make a real impact."

I nodded, feeling a surge of pride for him. His passion was infectious, and I could see how much this meant to him. Yet, there was a part of me that was aware of the potential implications of such a move. It wasn't just about a career opportunity; it was about how it would fit into the larger puzzle of our lives. "It sounds incredible," I said softly, reaching out to squeeze his hand. "But how do you feel about the balance between this new project and our personal life? We've both worked so hard to create a space where we can thrive together."

Ethan's expression softened, and he turned to face me fully. "That's exactly what I've been thinking about. I want to ensure that whatever step I take professionally doesn't come at the cost of our relationship. We've built something so beautiful together, and I don't want to jeopardize that for the sake of a career move."

His words resonated deeply with me, and I could feel the weight of our shared commitment. "I appreciate that," I said, my voice steady with conviction. "It's important to me, too. I've been reflecting on my own goals, and there's so much I want to explore professionally. I've always dreamed of taking on more significant projects and perhaps even pursuing further education. I want us both to grow, but it's crucial that we do it in a way that supports each other."

The conversation continued, each of us laying out our hopes and dreams with a sense of both vulnerability and excitement. We discussed the possibility of starting a family, something that had been on our minds for a while. It was a topic that brought a mixture of anticipation and anxiety. The idea of nurturing a new life together was incredibly appealing, but it also came with its own set of challenges and adjustments.

"We've always talked about having children," Ethan said, his voice tinged with both hope and uncertainty. "But now, it feels like the right time to seriously consider it. I imagine us creating a home filled with laughter and love, but I also want to make sure we're prepared for the responsibilities that come with it."

I could see the depth of his commitment and the care with which he approached this subject. "I feel the same way," I replied. "I want to be ready for this next chapter, not just emotionally but also practically. We've built a strong foundation, and I believe we can handle whatever comes our way. It's about finding the right balance and ensuring that we support each other every step of the way."

As the night wore on, our discussion evolved into dreams of personal growth and adventure. We talked about traveling to new places, exploring different cultures, and continuing to challenge ourselves. Each idea was a testament to the life we wanted to build—a life filled with exploration, learning, and shared experiences.

The more we talked, the clearer it became that our future was not just about reaching specific milestones but about embracing the journey together. We envisioned a life where we could both pursue our passions while nurturing our relationship. The excitement in our voices was palpable, and it was evident that our love was a driving force behind our ambitions.

By the time we finally drifted off to sleep, our hearts were full of optimism and anticipation. The future was unfolding before us, and it was a canvas we were eager to paint together. Our dreams were not just about what we wanted to achieve individually but about how we could grow and thrive as a couple. As we snuggled under the covers, the warmth of our shared dreams wrapped around us like a comforting embrace, and we knew that whatever challenges lay ahead, we would face them together, with love and unwavering commitment.

The days slipped by in a gentle blur of anticipation and planning, each moment adding a brushstroke to the canvas of our future. Ethan and I embraced the newfound energy that came with envisioning our lives together, our discussions often stretching into the late hours of the night, fueled by coffee and the warmth of our shared dreams.

One evening, as we lounged in our living room surrounded by the soft glow of our carefully chosen lamps, Ethan brought up the idea of expanding our family. It wasn't a sudden thought but rather a culmination of our many conversations and a natural evolution of our relationship. I watched as he spoke, his eyes bright with a mix of excitement and vulnerability.

"I've been thinking," he began, his tone thoughtful, "about what it would be like to bring a child into our lives. It's something we've talked about before, but now it feels more real. I can picture it—the little things, like bedtime stories and morning routines, and the big moments, like watching them grow and explore the world."

I felt a flutter of emotion at his words. The idea of starting a family was both exhilarating and daunting, but hearing Ethan's heartfelt reflection made it feel tangible and possible. "I've thought about it too," I admitted, my voice soft but steady. "I imagine us navigating the highs and lows of parenthood together, supporting each other and learning as we go. It's a big step, but I believe we're ready for it."

The thought of expanding our family was interwoven with discussions about our careers and personal growth. Ethan's new job opportunity was an exciting development, and we both recognized the importance of aligning his professional ambitions with our personal goals. We talked about the possibility of me pursuing further education or taking on new challenges in my own career, each idea adding a layer to the life we were planning.

"It's important for both of us to continue growing," I said one evening, as we sat at the kitchen table, surrounded by plans and lists. "We've always supported each other's dreams, and I think that's a big part of what makes our relationship so strong. I want us to be able to chase our goals while also building a life together that's fulfilling and balanced."

Ethan nodded, his expression thoughtful. "I agree. And that balance is crucial. It's about finding ways to integrate our personal and professional lives so that we're not just coexisting but truly thriving together. I want us to look back on this time and feel proud of what we've accomplished, both individually and as a couple."

We spent hours discussing potential scenarios, imagining different paths our lives could take. We dreamed about traveling to far-off places, experiencing new cultures, and continuing to grow both personally and professionally. Each idea was met with enthusiasm and a sense of adventure, underscoring the love and excitement we felt for our shared future.

One afternoon, as we walked hand in hand through a nearby park, the reality of our conversations felt even more vivid. The trees were lush and green, the sun casting dappled shadows on the path, and the world seemed to echo the promise of our dreams. We talked about how we could make time for our relationship amid our busy lives, ensuring that we remained connected and in tune with each other.

"We have to remember," Ethan said, his voice steady and reassuring, "that while we're planning for the future, it's also important to enjoy the present. We've worked so hard to get to this point, and I want us to savor these moments together, to find joy in the everyday as we move forward."

His words resonated deeply with me, and I felt a wave of gratitude for the life we were building together. The future was an open road, full of possibilities and challenges, but with Ethan by my side, I felt a profound sense of confidence and optimism. We had faced so much already, and our shared commitment and love made me believe that we could navigate whatever came our way.

As we continued to plan and dream, our hearts were full of hope and excitement. Each day was a step closer to realizing our vision, and the journey itself was as important as the destination. We embraced the love and adventure that our second chance had brought us, and with each conversation and shared moment, we solidified the foundation of our future.

In the quiet of our home, surrounded by the evidence of our dreams and plans, I felt an overwhelming sense of peace. We were building a life together, one that reflected our passions, values, and aspirations. The future was unfolding before us, and with Ethan's hand in mine, I knew that whatever challenges lay ahead, we would face them with unwavering love and a shared sense of purpose.

The days of routine began to blur into one another, a rhythm that felt both comforting and predictable. It was then that Ethan and I decided it was time to shake things up, to venture beyond our familiar comfort zones and explore new horizons. The idea of diving into uncharted territory—together—seemed both exhilarating and daunting, yet it promised a refreshing change from the mundane.

We started with painting, something neither of us had ever seriously considered before. I remember the first day we walked into the art studio, a modest space bathed in soft, natural light. The scent of acrylic paint and turpentine hung in the air, mingling with the faint hum of classical music that played softly in the background. We were handed smocks and shown to our canvases, each blank and inviting.

Ethan's initial apprehension was palpable. He approached the canvas with the same caution he might have had with a new recipe, his brush trembling slightly in his hand. I couldn't help but smile at his tentative strokes. There was something profoundly intimate about witnessing him step into this new world, his creativity unfolding with each brushstroke.

As for me, I was no less tentative. My first attempts were clumsy, my colors muddled and shapes uncertain. But there was something magical about the process—the way our imperfections blended into something uniquely ours. We spent hours in that studio, our conversation a mixture of artistic critique and shared laughter. It was a testament to our willingness to embrace new experiences, and with each session, we found ourselves growing closer, our bond deepened by the creative chaos we shared.

Next on our list was hiking, an activity neither of us had explored with any seriousness. We chose a trail that promised a moderate challenge, a path winding through lush forest and rocky terrain. Our early morning trek began with the crisp, cool air brushing against our faces. The ascent was steeper than we anticipated, and as we trudged upward, our breaths came in puffs of mist.

Ethan's determination was impressive, though he occasionally paused to catch his breath and offer me a supportive smile. I admired his resilience and the way he cheered me on as I struggled with the uneven ground. Together, we encouraged each other, our shared effort turning the hike into an adventure of mutual support and encouragement.

When we reached the summit, the view was breathtaking—an expansive vista of rolling hills and distant mountains, the sun casting golden light across the landscape. We stood together, the wind tousling our hair, and felt a profound sense of accomplishment. It wasn't just the physical challenge we had overcome, but the experience of facing it together, navigating new terrain, and discovering our own limits.

Cooking classes were another venture that drew us in with equal parts curiosity and excitement. The culinary world was uncharted territory for us both, and each class brought its own set of surprises. We learned to prepare dishes from various cuisines, our initial attempts often leading to more laughter than culinary mastery. Yet, each meal we prepared together became a celebration of our efforts, a reminder of our willingness to embrace the unfamiliar.

Our kitchen adventures were filled with playful banter and shared moments of triumph, like the time Ethan managed to perfect a delicate soufflé, or when I successfully recreated a spicy Thai curry. These experiences, though seemingly mundane, were a reflection of our journey together—each new recipe, a testament to our ability to grow and learn from one another.

Through these shared activities, we discovered more than just new hobbies. We uncovered hidden aspects of ourselves and each other, finding joy in the unexpected and delight in the process of exploration. Each venture into uncharted territory brought us closer, revealing new layers of our relationship and deepening our connection.

The act of exploring together—whether it was creating abstract art, conquering hiking trails, or mastering culinary techniques—became a metaphor for our life together. It was a reminder that our journey was not just about maintaining the status quo but about continually seeking growth and embracing new experiences.

Our exploration into these new territories wasn't merely about the activities themselves but about the shared moments, the laughter, and the occasional frustrations. It was about how we navigated the unknown together, supporting and encouraging each other, and discovering that the adventure was just as important as the destination.

In the midst of these new experiences, we found ourselves not only enriched by the activities but by the deeper understanding of our partnership. Each new challenge, whether a stroke of paint or a hike up a mountain, became a chapter in our shared story—a testament to the strength of our bond and the beauty of our shared journey into uncharted territory.

The process of immersing ourselves in these new hobbies brought us both a sense of exhilaration and vulnerability. Each activity was a window into a world neither of us had ventured into, revealing not only our own hidden talents but also deepening our appreciation for each other's qualities. It was a time of discovery—both of our individual selves and of each other.

Painting, for instance, started as a mere curiosity but quickly evolved into a ritual of sorts. As we continued to attend the art classes, I found myself captivated by the transformation taking place on the canvas. Each session became a journey through color and texture, a dialogue between our creative spirits. Ethan, once hesitant and unsure, grew more confident with each brushstroke. His paintings, initially timid and restrained, began to express a depth and intensity that surprised him. I watched him evolve from a reluctant participant to an enthusiastic artist, his eyes lighting up with each new creation.

Our evenings spent at the studio were often punctuated with laughter, debates over color choices, and playful arguments about which shade best represented our emotions. Yet, amid the mess of paints and the chaos of our artistic endeavors, there was a profound connection forming. The act of painting together became a metaphor for our relationship—an ongoing process of exploration and expression, where each stroke on the canvas mirrored our growing understanding and acceptance of one another.

Hiking presented a different set of challenges and rewards. Each trail we chose tested our endurance and resilience, yet it also offered moments of pure, unfiltered beauty. I remember one hike in particular, where we stumbled upon a secluded waterfall. We had been climbing for hours, our legs weary and our spirits slightly deflated. But as we reached the clearing and the sound of cascading water filled the air, it was as though we had discovered a hidden treasure.

Ethan's eyes sparkled with excitement as he waded into the cool, clear water, pulling me along with him. The thrill of our discovery, combined with the physical exertion, brought a sense of triumph and exhilaration that only deepened our bond. We stood together beneath the waterfall, the spray misting our faces, and I felt an overwhelming sense of gratitude for these shared moments. The hike had been challenging, but the reward of experiencing something so beautiful together was worth every step.

Cooking classes, too, were a revelation. Our culinary experiments ranged from the simple to the sophisticated, often with results that were far from perfect. But the kitchen became a stage for our collaboration, our mishaps, and our triumphs. We found ourselves immersed in the scents and sounds of the culinary world, from the sizzle of onions in a pan to the aromatic spices that wafted through the air.

There was a certain magic in preparing meals together, in the way our hands moved in tandem, chopping, stirring, and tasting. Our cooking sessions were filled with shared smiles and occasional spills, a dance of sorts between us and the ingredients. The camaraderie we developed in the kitchen extended beyond the cooking itself; it was in the way we navigated the messes and the successes, supporting each other and reveling in the joy of creating something together.

Through these new experiences, Ethan and I discovered aspects of ourselves that we had not previously known. We learned to appreciate each other's strengths and weaknesses, to embrace the imperfections and celebrate the growth. Our adventures into painting, hiking, and cooking were more than just activities—they were explorations of our relationship and our individual selves.

The excitement of these uncharted territories brought a fresh perspective to our lives. They reminded us of the importance of curiosity and exploration, of pushing boundaries and venturing into new experiences. Each activity became a chapter in our ongoing story, a testament to our willingness to grow together and embrace the unknown.

Our shared journey through these hobbies not only strengthened our bond but also provided a deeper understanding of each other. We found joy in the process of discovery, in the way our lives intertwined with each new experience. It was a reminder that our relationship was not just about maintaining a comfortable status quo but about continually seeking new adventures and opportunities for growth.

In the end, exploring these new territories became a celebration of our love and commitment. It was a testament to our willingness to step out of our comfort zones and embrace the unknown, together. The joy and connection we found in these experiences became a reflection of the strength and resilience of our relationship, reinforcing our belief in the beauty of discovering new facets of ourselves and each other.

The journey through these new hobbies began to weave its way into the fabric of our daily lives, intertwining with our routines and creating a rhythm of discovery and growth. Each activity brought its own set of challenges and triumphs, transforming ordinary moments into extraordinary experiences.

One rainy afternoon, we decided to experiment with a cooking class we had been hesitant to try. The class was meant to teach us how to make intricate pastries—something neither of us had ventured into before. The kitchen was filled with the comforting hum of conversation and the clinking of utensils. We were paired up with other couples, each one filled with the same mix of excitement and apprehension that we felt.

As we rolled out dough and crafted delicate layers of puff pastry, Ethan and I found ourselves laughing at our initial clumsiness. The dough was stubborn, refusing to cooperate, and our attempts at perfect folds led to a series of delightful disasters. But rather than feeling frustrated, we embraced the chaos. The kitchen became a playground of flour clouds and sweet aromas, and through it all, we found ourselves drawn closer by our shared perseverance.

The final product, a tray of less-than-perfect pastries, was far from what we had envisioned. But as we tasted our creation, there was an undeniable sense of satisfaction. The pastries were delicious, not because of their appearance but because of the love and effort we had poured into them. We celebrated our imperfections, savoring each bite as a testament to our journey together—a journey filled with laughter, resilience, and a touch of sweetness.

Our hikes, on the other hand, offered a different kind of adventure. The trails became our escape from the hustle and bustle of daily life, a sanctuary where we could leave behind the worries and immerse ourselves in the serenity of nature. Each hike was a new chapter, filled with breathtaking views and moments of introspection.

One particularly memorable hike took us to a mountaintop, where the world below seemed to dissolve into a tapestry of colors and shapes. We sat together on a rock, our legs dangling over the edge, and took in the panoramic view. The silence was profound, broken only by the gentle rustle of leaves and the distant call of birds.

In that moment, the vastness of the landscape mirrored the expanse of our own journey. We talked about our hopes and dreams, about the future we envisioned together. It was a moment of deep connection, where the beauty of the natural world seemed to reflect the beauty of our relationship. We marveled at how far we had come, how much we had grown, and how our shared experiences had shaped us into who we were.

Painting, too, became a metaphor for our evolving relationship. The canvas was our blank slate, a space where we could express our innermost thoughts and emotions. Each session in the studio was an opportunity to explore new facets of ourselves and each other. We experimented with colors and techniques, finding joy in the process of creation.

One painting session stands out in my memory. We had decided to create a collaborative piece, a blend of our individual styles. As we worked side by side, our brushes moving in harmony, the painting began to take shape. It was a reflection of our combined creativity, a visual representation of our journey together. The process was as important as the finished piece, and the canvas became a symbol of our partnership.

Through the smudges of paint and the layers of color, we discovered new ways to communicate and connect. Our artwork became a testament to our growth, to the way we had learned to blend our differences into something beautiful. Each brushstroke was a reminder of the strength of our bond, of our ability to navigate uncharted territory and emerge stronger.

As the days turned into weeks, and the weeks into months, we continued to embrace the uncharted territory of our lives. The new hobbies and experiences had become integral to our relationship, a testament to our willingness to explore and grow together. Each adventure was a step toward understanding ourselves and each other more deeply.

In the end, the journey through painting, hiking, and cooking was more than just a series of activities. It was a celebration of our love, of our shared curiosity, and of our commitment to discovering new aspects of ourselves and our relationship. It was a reminder that, even in the midst of the familiar, there is always room for adventure and growth. And as we continued to explore, we knew that the love and connection we had forged would guide us through every uncharted territory we encountered.

# Chapter 22: Family Ties

The anticipation of expanding our family brought a new layer of excitement to our lives, tinged with the weight of important decisions. As Ethan and I navigated this new chapter, our conversations often turned to the delicate balance we would need to strike between our cultural traditions and the future we envisioned for our children.

One crisp autumn evening, as the golden light of the setting sun filtered through our living room windows, Ethan and I sat on the sofa, our fingers intertwined. We had been mulling over the many questions that had surfaced about how to incorporate our cultural heritages into our future family life. The warmth of the room contrasted with the cold uncertainty of our thoughts.

"How do you envision blending our traditions?" Ethan asked softly, his gaze fixed on a spot just beyond the horizon, lost in thought.

I took a deep breath, feeling the gravity of the question. My own heritage was deeply rooted in customs that had been passed down through generations, each celebration infused with rituals and meanings that I cherished. Ethan's culture, too, was rich with its own set of traditions that he had grown up with and held dear. Merging these would not only be a challenge but also a beautiful opportunity to create something unique.

"It's not just about merging two sets of traditions," I began, searching for the right words. "It's about creating a tapestry that reflects both of us, our pasts, and the future we want for our children."

Ethan nodded, his expression thoughtful. "I agree. But what if our families have different expectations about how things should be done?"

The concern in his voice was palpable, and I knew it was something we both felt deeply. Our families had been incredibly supportive throughout our relationship, but the prospect of blending our cultures in new ways brought with it a range of opinions and expectations.

Later that week, we gathered with our families for a dinner, a casual affair that belied the importance of the conversations that were about to unfold. The table was set with a combination of dishes from both our heritages—fragrant biryani, savory tamales, and a few experimental recipes we had tried out. The atmosphere was light, filled with laughter and the clinking of glasses, but beneath it lay an undercurrent of tension.

As the evening progressed, our conversation naturally veered toward the topic of our future family. The initial responses were warm and supportive, with both our parents expressing their excitement and enthusiasm. But as we delved deeper into specifics, the undercurrents of differing expectations began to surface.

Ethan's mother, with her gentle demeanor, shared her hope that our children would embrace the traditions she had nurtured. She spoke of the rituals that had been a part of her life and the ways she envisioned passing them on. Her words were filled with a sincere desire to keep her cultural heritage alive, and I could see the depth of her affection for her son and future grandchildren in every word.

My own parents, too, had strong feelings about preserving our traditions. My mother's voice was tinged with a mix of pride and concern as she talked about the customs that defined our family celebrations. Her passion for these traditions was evident, and she conveyed how important it was for her to see them continue through the generations.

The discussions were heartfelt but also highlighted the challenges we faced. Each side presented valid points, and as much as we wanted to honor both cultures, the logistics of integrating them into a cohesive upbringing seemed daunting.

Ethan and I spent many nights discussing these conversations, weighing the points our families had made and how we could create a balanced approach. We wanted to respect and integrate both sets of traditions, but it was clear that we needed to find a way to blend them without losing sight of what was important to us as a couple.

One of the key moments in our discussions was realizing that our approach didn't have to be perfect or exhaustive. Instead, it could be a journey of discovery and adaptation. We started thinking about ways to introduce our children to both cultures gradually, celebrating key traditions from each while creating new ones that were uniquely ours.

We began drafting ideas for how to celebrate holidays and special occasions, ensuring that each cultural aspect was represented. We also looked into educational resources and community events that could provide a deeper understanding of both cultures, allowing our children to explore their heritage in meaningful ways.

In the end, the journey was about more than just navigating family expectations. It was about embracing the love and respect we had for each other's cultures and finding a way to weave them into the fabric of our future family life. It was a process of growth and compromise, one that brought us closer together as a couple and enriched our understanding of what it meant to build a life together.

As we moved forward, our commitment to each other and our future family remained steadfast. We knew that the path would not always be smooth, but with each discussion and decision, we were building a foundation of mutual respect and love that would support us through every challenge and triumph.

As the days turned into weeks, the reality of our conversations with our families began to settle into our everyday lives. The initial excitement of planning for our future was now tinged with the complexity of merging our cultural traditions. Ethan and I found ourselves wading through a sea of expectations, both our own and those of our families, trying to find a way forward that honored both sides.

One chilly afternoon, we decided to visit a local cultural festival, a vibrant celebration that showcased a variety of traditions from around the world. We hoped that immersing ourselves in this diverse environment might offer some clarity and inspiration. The festival was a sensory overload of colors, sounds, and aromas. Stalls lined the streets, each offering a glimpse into different cultures through food, music, and art.

As we walked hand in hand through the bustling crowds, Ethan's enthusiasm was palpable. He was particularly drawn to a booth that featured intricate handwoven textiles from his cultural background. He pointed out the patterns, explaining their significance and the stories behind them with a pride that was both endearing and enlightening.

I watched him, my heart swelling with affection. It was in these moments of shared discovery that I felt the depth of our connection. We were not just navigating this journey together; we were learning and growing as partners, bound by a shared curiosity and respect for each other's histories.

Later, we found ourselves at a cooking demonstration where a chef prepared traditional dishes from my culture. The aromas of spices and herbs filled the air, and I felt a pang of nostalgia mixed with excitement. Watching the chef expertly blend ingredients, I imagined how these same dishes might someday be a part of our family gatherings.

Ethan watched me with a warm smile, sensing my emotional response. "This looks amazing," he said, his voice gentle. "I can see why these traditions are so important to you."

His words were a balm to my soul, a reassurance that he truly understood the significance of what was unfolding. It was in these quiet, unspoken moments that we built the foundation for our future together—a future where both our cultural legacies could coexist and thrive.

As we left the festival, our minds were abuzz with ideas. We spent the evening at home, discussing how we might incorporate elements from both our cultures into our daily lives. It was clear that while the process would require effort and compromise, it was also an opportunity to create something uniquely ours.

Our conversations turned to specific traditions and how we could celebrate them in a way that felt authentic and inclusive. We began drafting a plan that included key holidays and customs from both backgrounds, setting aside special times to honor each tradition. We talked about how to integrate aspects of each culture into our home—perhaps by decorating with elements from both sides or blending traditional recipes into our meals.

The discussions weren't always easy. There were moments of disagreement, and the weight of family expectations sometimes felt heavy. But through every challenge, we reminded ourselves of our shared goal: to build a family that was rich in heritage and full of love.

One particularly poignant moment came when we had a heart-to-heart with our parents, sharing our vision for blending traditions. We approached the conversation with an open heart, expressing our desire to honor both cultures while also creating new traditions that reflected our journey as a couple.

The reactions were mixed. Some family members were supportive and understanding, eager to see how our plans would unfold. Others were more hesitant, concerned that the blending of traditions might dilute the essence of their cultural practices. We listened with empathy and reassured them that our aim was not to diminish any tradition but to weave them together in a way that celebrated all aspects of our backgrounds.

As we continued to navigate these discussions, Ethan and I found solace in the knowledge that we were building a foundation for our family based on mutual respect and love. Each step forward, each compromise, brought us closer together and strengthened our commitment to one another.

Through it all, our shared vision remained clear: to create a family life that embraced both our cultural heritages while forging new traditions that were uniquely ours. We knew that this journey would be an ongoing process, one that required patience, understanding, and an open heart.

In the quiet moments of reflection, as we looked out over the city lights from our cozy home, we felt a deep sense of gratitude. We were embarking on a path that, while challenging, was also filled with promise. Our love and our shared dreams guided us, and we were ready to face whatever lay ahead, knowing that together, we could build a future that honored the past and embraced the possibilities of tomorrow.

The conversation with our families lingered in our minds as we settled into the rhythm of our days. Each meeting, each phone call brought new insights and, occasionally, new tensions. Yet amidst the ebb and flow of family dynamics, Ethan and I discovered a deeper understanding of our own desires and dreams. We were navigating uncharted waters, but with every step, we were learning how to steer our course together.

One chilly winter evening, we decided to host a small gathering in our home—a chance to share a meal and discuss our plans with both sides of our family in a more informal setting. We hoped the warmth of the evening and the comfort of good food would ease some of the underlying tension and open up more meaningful conversations.

The house was filled with the rich aromas of a fusion dinner: spicy curries alongside hearty stews, savory pastries paired with delicate pastries. The table was a visual feast, reflecting the blending of our cultural backgrounds. We had carefully curated the menu to showcase dishes that represented both sides, hoping to create a space where everyone could feel included and appreciated.

As our family members arrived, the initial awkwardness quickly melted away. Laughter and conversation flowed more freely as we all gathered around the table. I watched with a soft smile as Ethan and my family members engaged in animated discussions about the food. They marveled at the flavors and the intricacies of the dishes, which seemed to break down barriers and build bridges between us.

During the meal, Ethan and I took turns sharing our vision for our future family. We spoke candidly about our desire to honor both of our cultures while creating new traditions that would be meaningful to our children. We talked about celebrating both our heritage and embracing the new experiences that life would bring.

It was clear that our families were still processing the idea of merging traditions. Ethan's parents expressed their concerns about losing the essence of their cultural practices, while my family worried about the potential dilution of the traditions they had cherished for generations. We listened with empathy, acknowledging their feelings and reassuring them that our intention was to honor the past while forging a path that was uniquely our own.

Throughout the evening, the conversations grew more constructive. We shared specific ideas for how we might integrate our traditions into our family life. We proposed celebrating certain holidays with a combination of both cultural practices, blending festive customs and culinary delights to create a rich tapestry of shared experiences.

The most poignant moment came when Ethan's mother, with a thoughtful look in her eyes, shared a story from his childhood—one that was steeped in the traditions of his family. Her voice trembled with emotion as she spoke, and it became evident how deeply rooted these customs were in her heart. Ethan's father, who had been quietly listening, nodded in agreement, and there was a visible shift in the room. The shared history and the personal connections began to bridge the gap between our differing viewpoints.

By the end of the evening, there was a new sense of mutual respect and understanding. Our families had witnessed firsthand the love and commitment we shared and saw how our vision for the future was not about replacing traditions but about embracing and enriching them. The walls that had seemed so formidable now appeared more porous, allowing for the possibility of blending our cultures in a way that honored everyone involved.

As our guests departed, Ethan and I stood together in the dim glow of the kitchen, surrounded by the remnants of our successful gathering. The house felt warmer than it had before, not just from the evening's meal but from the newfound connections and the shared resolve to move forward with our plans.

In the quiet moments that followed, we reflected on the journey we had undertaken. It wasn't just about creating a home and a family but about weaving together the threads of our individual histories into something that was greater than the sum of its parts. We understood that the road ahead would require ongoing dialogue and compromise, but we were more confident than ever that we could navigate it together.

With each conversation, each shared experience, we grew closer—not just as a couple but as a family united by love and respect for our diverse backgrounds. The future was still unfolding, but we faced it with a sense of hope and excitement, knowing that we were building something truly special. And as we looked ahead, hand in hand, we felt ready to embrace whatever came next, confident in the strength of our bond and the love that had brought us together.

# Chapter 23: A Test of Faith

The news came on an ordinary Tuesday, when the world seemed to be humming along in its usual rhythm. Ethan and I were making dinner, our kitchen filled with the comforting aroma of garlic and herbs. We laughed over a shared joke, our spirits light and carefree, when the phone rang, slicing through the tranquility with an unexpected urgency.

Ethan's face changed as he glanced at the caller ID. The smile that had been playing at the corners of his lips faded, replaced by a look of concern. He excused himself and answered the call in the other room, leaving me to stir the pot on the stove. The silence stretched, a palpable weight that pressed against my chest. The minutes ticked by slowly, each one stretching into an eternity.

When he finally re-entered the kitchen, his expression was unreadable, and I could see the worry etched into his features. He sat down at the kitchen table, his movements slow, deliberate. I felt a pang of anxiety. Ethan's eyes met mine, filled with a mix of sadness and determination.

"It's my father," he said quietly. "He's been diagnosed with a serious health condition. They don't know the full extent yet, but it's going to require immediate surgery and a lot of follow-up treatment."

My heart sank. The world outside seemed to blur as I focused solely on Ethan's face, trying to read the emotions there. We had both faced challenges before, but this felt different. The vulnerability in his eyes, the tremor in his voice—it was clear that this was a test we hadn't anticipated.

We spent the evening trying to process the news, our conversations shifting between practicalities and emotional support. Ethan was naturally inclined to shield his family from his own fears, but the cracks in his façade were evident. He spoke of the logistical details—trips back and forth, financial implications, and how to manage the time away from work. Yet beneath the surface of these practical concerns lay a sea of uncertainty and fear.

In the days that followed, our routine was overtaken by the demands of the situation. We found ourselves thrust into a whirlwind of hospital visits, phone calls with family members, and endless planning. Ethan was a rock for his family, managing every detail with meticulous care. I watched him navigate this storm with a grace that both impressed and worried me. His strength was undeniable, but I could see how it was wearing him down.

Throughout this period, I struggled to balance being a source of support with managing my own feelings of helplessness. I wanted to be the anchor Ethan needed, but there were moments when the weight of the situation felt unbearable. The stress of seeing him so distressed, coupled with the uncertainty of his father's health, was a strain on both of us.

One night, after a particularly grueling day, we sat together in our dimly lit living room. The quiet was heavy, filled with unspoken words. Ethan had fallen silent, his eyes fixed on the distant flicker of a candle. I reached out and took his hand, squeezing it gently. We didn't need words at that moment; our connection spoke volumes.

"I don't know what the future holds," Ethan said softly, his voice trembling. "But I do know that I'm grateful you're here with me."

"I'm not going anywhere," I replied, my voice steady despite the lump in my throat. "We'll face this together, no matter what."

The ordeal became a crucible for our relationship. Each day tested our patience, our resilience, and our ability to lean on one another. We found solace in the little moments of connection—a shared cup of coffee, a touch on the shoulder, a quiet walk through the park. These small acts of kindness became the lifeline that kept us grounded.

As the days turned into weeks, we began to find our footing again. The initial shock began to fade, replaced by a cautious optimism. Ethan's father's surgery was successful, and though the road to recovery was long and uncertain, there was hope. We faced each challenge with a newfound strength, guided by the love and trust that had deepened through this trial.

In the midst of the struggle, we discovered something profound. Our relationship, forged in the fires of adversity, was stronger than we had imagined. The experience had stripped away any remaining illusions, revealing the core of our commitment to each other. We learned to lean on each other more fully, to communicate more openly, and to cherish every moment of togetherness.

The road ahead was still uncertain, but as we walked it hand in hand, we knew that we had weathered a storm that had tested the very foundations of our relationship. The love that had brought us together had been tempered by hardship, emerging not only intact but strengthened. And as we looked toward the future, we did so with a profound appreciation for the depth of our bond and the faith that had carried us through the darkest of times.

The weeks that followed were a turbulent blend of hope and anxiety. Each day seemed to unfold with a new challenge, a fresh round of tests for our patience and resilience. Ethan's father's health remained precarious, a constant shadow over our daily lives. I found myself navigating between being a supportive partner and dealing with my own swirling fears.

Every morning, Ethan would rise before the sun, his mind already consumed with worry. He'd sip his coffee in silence, the weight of the world pressing heavily on his shoulders. I watched him with a mixture of admiration and heartache, wishing I could ease his burden. The routines we once took comfort in now felt like distant memories. Our days were filled with hospital visits, phone calls to family, and countless hours spent trying to maintain some semblance of normalcy.

One evening, as we settled into our worn-out living room couch after another grueling day, Ethan finally broke the silence that had become our norm. "I keep thinking about everything that's happened," he said, his voice cracking under the strain. "It feels like we're living in a bad dream, and I'm afraid to wake up."

I could see the exhaustion in his eyes, the way the lines on his face had deepened. I moved closer, resting my head against his shoulder, trying to offer solace through my presence alone. "I know it's hard," I whispered. "But we're stronger than we realize. We've faced challenges before, and we've always come out the other side."

He sighed deeply, his breath a warm gust against my temple. "I just want things to go back to normal. I want to see my father healthy again, to not feel like we're living on the edge of something terrible."

His vulnerability was a reminder of the weight we both carried. We were no longer just two people in love; we were partners in a struggle that tested our very foundation. The fear of the unknown loomed large, but in the midst of it, we found unexpected moments of connection.

One night, after a particularly difficult visit to the hospital, we decided to cook dinner together—a simple act that had become a rare respite from our worries. As we chopped vegetables and stirred sauces, we joked and laughed, finding comfort in the normalcy of the task. The kitchen, once a place of everyday routine, became a sanctuary where we could escape, if only for a few hours, from the relentless pressure of the outside world.

During these moments, I saw glimpses of the man I fell in love with—the same humor, the same kindness that had drawn me to him. It was a bittersweet reminder of what we had built together, a beacon of hope amidst the storm.

Despite our efforts to maintain a semblance of normal life, there were days when the weight of the situation became too much. On one such day, Ethan's father's condition worsened, and we found ourselves in a holding pattern of waiting and hoping. The stress began to take a toll on both of us, manifesting in sleepless nights and quiet arguments over trivial matters.

One particularly fraught evening, as we sat together in the dimly lit bedroom, I reached out and took Ethan's hand. "We need to talk," I said gently. "This isn't just about your father. It's about us, too."

He looked at me, his eyes weary but filled with a flicker of understanding. "What do you mean?"

"I mean," I continued, "that we're in this together. We need to be honest about how we're feeling and what we need from each other. We can't let this situation pull us apart."

Ethan nodded slowly, his grip tightening around my hand. "I don't want to lose us in the process. I've been so focused on everything else that I forgot we're fighting this battle together."

The conversation marked a turning point. It was a reminder that, despite the chaos, our relationship was still the cornerstone of our lives. We began to make a conscious effort to support each other more openly, to express our fears and frustrations without letting them fester.

As Ethan's father slowly began to show signs of improvement, the relief was palpable. It was as if a cloud had lifted, and while the path to recovery was still uncertain, there was a glimmer of hope on the horizon.

In the midst of the trials, we found that our bond had deepened. We had navigated a storm that seemed insurmountable, and in doing so, we had discovered a new level of trust and commitment. The experience had tested us in ways we hadn't imagined, but it had also reaffirmed the strength of our love.

With each passing day, we learned to appreciate the small victories, to find solace in the moments of calm amidst the chaos. We emerged from the ordeal not just as survivors but as a stronger, more resilient couple. And as we looked toward the future, we did so with a renewed sense of gratitude for the love that had guided us through the darkest of times.

We spent many nights in that half-light of uncertainty, where the future seemed as foggy as the headlights on a rainy evening. The hospital room, with its beeping monitors and the sterile smell of antiseptic, became an unwelcome but necessary backdrop to our lives. Every day, Ethan and I found ourselves grasping at small victories—the encouraging news from doctors, a slight improvement in his father's condition, or even just the comfort of each other's presence.

There were days when it felt like we were wading through a mire of exhaustion and worry, but we had found solace in our unwavering support for one another. Our shared experiences of fear, vulnerability, and hope had intertwined our lives even more closely. We realized that facing such adversity had taught us more about ourselves and each other than we could have ever anticipated.

One evening, after what had felt like an endless series of bad news and sleepless nights, we found ourselves alone on the hospital's rooftop garden. The city lights below twinkled like a constellation of hopes and dreams, a stark contrast to the intensity of our recent days. We sat together on a bench, the cool night air a refreshing change from the stifling hospital environment.

Ethan leaned back, taking in the view with a weary sigh. "I never imagined we'd be here, facing something like this," he said, his voice a mix of exhaustion and reflection.

I reached for his hand, squeezing it gently. "Neither did I. But look at us now. We've managed to hold on, to keep moving forward even when it felt like we couldn't."

He turned to me, his eyes searching mine as if to find some deeper understanding. "It's strange how something so terrible can also show you just how strong you can be. I've learned a lot about us these past few weeks."

I nodded, feeling a surge of emotion. "Me too. I've seen sides of you I didn't know existed, and it's made me realize just how much I love you. The way you've handled everything—your strength, your patience—it's incredible."

Ethan's gaze softened, and he pulled me into an embrace. For a moment, the world seemed to shrink to just the two of us, the city lights below a distant memory. We held each other tightly, finding comfort in the warmth of our connection amidst the chaos.

In the days that followed, as Ethan's father began to show more significant signs of recovery, we started to reclaim pieces of our normal life. We resumed some of our routines, though now they were infused with a newfound appreciation for the simple joys. Cooking together became more than just a daily task—it was a way to reconnect and share in moments of lightness.

We also took time to reflect on what had transpired, discussing how the experience had changed us and what we wanted for the future. There were conversations about dreams, fears, and the lessons we had learned. Each dialogue was a testament to our commitment to understanding and supporting each other.

One particularly memorable evening, as we sat on the balcony watching the sunset, Ethan looked at me with a mix of gratitude and hope. "I don't know what the future holds, but I know that no matter what, we'll face it together. This experience has shown me just how resilient we are."

I smiled, feeling a warmth that came from both the setting sun and the depth of our bond. "I feel the same way. We've been through something that tested us in ways we never imagined, and we've come out stronger. I wouldn't have wanted to face it with anyone else."

The sunset painted the sky in hues of orange and pink, a beautiful reminder of the end of one chapter and the beginning of another. As we looked forward, we did so with a renewed sense of unity and hope. The trials had been daunting, but they had also strengthened our trust in each other. We had weathered a storm that had felt unrelenting, and in doing so, we had forged a deeper connection.

Our journey through this challenging period had reinforced something fundamental in our relationship—a commitment not just to weather life's storms, but to face them together with love and resilience. We had discovered that our bond was not just about shared dreams and joyful moments, but also about navigating through the tough times and emerging stronger.

As we prepared to move forward, we did so with the knowledge that while life would continue to bring its challenges, we had already proven our ability to overcome them. Our love had been tested, and it had proven to be a guiding light through even the darkest times. With this newfound strength and understanding, we faced the future not with trepidation, but with a shared sense of anticipation and readiness for whatever came next.

# Chapter 24: Renewed Vows

In the months following our challenging ordeal, Ethan and I found ourselves wrapped in a cocoon of renewal and reflection. The trials we had faced had brought us closer, solidifying a foundation of love and trust that we were eager to celebrate. With this newfound clarity, we decided to mark our journey with a renewed vow, a testament to the love that had weathered every storm.

As the date approached, our home became a flurry of activity. It was as though we were orchestrating a symphony of memories, each detail a note in a melody that spoke of our love story. We envisioned a ceremony that would not only honor our personal vows but also embrace the rich tapestry of our cultures. It was a task that brought us closer together, each decision made with a shared sense of purpose and affection.

The venue, a charming garden bathed in golden afternoon light, was a perfect canvas for our celebration. The flowers we chose—vibrant marigolds intertwined with delicate orchids—were symbolic of our diverse backgrounds, blending seamlessly into a beautiful harmony. The space was transformed into a haven of romance, adorned with lanterns and ribbons that fluttered gently in the breeze, as if echoing the whispers of our promises.

On the morning of the ceremony, I found myself immersed in a mixture of excitement and nostalgia. As I looked in the mirror at my reflection, adorned in a gown that combined elements of both my heritage and Ethan's, I felt a profound sense of gratitude. Each stitch in the fabric seemed to carry a piece of our journey, woven together into a garment that spoke of our shared history and future dreams.

Ethan, too, was a picture of grace and anticipation. Dressed in a suit that reflected his cultural roots and our shared tastes, he exuded an air of calm determination. As he adjusted his tie and glanced at his reflection, his eyes met mine through the mirror. There was a silent conversation between us, one of reassurance and unspoken promises.

The ceremony began with a gentle breeze carrying the sounds of laughter and conversation from our gathered guests. Family and friends, some of whom had traveled great distances, filled the garden with their presence, their joy palpable in the way they mingled and shared in our celebration. Their support was a testament to the community we had built around us, a reminder of the love and encouragement that had guided us through our toughest times.

As we stood before our loved ones, the air was thick with anticipation. Our officiant began the ceremony with words that captured the essence of our journey—how we had faced adversity with unwavering strength and how our love had become a beacon of hope. His words resonated with everyone present, each phrase a reflection of our shared experiences and the love that had carried us through.

When it was time to exchange our renewed vows, Ethan and I faced each other, our hands intertwined. There was a moment of silence as we looked into each other's eyes, our hearts beating in synchrony. With each word spoken, we reaffirmed our commitment, our promises echoing through the garden like a sacred song.

"I vow to cherish you," Ethan began, his voice steady and filled with emotion. "To stand by your side through every joy and challenge. Our journey has only made my love for you stronger, and I promise to honor and nurture that love every day."

As I listened to Ethan's vows, my heart swelled with emotion. When it was my turn, my voice wavered slightly, but it was steady with conviction. "I vow to love you deeply and unconditionally. Through every moment of happiness and every trial, I will remain by your side. Our love has grown in ways I never imagined, and I promise to continue growing with you."

The exchange of vows was followed by the traditional rituals that blended our cultural practices, each symbolizing the unity and harmony we sought in our lives together. As we completed the ceremony, the unity of our cultures and the depth of our love became a vibrant tapestry, woven together with threads of hope, respect, and understanding.

The reception that followed was a celebration of our love and the life we had built. The garden was filled with laughter, dancing, and heartfelt toasts. The food, a delightful mix of dishes from our backgrounds, was a feast for the senses, each bite a reminder of the beautiful diversity that we celebrated in our relationship.

As the evening drew to a close, Ethan and I found a quiet moment alone. The stars above seemed to shine a little brighter, as if in celebration of our renewed vows. We held each other close, reflecting on the day and the promises we had made.

In that quiet moment, amidst the lingering echoes of joy and love, we knew that our journey was far from over. Our renewed vows were not just a celebration of what we had achieved but a promise of the future we were excited to build together. With hearts full of hope and eyes set on the horizon, we embraced the future with the same love and dedication that had brought us to this beautiful moment.

The sun cast a golden hue over the garden, where the soft hum of conversation and the delicate strains of a string quartet filled the air with a warm, inviting atmosphere. The setting was nothing short of magical—an idyllic blend of elegance and intimacy that mirrored the essence of our relationship. As Ethan and I stood at the threshold of this new chapter, surrounded by the people who had witnessed our journey, it felt as though the world was holding its breath, waiting for the next beautiful moment to unfold.

The ceremony was a testament to the richness of our shared experiences and the depth of our connection. Each element was thoughtfully chosen to reflect not only our personal tastes but also the cultural traditions that had shaped us. The vows we exchanged were not mere words but a reflection of the lives we had lived and the dreams we held for the future.

When it was time to make our promises anew, Ethan took my hands in his, his eyes brimming with sincerity. The world seemed to narrow down to just the two of us, the bustling garden fading into a backdrop of muted colors. His voice was steady and full of emotion as he spoke, each word a pledge that resonated deeply within me.

"I vow to cherish you," he began, his gaze unwavering, "to stand by your side through every joy and every challenge. Our journey together has been a testament to our strength and love, and I promise to honor and nurture that love every day of our lives."

As he spoke, I felt a rush of warmth spread through me, mingling with the anticipation that had been building all day. I took a deep breath, searching for the right words to convey the depth of my feelings. When I spoke, my voice was tinged with the vulnerability that comes from baring one's soul.

"I vow to love you deeply and unconditionally," I said, my voice trembling slightly but filled with conviction. "Through every moment of joy and every trial, I will remain by your side. Our love has grown in ways I never imagined, and I promise to continue growing with you, embracing each new chapter of our lives together."

The vows, once spoken, seemed to hang in the air like a delicate, shimmering thread, binding us together in a renewed promise of forever. The ceremony was a celebration of not just our union but of the journey we had traveled to reach this point. The blend of cultural traditions, from the exchange of symbolic gifts to the ceremonial rituals, added a layer of meaning that spoke of our commitment to honor both our individual backgrounds and our shared future.

As the final words of the ceremony echoed through the garden, Ethan and I were enveloped in a sense of peace and contentment. We exchanged a look of profound understanding, a silent acknowledgment of the journey we had undertaken and the path that lay ahead. The garden, with its soft lights and gentle melodies, seemed to embrace us, creating a cocoon of warmth and love.

The reception that followed was a reflection of the joyous spirit that marked our renewal. The tables were adorned with vibrant flowers and candles that flickered softly, casting a romantic glow over the guests. The air was filled with the mingling scents of exquisite dishes, each one a blend of flavors that told the story of our diverse backgrounds.

Laughter and conversation flowed freely as our loved ones shared in the celebration, their smiles and well-wishes adding to the tapestry of our day. It was a moment of collective joy, where each toast and each heartfelt embrace spoke of the support and love that had surrounded us throughout our journey.

As the evening wore on, Ethan and I found ourselves taking a quiet moment away from the festivities, seeking solace in the peacefulness of the garden. The stars above seemed to twinkle with a special brilliance, as if they, too, were celebrating our renewed vows. We stood together, hand in hand, savoring the tranquility that followed the day's excitement.

In that serene moment, with the cool night air gently caressing our faces, we reflected on the significance of the day. The vows we had renewed were not just a reaffirmation of our love but a celebration of the strength and resilience that had carried us through every challenge. We knew that the future was full of possibilities, and as we stood together, we felt an overwhelming sense of gratitude for the journey that had brought us here.

The renewed vows were more than just a ceremony; they were a symbol of our unwavering commitment to each other and to the life we were building together. With hearts full of hope and eyes set on the horizon, we embraced the future with a renewed sense of purpose, ready to face whatever came next with the same love and dedication that had guided us thus far.

The evening carried on, each moment unfolding like a cherished memory in the making. As the sun dipped below the horizon, casting a soft, golden glow over the garden, Ethan and I reveled in the beauty of our surroundings. The gentle murmur of conversations and laughter intertwined with the soft strains of music, creating an atmosphere of pure, unfiltered joy.

The heart of the celebration was a series of toasts and speeches from our closest family and friends. Each story shared, each laugh echoed, was a testament to the journey we had taken together. Listening to the heartfelt words from those who had been with us through our highs and lows filled me with a profound sense of gratitude. Their support and love had been a constant thread in the tapestry of our lives.

When my best friend stepped up to speak, her voice trembling with emotion, I felt a lump rise in my throat. Her words were a reflection of the deep bond we shared, and as she recounted the early days of our relationship, it was impossible not to be overwhelmed by the passage of time and the distance we had traveled. Each anecdote painted a vivid picture of our love story, capturing both the laughter and the challenges that had shaped our journey.

Ethan's parents, too, offered their words of wisdom and encouragement. Their support had been unwavering, and their pride in our commitment was palpable. As they spoke of the importance of family and the strength found in unity, I felt a profound sense of belonging. The blending of our cultures, which had once seemed like a daunting challenge, now felt like a beautiful dance, each step harmonizing with the other to create something uniquely our own.

As the evening progressed, the ambiance shifted to one of carefree celebration. The laughter grew louder, and the dance floor filled with the joyful energy of our guests. Ethan and I joined them, our hearts light and our spirits high. Dancing together, I marveled at the depth of our connection—the ease with which we moved together, the unspoken understanding that bound us. It was as if the world had narrowed down to this single, perfect moment of shared happiness.

The culmination of the evening came with a special surprise that Ethan had planned—a slideshow of our journey together. As the images flickered across the screen, each photo told a story of our love, from the tender beginnings to the milestones we had celebrated. The laughter, the tears, the quiet moments of intimacy—all were captured in a visual tapestry that was as moving as it was beautiful. Watching the slideshow, I felt a rush of emotions, each image a reminder of the life we had built together and the future we were still creating.

As the final notes of the evening's music faded into the night, Ethan and I took a moment to step away from the crowd. The garden, now illuminated by soft, twinkling lights, seemed to embrace us in a cocoon of tranquility. We stood together, our fingers entwined, gazing out at the scene of our celebration.

"I can't believe how perfect today has been," Ethan said softly, his voice full of awe and contentment.

I leaned against him, savoring the warmth of his embrace. "It has been perfect," I agreed. "But more than that, it's been a testament to everything we've been through and everything we're yet to face."

We spoke quietly, reflecting on the significance of our renewed vows and the promises we had made to each other. The ceremony had been a beautiful affirmation of our love, but it was the quiet moments like this—when we were alone together, away from the noise and celebration—that felt the most profound. It was in these moments that we truly understood the depth of our commitment and the strength of our bond.

As we walked hand in hand through the softly lit garden, the stars above seemed to shine a little brighter, as if celebrating with us. The future stretched out before us, filled with possibilities and adventures yet to come. With hearts full of hope and a renewed sense of purpose, we embraced the journey ahead, knowing that whatever challenges we might face, we would face them together.

The evening was a beautiful reminder of the love and commitment that had always been at the heart of our relationship. As we headed back to the celebration, I felt a deep sense of peace and fulfillment. We had renewed our vows not just as a ceremonial gesture but as a reaffirmation of the life we had built together—a life rich with love, understanding, and endless possibilities.

In the end, it wasn't just about celebrating the past but about embracing the future with open hearts and unwavering commitment. And as we looked out at the world with a renewed sense of purpose, it was clear that our journey together was far from over. It was just beginning, and with each passing day, we would continue to write the story of our love, one beautiful chapter at a time.

# Chapter 25: Embracing Parenthood

The day we brought our child home was etched into my memory with a clarity that made every other moment seem distant. Ethan and I had spent countless hours preparing for this moment, assembling cribs and organizing tiny clothes, yet nothing could have truly prepared us for the profound shift that parenthood would bring to our lives. As we walked through the door of our home with our newborn, an overwhelming sense of responsibility and joy settled over us, and it was clear that our lives were about to change forever.

The first few weeks were a whirlwind of sleepless nights and endless feedings, each moment filled with a blend of exhaustion and exhilaration. Our little one, so small and delicate, became the center of our universe, drawing us closer in ways we had never imagined. Ethan and I found ourselves navigating the uncharted waters of parenthood together, our love and partnership evolving as we adapted to our new roles. Each time our baby let out a soft cry or cooed in their sleep, we exchanged glances that spoke volumes—words seemed inadequate to convey the depth of our emotions.

In the quiet moments between the chaos of feedings and diaper changes, we discovered new facets of each other. Ethan, with his gentle touch and calming presence, became a source of immense comfort. Watching him cradle our child, his eyes filled with a tenderness that only deepened my love for him, was a revelation. Parenthood revealed a side of him I had not fully seen before—a nurturing and patient side that made me fall in love with him all over again.

As we faced the daily challenges of parenthood, we leaned on each other for support. There were nights when we were both overwhelmed, unsure of how to handle a sleepless baby or a seemingly endless stream of concerns. During those times, we would sit together, exhausted but determined, finding solace in our shared commitment to our new family. Our conversations became a mix of practical strategies and dreams for the future, balancing the realities of parenthood with the hopes we held for our child.

Amidst the challenges, there were also moments of pure, unadulterated joy. The first time our baby smiled at us, a tiny, sleepy grin that seemed to light up the room, was a memory we both cherished. Ethan's laughter, genuine and hearty, filled the house as we marveled at our child's developing personality. Those simple, everyday moments became the fabric of our new life, stitching together our hopes and dreams with threads of love and shared experience.

Our relationship, while tested, grew stronger through this journey. The demands of parenthood required us to be more communicative and patient with each other. We learned to read each other's cues, offering support in unspoken ways. Whether it was taking turns during late-night feedings or simply sharing a quiet cup of coffee amidst the chaos, we found comfort in the rhythm of our new life together. Each act of kindness and understanding became a testament to the strength of our bond.

The dynamic of our relationship also shifted as we adapted to our roles as parents. Our conversations, once focused solely on our aspirations and dreams, now included plans for our child's future and the values we wanted to instill. We found ourselves discussing parenting philosophies and sharing our visions for the kind of upbringing we wanted to provide. These discussions, while sometimes challenging, brought us closer as we worked to align our goals and dreams for our family.

As we adjusted to the new rhythms of our life, we also made a conscious effort to nurture our relationship. Date nights, though rare and often impromptu, became cherished moments of connection. We would sneak away for a few hours, savoring the rare opportunity to reconnect as a couple. These moments were a reminder of the love that had brought us together and the importance of keeping that flame alive amidst the demands of parenthood.

With each passing day, we learned to embrace the chaos and find joy in the little things. The sight of Ethan gently rocking our baby to sleep, the sound of laughter filling the house as we played together, and the quiet moments of reflection as we watched our child sleep were all reminders of the love that anchored us. Parenthood had added a new dimension to our love story, one that was filled with both challenges and immense rewards.

As we looked at our child, so innocent and full of potential, we felt a renewed sense of purpose. Our love had grown and evolved, taking on a new depth and meaning. The journey of parenthood, though demanding, had enriched our lives in ways we had never anticipated. We faced each day with gratitude and anticipation, excited for the future and the many adventures that lay ahead for our growing family.

In the end, embracing parenthood was not just about adjusting to new responsibilities but about celebrating the love that had brought us to this moment. It was a testament to the strength of our bond and the beauty of the life we were building together. Through every challenge and every joy, we found that our love had not only survived but had flourished, growing stronger with each passing day.

The days quickly blurred into nights, each moment marked by the rhythmic dance of parenthood. Ethan and I found ourselves in a whirlwind of responsibilities, our lives now orchestrated around the needs of our tiny, demanding bundle of joy. Despite the exhaustion, there was an undeniable magic in these early weeks—a kind of wonder that came with each new discovery and milestone.

Our home was filled with the gentle hum of a lullaby playing in the background, a soothing sound that promised rest for our baby and, fleetingly, for us as well. The nursery, once a pristine and orderly room, now bore the marks of sleepless nights and late-night feedings. Yet, amidst the chaos, there was a profound sense of fulfillment. Each time we looked at our baby's serene face as they drifted off to sleep, the trials of parenthood seemed to fade into the background.

Navigating this new chapter, Ethan and I had to learn to recalibrate our relationship. The intimate moments we once shared were now punctuated by the soft cries of our baby, and our conversations frequently revolved around schedules, diapers, and feeding times. It was a shift we hadn't fully anticipated, but one we embraced with an open heart. We found solace in the small acts of support, the unspoken gestures that said, "I'm here with you, every step of the way."

Ethan's patience and care during those early days were nothing short of extraordinary. I often found myself overwhelmed by the constant demands of our new role, but Ethan's steady presence was a balm to my frayed nerves. Whether it was him gently taking the baby for a midnight feeding or offering to handle the laundry so I could catch a few moments of rest, his actions spoke louder than any words of reassurance. In those moments, I saw a side of him that deepened my love and admiration.

Our relationship was tested, yes, but it was also strengthened. The challenges of parenthood brought us face-to-face with our vulnerabilities and fears, but through every sleepless night and every uncertain decision, we discovered the depth of our commitment to each other. Our shared experience of becoming parents created a new layer of understanding between us, one that was built on trust and mutual respect.

Even though our days were filled with the demands of a newborn, we made a conscious effort to find moments of connection. A quick kiss before rushing off to work, a lingering touch as we exchanged shifts during nighttime feedings, and stolen glances over the baby's crib—all these small moments were reminders of the love that had brought us together and the love that continued to grow.

Parenthood, while a beautiful experience, also required us to reassess our priorities. We learned to juggle our responsibilities, carving out time for each other amidst the demands of our new roles. The balance was delicate, often precarious, but it was something we navigated together. Each evening, after the baby was finally asleep, we would sit together, sharing stories from our day and planning for the future. These conversations became our refuge, a place where we could reconnect and dream together, even in the midst of exhaustion.

The joy of watching our baby grow and change brought a renewed sense of purpose. Each milestone, from the first smile to the first tentative steps, was a celebration of our collective journey. We reveled in these moments, savoring the simple, profound joys that parenthood brought. As we observed our child's personality emerging, we marveled at the unique blend of traits and quirks that made them who they were. Our baby was a reflection of us, and yet, they were entirely their own person.

We also learned to lean on our support network, accepting help from family and friends who offered their love and assistance. Their presence was a reminder that we were not alone in this journey. The occasional date night or weekend visit from loved ones provided a much-needed respite, allowing us to recharge and reconnect. These moments of respite were like little islands of peace in the storm of parenthood, offering us both relief and a renewed appreciation for the family we were building.

The challenges of parenthood, while demanding, were also profoundly rewarding. Each day brought new experiences, new lessons, and a deeper connection between Ethan and me. The love we had for each other was now intertwined with our love for our child, creating a rich tapestry of emotions and experiences. Parenthood had become a shared adventure, one that enriched our relationship and deepened our bond.

As we navigated this new chapter of our lives, we found that our love story was not only about the romantic moments we had shared but also about the everyday acts of kindness, the quiet support, and the shared dreams for our future. Parenthood had added a new dimension to our love, one that was filled with both challenges and immeasurable joy. Through it all, Ethan and I remained steadfast in our commitment to each other, finding strength and solace in the shared journey of raising our child.

As the days turned into weeks, Ethan and I began to find a rhythm in our new lives as parents. The early chaos of sleepless nights and endless feedings gradually gave way to a more manageable routine. Each day presented its own set of challenges, but also small victories that reassured us we were doing okay.

We found comfort in the routine we were establishing, though it was far from perfect. Mornings were a flurry of activity—Ethan often took the first shift, coaxing our baby into the day with soft songs and gentle cuddles while I grabbed a few extra moments of sleep. It was a small but significant act of support, one that allowed me to face the day with a bit more energy. By the time I emerged, bleary-eyed but grateful, the house was already infused with a sense of calm.

Evenings, too, became a cherished time. After the baby was fed and settled, Ethan and I would collapse onto the couch, our bodies weary but our spirits renewed by the quiet. These moments of stillness, when the world seemed to pause and we were alone with each other, became sacred. We talked about our day, shared our hopes and fears, and planned for the future. Our conversations were no longer just about our own dreams but now included the dreams we held for our child.

The joys of parenthood were often found in the simplest of moments. The way our baby's eyes would light up with recognition when Ethan walked into the room, the soft giggles that erupted during bath time, and the tender moments of rocking our child to sleep—each was a reminder of the profound love that had grown between us. Parenthood, while challenging, was also incredibly rewarding, a testament to the strength of our bond and our commitment to each other.

Balancing our roles as parents with our relationship required constant effort. We had to be intentional about nurturing our connection, even when it felt like there was little time left in the day. Date nights, once frequent and spontaneous, became planned events, carefully scheduled between feedings and naps. These moments of romance, though less frequent, were no less meaningful. They were a reminder of who we were before parenthood and the love that had brought us together.

We also learned to appreciate the small gestures of support that often went unnoticed. A reassuring touch, a shared smile over a sleepless night, or simply the act of listening when the other needed to vent—these moments became the threads that wove us closer together. They were the silent affirmations of our love and our dedication to one another.

The challenges of parenthood, while testing us, also brought us closer. We learned to navigate the difficulties together, facing each new hurdle as a united front. The exhaustion, the uncertainty, and the occasional frustration were all tempered by the knowledge that we were in this together. Each obstacle we overcame strengthened our bond and reinforced the trust we had in each other.

As our baby grew, so did our appreciation for the role we played in their development. Watching them reach new milestones—rolling over, taking their first steps, uttering their first words—was a profound experience. Each new achievement was a reflection of the love and care we had poured into their upbringing, and each moment of growth was a testament to our shared journey.

Parenthood had brought a new dimension to our love story, one that was rich with both challenges and triumphs. It was a journey that tested our patience, but also revealed the depths of our love and commitment. The connection we shared had deepened in ways we hadn't anticipated, as we faced the trials of parenthood together.

Through the sleepless nights and the long days, the shared responsibilities and the quiet moments of rest, we discovered that our love was not only enduring but evolving. Parenthood had added a new layer to our relationship, one that was built on the foundation of trust, support, and a deep, abiding love. Each day, as we navigated the joys and challenges of raising our child, we were reminded of the strength of our bond and the incredible journey we had embarked upon together.

# Chapter 26: Cultural Fusion

The soft glow of the afternoon sun filtered through the kitchen window, casting a warm, inviting light over the room. Ethan and I were engaged in one of our favorite family traditions: cooking together. Today, it was a special kind of fusion—combining elements of both our cultures into a single meal that was as much a celebration of our heritage as it was a testament to our life together.

He was expertly chopping vegetables, his movements a dance of practiced precision. I was at the stove, stirring a fragrant pot of curry while occasionally adding a pinch of spices. Our kitchen had become a canvas, where the vibrant colors and scents of our respective cultures mingled in a harmonious symphony. It was here that our shared journey unfolded, a testament to the unique blend of our backgrounds.

Ethan glanced over at me, a playful smile tugging at his lips. "I think this might be the best fusion we've done yet. The blend of spices is just perfect."

I laughed, feeling a rush of warmth at his words. "I agree. I think we're getting better at this every time we try."

Our conversations during these cooking sessions were often filled with stories from our childhoods—tales of holiday traditions, family gatherings, and the little quirks that made each of our cultures special. It was a way to weave our individual histories into the fabric of our daily lives, ensuring that the traditions we cherished wouldn't be lost but would instead evolve into something new and meaningful.

As we set the table, the dining area became a reflection of our journey together. Our table settings were a medley of traditional and modern elements. Ethnic tablecloths were paired with contemporary dinnerware, and the mix of traditional dishes with new recipes created a feast that was as much a celebration of our pasts as it was a nod to our shared future.

Family dinners had become a time to showcase this cultural fusion, blending recipes from both our heritages into a meal that was uniquely ours. We celebrated holidays with a similar spirit, integrating the rich traditions of our respective cultures into each festive occasion.

The winter holidays were a particularly joyful time. Our home would come alive with decorations that reflected both our backgrounds—brightly colored lanterns from one culture hung alongside traditional garlands from the other. We combined our holiday customs into a single celebration, creating new rituals that honored our histories while adding fresh traditions that spoke to our blended family.

One year, we introduced a holiday exchange where we exchanged traditional gifts from each culture. It was an exercise in understanding and appreciation, as we learned the significance behind each item and its place in our combined celebration. The joy on our family's faces as they opened gifts and experienced the blending of our traditions was a reminder of the beauty in our cultural fusion.

Daily rituals were similarly infused with our cultural blend. Our mornings began with a harmonious mix of traditional breakfasts from both sides of the family. The aroma of freshly brewed coffee mingled with the scent of spices, creating a unique start to our days. The lullabies we sang to our child at bedtime combined melodies from both our backgrounds, crafting a bedtime routine that was both comforting and culturally rich.

As we navigated these blended traditions, we found that each small choice contributed to a greater tapestry—a rich, intricate pattern woven from the threads of our separate histories. It wasn't always easy; there were moments of negotiation and compromise.

But each decision, each new tradition, became a testament to our commitment to honoring both our pasts while building a future together.

The joy of this fusion extended beyond our own family. We included friends and extended family in our celebrations, sharing the unique blend of traditions we had created. These gatherings became opportunities to showcase our cultural integration, and they were met with enthusiasm and admiration. Our loved ones appreciated the effort we put into blending our traditions, and it fostered a sense of unity and understanding among all who joined us.

Our journey of cultural fusion was more than a celebration of our backgrounds; it was a living, evolving testament to our relationship. It represented our commitment to each other and our dedication to creating a life that honored both our histories while embracing the future we were building together.

As I looked around the room, taking in the sight of our blended traditions and the warmth of our shared space, I felt a deep sense of contentment. Our home was a reflection of who we were—a vibrant tapestry of cultural threads that came together to create something beautiful and unique. Each meal we shared, each holiday we celebrated, and each daily ritual was a reminder of the love and respect that had guided us through our journey together.

The rhythm of our blended lives continued to find its own steady beat, like a song composed of our unique experiences and backgrounds. Our days were colored with the vibrant hues of both our cultures, each new tradition a note in the melody of our family life. We had learned to navigate the delicate balance of honoring our separate histories while creating a shared future, and it had become an adventure in itself.

One evening, as the first hints of spring began to breathe new life into the world outside, Ethan and I found ourselves in the midst of planning another celebration that would blend our traditions. This time, it was to be a birthday party for our little one. The occasion was an opportunity to meld our festive customs into a celebration that was distinctly our own.

We sat together at the kitchen table, surrounded by sketches of decorations and lists of potential activities. The room was filled with a comfortable hum of our collective creativity, each of us contributing ideas and suggestions. Ethan suggested incorporating traditional music from his culture, while I proposed adding a dance that my family used to perform during special events. It was an exhilarating process, each idea sparking new inspiration as we crafted a celebration that honored both of our heritages.

As we worked, our conversations meandered through fond memories of past celebrations—stories of laughter and joy, of family gatherings that had once seemed so ordinary but now felt like precious relics of our past. These shared memories not only enriched our planning but deepened our appreciation for the way our backgrounds had shaped us.

The party itself was a kaleidoscope of color and sound, a joyous fusion of traditions that reflected the beautiful complexity of our lives. The decorations were a blend of vibrant patterns and elegant designs, representing the two cultures that had come together to form our family. Music from both traditions played softly in the background, weaving a soundtrack that was both familiar and fresh.

The centerpiece of the celebration was a carefully crafted cake that combined elements from both our backgrounds. It was a masterpiece of confectionery art—a blend of flavors and designs that spoke to the heart of our fusion journey. Each bite was a delightful surprise, a reminder of the delicious blend of cultures that defined our family.

Guests arrived, their faces lighting up with curiosity and delight as they experienced the fusion of traditions for themselves. Conversations flowed easily, a testament to the way our combined heritage had created a space where diverse backgrounds came together in harmony. We shared stories, laughter, and a sense of connection that transcended cultural boundaries.

In the midst of the celebration, as I looked around at the happy faces of our friends and family, I was struck by a profound sense of gratitude. Our journey of cultural integration had been filled with its share of challenges, but moments like these made every effort worthwhile. The joy of seeing our loved ones embrace and celebrate the unique blend of our traditions was a powerful reminder of the beauty in our shared experiences.

As the evening drew to a close and the last of the guests departed, Ethan and I found a quiet moment alone together. We stood side by side, watching as the remnants of our celebration were gently tidied away. The room was filled with the soft glow of candlelight, and the air was rich with the lingering aromas of our festive meal.

Ethan took my hand in his, his eyes reflecting the warmth and love that had been so evident throughout the evening. "Tonight was perfect," he said softly. "I couldn't have asked for a better way to celebrate our journey."

I squeezed his hand gently, feeling the same sense of fulfillment that radiated from him. "It was," I agreed. "Every moment was a testament to the life we've built together—a life that honors our past while celebrating our present."

In that quiet moment, surrounded by the echoes of laughter and the remnants of our celebration, I felt an overwhelming sense of contentment. Our journey had been one of discovery and adaptation, of blending traditions and creating new ones. It was a journey that had deepened our bond and enriched our lives in ways we had never imagined.

As we looked forward to the future, we knew that our path would continue to be shaped by the rich tapestry of our cultures. Each new celebration, each shared tradition, would be a reflection of our ongoing commitment to honor our backgrounds while embracing the new dimensions of our life together. And through it all, we would continue to build a family story that was uniquely ours—a beautiful fusion of heritage and love.

In the quiet of our home, surrounded by the subtle hum of life unfolding, Ethan and I continued to weave our cultural tapestries into the everyday fabric of our family life. The mornings began with the aroma of blended spices and coffee brewing in the kitchen, each scent a reminder of our shared journey. Our breakfast table, once a canvas of single traditions, had transformed into a vibrant spread of dishes that celebrated the best of both worlds. We reveled in the unique joy of introducing our children to flavors and customs from both of our heritages, their curious little faces lighting up with each new experience.

The rituals that had once been confined to our individual histories now coexisted in beautiful harmony. On weekends, our home was a symphony of cultural celebrations. Mornings began with laughter and music, as we mixed traditional songs from both cultures into a joyful medley that had become a favorite part of our routine. The afternoons were often filled with the clatter of pots and pans, as we prepared meals that fused recipes and techniques from our respective backgrounds into something uniquely ours.

The holidays, once a time of singular focus, had transformed into vibrant celebrations that blended the richness of our cultures. For example, during the winter holidays, we embraced the tradition of decorating with ornaments from both backgrounds, creating a dazzling display that reflected the warmth and diversity of our family. Our Christmas tree was adorned with colorful decorations that told stories from both our heritages, each ornament representing a piece of our collective history.

As we navigated these new traditions, we also faced moments of reflection and adjustment. Some practices clashed or needed refinement to fit our evolving family dynamic. For instance, when it came to special ceremonies, finding a balance between different customs required thoughtful negotiation and creativity. One memorable occasion was when we prepared for our children's first major cultural festival. We wanted to honor both traditions in a way that felt authentic and meaningful. After many discussions, we found a beautiful compromise: a ceremony that began with the rituals of one culture and transitioned into the celebratory practices of the other. The result was a truly unique event, blending old and new, familiar and foreign, into a seamless celebration of our family's identity.

These experiences often sparked deep conversations between Ethan and me about the essence of our individual cultures and the meaning of our shared experiences. Late at night, when the house was quiet and the children were asleep, we would sit together, reflecting on how far we had come and envisioning the future. We spoke of our hopes for our children, wondering how they would navigate their own identities as they grew up in this fusion of backgrounds. We dreamed of the day when they would carry forward these traditions, not as burdens of expectation but as cherished parts of their heritage.

The journey of blending our cultures was not always smooth. There were moments of misunderstanding and disagreement, as each of us occasionally clung to certain traditions more fervently than the other. These moments, however, were opportunities for growth and learning. Through honest dialogue and compromise, we learned to approach our differences with empathy and respect. Our conversations often ended with laughter and a renewed appreciation for the beauty of our shared life.

One particularly touching moment was when we hosted a family gathering that brought together relatives from both sides. The event was a celebration of our journey and a chance to showcase how we had blended our traditions into something new and beautiful. As family members marveled at the way we had combined cultural elements, there was a palpable sense of pride and acceptance. The gathering became a testament to our commitment to honoring both heritages while creating a new narrative that was uniquely our own.

In these celebrations and everyday moments, we found not just a balance between our cultures but a deepened connection to each other. The blending of our traditions had become a metaphor for our relationship—a continuous journey of adaptation and discovery. Each new tradition was a piece of our shared story, a reminder of the love and commitment that had brought us together and continued to sustain us.

As our family grew and evolved, so too did our understanding of what it meant to merge our backgrounds into a cohesive whole. We realized that the process was not about erasing our pasts but about building a future that embraced the best of both worlds. Our home had become a sanctuary of cultural fusion, a place where every tradition was celebrated and every story honored. And as we looked forward to the future, we knew that this journey of integration and celebration would continue to be a central part of our lives, enriching our family and deepening our love.

# Chapter 27: Facing the Future

The soft light of dawn filtered through the curtains, casting a golden hue over our quiet bedroom. Ethan and I lay in bed, our conversation drifting from the mundane to the profound. The rhythms of our lives had settled into a comfortable routine, but beneath the surface, we both felt a gentle pull toward the future, an unspoken desire to build something enduring together.

We began to talk about our dreams, those elusive visions of what we wanted our lives to become. The conversation started casually, over coffee on a sleepy Sunday morning, but soon grew into something deeper. Our goals for the future unfolded like a delicate flower, each petal revealing new layers of ambition and hope.

Ethan spoke first, his voice filled with the excitement of new possibilities. He envisioned expanding his career, pushing boundaries and reaching new heights. It wasn't just about professional success for him; it was about making a difference, contributing something meaningful to the world. He shared his dreams of mentoring others, helping them achieve their own goals and dreams. The passion in his voice was contagious, and I found myself imagining the ways we could support each other in these aspirations.

As we talked, our discussions naturally shifted to personal growth. We both recognized the importance of evolving as individuals, of continuing to learn and grow even as we faced the demands of daily life. For Ethan, this meant pursuing new hobbies and expanding his knowledge in areas he had always been curious about. For me, it was about nurturing my creative side, finding time to write and explore new artistic ventures. Our conversations were peppered with laughter and shared excitement as we envisioned ourselves taking on new challenges and embracing opportunities for self-discovery.

But our dreams weren't confined to personal achievements. We also began to talk about the impact we wanted to have on our community. Our discussions grew more earnest as we considered the ways we could give back, leaving a positive mark on the world around us. We spoke of volunteer work, of supporting causes we were passionate about, and of creating initiatives that would make a difference. These conversations were filled with a sense of purpose, a shared commitment to making our corner of the world a better place.

As we brainstormed and planned, our hearts swelled with a renewed sense of possibility. It was as if we were mapping out a new chapter of our lives, one that was rich with promise and potential. We imagined the legacy we wanted to leave behind, not just for ourselves but for our children and future generations. The idea of building something lasting, something that would endure beyond our time, gave us a profound sense of fulfillment.

In the quiet moments between our discussions, we reflected on the journey that had brought us here. We had faced challenges and celebrated triumphs, navigated the complexities of blending our lives and cultures. And now, as we looked toward the future, we felt a deep sense of gratitude for the path we had traveled together. Our love and commitment had been the foundation of our journey, and it would continue to guide us as we faced the road ahead.

The dreams we shared were not just about achieving personal milestones or professional success. They were about building a life that was meaningful and fulfilling, a life that reflected our values and aspirations. We talked about creating a home that would be a haven of love and warmth, a place where our family could thrive and grow. We envisioned traditions and rituals that would be passed down through generations, a legacy of love and connection that would endure.

As we continued to dream and plan, our conversations were infused with a sense of hope and determination. We were united in our vision for the future, committed to supporting each other in every endeavor. Our shared goals became a source of inspiration, fueling our drive to make our dreams a reality.

In the evenings, as we sat together, our hands entwined, we would revisit our plans, fine-tuning our vision and setting new goals. The journey ahead was filled with uncertainty, but we faced it with confidence and optimism. Our love had been tested and proven, and it was now the bedrock upon which we built our future.

Our conversations about the future were more than just dreams and aspirations; they were a reflection of our shared commitment to each other and to the life we wanted to create. Each discussion brought us closer, deepening our connection and strengthening our resolve. As we faced the future together, we knew that the path we chose would be shaped by our love, our dedication, and our unwavering belief in the possibilities that lay ahead.

In the soft glow of the evening, the warmth of our home wrapped around us like a comforting embrace. The kids had finally settled into their bedtime routine, their laughter fading into the background as the house fell into a serene quiet. Ethan and I sat together on the porch, the gentle hum of cicadas filling the air as we turned our thoughts toward the future. It was during these peaceful moments, away from the rush of daily life, that our dreams and plans seemed to crystallize with the most clarity.

We leaned into each other, the weight of our shared experiences giving depth to our conversations. As we discussed our career aspirations, Ethan's eyes sparkled with excitement. He spoke of ambitious goals and innovative projects, his voice a mix of passion and determination. I could see the fire in him, the drive to make a mark that was uniquely his. Each dream he shared was like a piece of a puzzle, fitting seamlessly into the larger picture of our life together.

It was not just about achieving personal success; it was about creating something that would benefit others, leaving a legacy that reflected our values and aspirations.

I listened intently, my own ambitions intertwining with his as we mapped out our professional futures. I spoke of my own dreams, of the impact I hoped to make in my field, and the ways I wanted to grow both personally and professionally. The support we offered each other was palpable, a testament to the strength of our partnership. Our conversations were not merely about setting goals; they were about fostering an environment where our individual dreams could flourish side by side.

The topic of personal growth was equally significant in our discussions. We both felt the need to continue evolving, not just for ourselves, but for the sake of our family. Ethan shared his interest in exploring new hobbies and deepening his knowledge in areas he was passionate about. I, too, expressed a desire to nurture my creative side, to find time for writing and other artistic pursuits that had long been on the back burner. There was a shared understanding that personal fulfillment was a key component of our overall happiness. We made plans to support each other in these endeavors, promising to carve out time and space for our individual passions.

But our dreams extended beyond our personal and professional lives. We spent many nights discussing the kind of impact we wanted to have on our community. These conversations were filled with a sense of purpose and a desire to contribute to something greater than ourselves. We talked about volunteer work, charitable initiatives, and ways to use our resources to support causes we were passionate about. Each idea was met with enthusiasm and commitment, a reflection of our shared belief in the power of giving back.

As we delved into these discussions, we found ourselves envisioning a future that was rich with possibility. We imagined creating programs that could help others achieve their own dreams, providing support and mentorship to those in need. We saw ourselves as active participants in our community, using our skills and resources to make a tangible difference. The vision we crafted was one of hope and positive change, a testament to the values we held dear.

The process of planning our future also involved reflecting on our past and present. We talked about the experiences that had shaped us and the lessons we had learned along the way. Our journey had been filled with highs and lows, moments of joy and challenges that tested our resolve. Through it all, our love had been the constant, guiding us through difficult times and celebrating with us during triumphs. As we looked ahead, we felt a deep sense of gratitude for the path we had traveled together.

Our future plans were not just a list of goals and aspirations; they were a reflection of our shared values and our commitment to building a life that was meaningful and fulfilling. Each conversation was a step toward creating a legacy that would endure, a testament to the strength of our bond and our dedication to making a positive impact.

In the quiet moments between our discussions, we would often sit in comfortable silence, simply enjoying each other's company. The weight of our dreams and plans settled into a comforting rhythm, a reminder of the journey we were on together. Our love, unwavering and true, was the foundation upon which we built our future. And as we faced the uncertainty of what lay ahead, we did so with the confidence that, no matter what challenges we might encounter, we would face them together, hand in hand, with hearts full of hope and determination.

As the weeks turned into months, our conversations about the future began to take on a more tangible shape. We found ourselves diving deeper into the specifics of our plans, turning dreams into actionable steps. The initial excitement gave way to a more measured approach, as we outlined the milestones we hoped to achieve and the ways we would support each other along the way.

One evening, as the sun dipped below the horizon and cast a golden glow across our living room, Ethan and I sat at the dining table with a stack of notebooks and a laptop open between us. We had decided to formalize our plans, not just as a mental exercise, but as a concrete blueprint for our future. The process was both exhilarating and daunting, but it felt right to give our dreams a structure that matched the intensity of our aspirations.

Ethan's enthusiasm was infectious as he laid out his career goals with meticulous detail. He spoke about advancing in his field, taking on new challenges, and leaving a mark that would extend beyond his immediate work. His vision included mentoring younger professionals and contributing to industry innovations that could benefit the broader community. His eyes lit up as he described each step, his passion evident in every word. It was clear that his professional journey was as much about personal fulfillment as it was about making a positive impact on others.

I, too, found myself immersed in the process, reflecting on my own goals with equal fervor. My aspirations were centered around growing in my career, but also finding a balance that allowed me to nurture my creative side. I envisioned launching projects that combined my professional skills with my artistic passions, creating something unique and meaningful. Our conversations often veered into brainstorming sessions, where ideas flowed freely and possibilities seemed endless. We plotted out timelines, identified resources, and set achievable targets, each plan underscored by the support we promised to give one another.

As we turned our attention to personal growth, the conversations became even more intimate. We talked about the ways we wanted to evolve as individuals and as a couple. Our goals included not just professional achievements but also personal milestones. We envisioned traveling to new places, exploring hobbies that intrigued us, and continuing to learn and grow together. Each dream was interwoven with the threads of our shared experiences, creating a rich tapestry of our future aspirations.

The discussions about our impact on the community were particularly profound. We delved into the kind of legacy we wanted to create, exploring various avenues through which we could contribute positively. Our ideas ranged from supporting local initiatives to launching charitable projects that aligned with our values. We considered the ways in which we could use our skills and resources to make a difference, whether through volunteer work, mentorship, or financial support for causes we cared about. The sense of purpose in these discussions was palpable, as we recognized the opportunity to extend our impact beyond our immediate circle and into the broader community.

As we solidified our plans, we also made space for flexibility. We understood that the future was unpredictable and that our journey would likely involve detours and adjustments. The key was to remain adaptable, to embrace the changes that life would inevitably bring, and to continue supporting each other no matter what challenges arose. Our commitment to each other was the cornerstone of our plans, and it was this unwavering dedication that gave us the confidence to pursue our dreams with both courage and optimism.

In quiet moments of reflection, we often found ourselves marveling at how far we had come and how much we had accomplished together. The process of planning for the future had strengthened our bond, deepening our understanding of one another and reinforcing the trust that had always been the foundation of our relationship. It was a testament to the strength of our partnership, a reminder that, together, we were capable of achieving remarkable things.

As we continued to navigate the complexities of life and plan for the future, the sense of hope and determination remained a constant companion. Our dreams were not just aspirations; they were reflections of our shared values and our commitment to building a life that was rich, fulfilling, and meaningful. With each conversation, each plan, and each step forward, we embraced the future with a sense of excitement and possibility, knowing that, no matter what lay ahead, we would face it together, hand in hand, with hearts full of love and unwavering resolve.

# Chapter 28: Community Connections

When we first moved to this vibrant neighborhood, there was always an unspoken promise between us to dive deeply into our new community. It wasn't merely about blending in or becoming familiar with the local customs; it was about weaving ourselves into the very fabric of the place, offering our hearts and hands to those around us. We wanted to create something meaningful, both for ourselves and for the people whose lives would intersect with ours. It was with this intent that we embarked on our journey of community involvement.

Our initiation into community life began with modest steps. Ethan and I attended neighborhood meetings, eager to understand the pulse of our new home. The meetings, though initially overwhelming with their flood of information and faces, became the first threads in the tapestry of our local connections. We listened to stories of longstanding residents, their voices rich with nostalgia and pride. They spoke of traditions and local heroes, of annual events that were the lifeblood of the community.

In these gatherings, we found our first opportunities to contribute. We volunteered for local events, from street fairs to charity fundraisers. Our participation was not just about being present; it was about engaging with genuine enthusiasm. Ethan's knack for organization and my love for creative projects made us a dynamic pair. Whether it was setting up booths, preparing materials, or simply offering a warm smile, we immersed ourselves fully. These events became our way of learning and giving back simultaneously.

One particular event that captured our hearts was the annual cultural festival. It was a celebration of diversity, and it resonated deeply with our own commitment to honoring our heritage while embracing others. We took on the challenge of organizing a booth that showcased a blend of our cultural backgrounds. From traditional dishes to handcrafted artifacts, the booth was a colorful representation of our journey together. The feedback was overwhelmingly positive, and it sparked conversations with many who were eager to learn about our traditions. It felt like a bridge had been built between us and our new neighbors, one that was strengthened with each shared story and exchanged recipe.

As we grew more comfortable, we began to seek out opportunities to support specific causes. We joined forces with local organizations focused on education, environmental sustainability, and social justice. Each cause was a chance to delve deeper into the issues that mattered to us and to contribute meaningfully. Our weekends were often filled with community clean-ups, tutoring sessions, and advocacy meetings. The work was sometimes exhausting, but it was also profoundly rewarding. We found ourselves surrounded by like-minded individuals, each passionate about making a difference. These shared experiences fostered friendships that extended beyond the boundaries of our volunteer work.

Our involvement also led to a new understanding of the diverse tapestry that made up our community. We discovered stories of resilience and innovation, tales of struggles and triumphs that were both inspiring and humbling. Engaging with people from different walks of life expanded our perspectives and deepened our appreciation for the collective strength of our neighborhood. It became evident that our contributions were not just about what we gave but also about what we received in return—a richer, more nuanced view of the world.

Through our efforts, we began to forge lasting relationships. The people we met along the way became more than just acquaintances; they became friends and allies in our shared mission. We hosted gatherings at our home, where conversations flowed freely, and laughter echoed through the rooms. These gatherings were a celebration of our growing connections, a way to acknowledge the bonds we had built and to continue nurturing them. Our home became a hub of activity, a place where ideas were exchanged, and plans were made.

Our commitment to community also reflected back on us, enriching our own lives in ways we had not anticipated. The sense of belonging we found in these connections was deeply fulfilling. It was as if, through our collective efforts, we had found a new family—a network of support and encouragement that enhanced our own journey. The friendships we cultivated provided a sense of stability and joy, reminding us of the importance of nurturing relationships beyond the confines of our immediate circle.

In our quiet moments, when we looked around at the community we had become a part of, we felt a profound sense of accomplishment. We had not only embraced our new home but had also left a mark on it, contributing to its vibrancy and strength. It was a reminder that community connections were not just about giving but also about growing and evolving together. Each interaction, each shared experience, added a layer of depth to our understanding and appreciation of the world around us.

As we continued to navigate our lives within this community, we did so with a renewed sense of purpose and gratitude. The bonds we had formed and the impact we had made were testaments to the power of connection and the beauty of shared experiences. It was a journey of mutual discovery and growth, one that had enriched our lives and had forever changed the way we saw our place in the world.

Our immersion into the community wasn't just about giving back; it was a transformative experience for us, a journey of rediscovery and connection. We found ourselves drawn to the little things—the spontaneous neighborhood cookouts, the impromptu book clubs, and the annual talent shows that brought out the best of everyone's creativity. Each event was an opportunity to weave ourselves further into the social fabric of our town, and it quickly became clear how much joy these connections brought to our lives.

One of the most unexpected joys was joining a local gardening group. The group met weekly at the community garden, a lush expanse of greenery that seemed to flourish as a result of the collective care of its members. Ethan, with his love for hands-on projects, took to the role of cultivating the soil with fervor. I was more tentative, unsure of my green thumb, but the shared labor of planting, weeding, and watering became a metaphor for our growing relationships. As we tended to the garden, we nurtured friendships, learning from each other and celebrating each bloom and harvest together.

The garden became a sanctuary, a place where our busy lives slowed down and the simple act of planting seeds took on a deeper meaning. It was here, amidst the scent of fresh earth and blooming flowers, that we found a new rhythm in our relationship. We talked about our dreams and aspirations while our hands worked the soil, discovering new layers of understanding and support in each other. The friendships we forged in this setting were grounded in shared experiences and mutual respect, creating a network of support that felt as nourishing as the garden itself.

Through our involvement in the community, we also became active in supporting local schools. We volunteered for various programs, from tutoring sessions to extracurricular activities. Seeing the students' enthusiasm and curiosity reinvigorated our own sense of purpose. It was an opportunity to contribute to the future, to help shape young minds and provide support where it was needed most. These interactions reminded us of the impact we could have, not just in our own lives but in the lives of those around us.

Our commitment to supporting education extended to organizing fundraisers and educational workshops. The enthusiasm and creativity that emerged from these events were invigorating. We collaborated with local artists and educators to create events that were both fun and educational, blending entertainment with learning in ways that resonated deeply with the community. Each event was a celebration of collective effort, showcasing the power of coming together for a common cause.

The cultural aspect of our involvement also grew richer. We organized events that highlighted various cultural traditions, blending our backgrounds with those of our neighbors. Festivals, workshops, and storytelling sessions became a regular feature of our calendar. These gatherings weren't just about celebrating diversity; they were about creating spaces where everyone felt seen and valued. We shared traditional recipes, music, and stories, and in doing so, we created a vibrant tapestry of cultural exchange that was as enriching as it was enlightening.

In these moments, we saw how our own cultural traditions were embraced and appreciated by others. The respect and interest from our neighbors made us feel that our efforts were making a difference. The community was not just accepting our contributions but was actively engaging with them, reflecting a genuine interest in the richness of our shared experiences. This mutual exchange fostered a sense of unity that went beyond mere coexistence; it was a deep, meaningful connection.

Our involvement in the community also became a source of inspiration for our family. Our children saw firsthand the value of giving back and the joy that comes from being part of something larger than oneself. We included them in our activities, from helping at fundraisers to participating in cultural events. They learned the importance of empathy, collaboration, and the joy of making a difference. It was a legacy we hoped to pass on, a way to show them that every small action contributes to a larger impact.

As we reflected on our journey, it became clear how much we had gained from our community involvement. The friendships we formed, the sense of belonging we cultivated, and the positive impact we made all contributed to a profound sense of fulfillment. Our initial efforts to integrate into the community had blossomed into a deeply rewarding experience, enriching our lives in ways we hadn't fully anticipated.

The community had become more than just a backdrop to our lives; it was a vibrant, living entity that we were proud to be a part of. Our connections with our neighbors and our shared experiences had created a network of support that felt both intimate and expansive. It was a testament to the power of community, to the ways in which we can come together to build something greater than ourselves.

Looking forward, we knew that our journey with the community was far from over. The relationships we had built and the impact we had made were just the beginning. We were excited about continuing our involvement, to further deepen our connections, and to contribute to the ongoing growth and vitality of our neighborhood.

The months rolled on, and with them came the rhythms of community life that had become so entwined with our own. We found ourselves looking forward to each new project, each new opportunity to connect and contribute. Our weekends were often spent at local events, from farmers' markets to neighborhood clean-ups. Each event felt like a piece of a larger mosaic we were helping to create, a testament to the collective spirit of our community.

One particular initiative that became close to our hearts was a community mentorship program. It paired local professionals with high school students who were eager to explore career options. Ethan, with his background in engineering, eagerly volunteered his time, guiding students through the complexities of his field and sharing his passion for problem-solving. I took on a role in organizing workshops and helping students with college applications, finding joy in the little victories of each application submitted and each acceptance letter received.

The mentorship program quickly blossomed into a cornerstone of our community's efforts to empower its younger generation. The sense of accomplishment we felt as we watched these students grow, find their paths, and begin to imagine their futures was immeasurable. It wasn't just about the professional advice; it was about showing them that their dreams were achievable, that someone believed in their potential. The reciprocal nature of these relationships enriched us as much as it did them, reinforcing the idea that giving back is a path to personal growth and fulfillment.

Our children, now more involved in community activities, were blossoming in this environment. They participated in the local youth council, where they learned the ins and outs of civic engagement and the importance of local governance. It was heartening to see them take on responsibilities and voice their ideas, growing into young individuals with a deep understanding of their role in shaping the world around them. Their excitement for the council meetings and their eagerness to contribute to community projects were reflections of the values we had hoped to instill in them.

We also began to host our own gatherings, inviting neighbors over for cultural exchange dinners and informal discussions on various topics of interest. These dinners were not just about sharing food; they were about sharing stories, traditions, and experiences. We found that such events provided a platform for deeper understanding and appreciation among diverse groups. Conversations flowed as easily as the wine, touching on everything from family traditions to current events. These dinners became a symbol of our commitment to bridging gaps and fostering a sense of unity within our neighborhood.

One particularly memorable event was a multicultural fair we organized. It was a celebration of the rich tapestry of cultures that made up our community. From food stalls representing cuisines from around the world to performances showcasing traditional music and dance, the fair was a vibrant display of diversity. It was an opportunity for everyone to share a piece of their heritage and learn about others. The fair was more than just a festival; it was a testament to the strength that comes from embracing and celebrating our differences.

Through these shared experiences, we found that our community connections were deepening in ways we had not anticipated. The friendships we had forged were not just casual acquaintances; they were meaningful relationships built on trust, respect, and shared values. We supported each other through personal milestones, celebrated each other's successes, and offered comfort during challenging times. The sense of belonging we had hoped to create was now a living reality, a testament to the power of genuine community engagement.

As we continued to integrate ourselves into the fabric of our community, we recognized the profound impact this involvement had on our lives. It had strengthened our relationships, broadened our perspectives, and enriched our sense of purpose. Each new project, each new connection, added a layer of fulfillment to our lives, reminding us of the importance of contributing to something greater than ourselves.

The sense of fulfillment we derived from our community involvement was not just about the tangible outcomes of our efforts but also about the intangible rewards of shared experiences and mutual support. Our lives had become richer and more meaningful through these connections, and we were deeply grateful for the opportunity to be part of such a vibrant, engaged community.

Looking ahead, we were excited about the possibilities for further involvement and growth. The community had become an integral part of our lives, a source of inspiration and connection that we cherished deeply. We were committed to continuing our efforts, to building on the relationships we had formed, and to contributing to the ongoing development and vitality of our neighborhood.

Our journey had shown us that community connections were not just about participating in events but about fostering a sense of belonging and contributing to a shared vision of growth and unity. It was a journey of mutual discovery and collective effort, one that had enriched our lives and left us with a deep sense of gratitude and hope for the future.

# Chapter 29: Reflections and Growth

As the days turned into months and the seasons danced through their endless cycle, Ethan and I found ourselves drawn to moments of quiet introspection. Life, with its relentless pace and constant demands, often swept us up in its current. But there, amid the whirlwind of our routines and responsibilities, we carved out pockets of stillness to reflect on the journey that had brought us to this point.

We sat together on our porch, the late afternoon sun casting a warm, golden hue over our home. The world outside was alive with the sounds of summer—the distant laughter of children, the gentle rustling of leaves, and the occasional chirping of cicadas. It was a symphony of serenity that enveloped us as we sipped our coffee, each of us lost in thought.

Our conversations were meandering paths, leading us to revisit the milestones we had crossed. We talked about the challenges we had faced and the triumphs we had celebrated. Our discussions were punctuated by laughter and moments of poignant silence, as we both marveled at how far we had come.

It wasn't just about the big achievements—the career advancements, the community projects, or the personal goals we had ticked off our lists. It was also about the small victories, the quiet moments of understanding, and the daily acts of love that had stitched the fabric of our shared life together. These were the threads that, though invisible to the casual observer, had woven a tapestry rich with meaning and emotion.

We found ourselves reflecting on the lessons learned through the trials and triumphs. There was a profound sense of accomplishment in recognizing how much we had grown—not just as individuals, but as partners. Our journey had been one of evolution, a continuous process of discovering new facets of ourselves and each other. We had navigated through storms and basked in sunshine, and through it all, our bond had only strengthened.

Ethan spoke of how our experiences had reshaped his perspective. He talked about the clarity he had gained regarding his career aspirations and personal values. It was clear that his journey had been marked by a deeper understanding of what truly mattered to him. He had learned that success wasn't just about professional accolades but about finding fulfillment in the everyday moments and the relationships that enriched his life.

For me, the reflections brought a similar sense of growth. I looked back at the woman I had been when we first started this journey—eager, perhaps a bit naive, but filled with dreams and determination. Over time, I had evolved into someone who understood the value of patience, resilience, and the importance of nurturing relationships. The path I had walked had taught me to appreciate the beauty in the mundane and to find joy in the small things that often go unnoticed.

We celebrated these insights with a quiet, shared smile, knowing that our growth was intertwined with the love and support we had offered each other. The journey had been far from perfect, but it had been ours, filled with moments of challenge and beauty, of doubt and certainty. And through it all, we had emerged stronger, more connected, and more appreciative of the life we had built together.

In our reflections, we also took time to acknowledge the people who had been part of our journey. Our family and friends, with their unwavering support and encouragement, had played an integral role in shaping our experiences. We expressed our gratitude for their presence in our lives, recognizing that their love and guidance had been a steadying force as we navigated through the highs and lows.

As we looked forward, we did so with a sense of anticipation and optimism. The future stretched out before us like an open road, full of possibilities and new adventures. We knew that while the road ahead would undoubtedly hold its own set of challenges, we faced it with a strengthened resolve and a deeper understanding of ourselves and each other.

Our reflections were not just a look back at what had been but a celebration of the journey that lay ahead. They were a reminder of the love that had guided us, the lessons that had shaped us, and the dreams that continued to inspire us. And as we sat together, holding hands and looking out at the horizon, we did so with a deep sense of gratitude for the life we had created and the endless potential that still lay before us.

The evening light was softer now, casting a gentle glow over our living room as we continued our reflections. Ethan and I had moved from the porch to the cozy embrace of our sofa, where we sank into the familiar comfort of each other's presence. The conversation flowed effortlessly, each word a testament to the deep bond we had nurtured over the years.

Our journey together had been a mosaic of experiences, each piece adding to the rich tapestry of our shared life. We recounted the days when we were just beginning, the early struggles that seemed insurmountable at the time but now felt like distant echoes. Those initial challenges had been the crucible in which our relationship was forged, shaping us into the partners we were today.

Ethan's eyes sparkled with a mixture of nostalgia and pride as he spoke of our early days. He remembered the uncertainty and the excitement of starting a life together, the late-night talks about our dreams and the way we clung to each other in moments of fear. There was a softness in his voice, a reverence for how far we had come from those tentative beginnings. His words painted vivid pictures of the growth we had both experienced, and his admiration for our journey was palpable.

I listened, my heart swelling with gratitude as I reflected on the countless ways Ethan had been my anchor. He had been my constant support, my cheerleader, and my confidant. The growth we had achieved wasn't solely the result of our individual efforts but a testament to the strength of our partnership. Each challenge we faced had been met with a united front, each success celebrated as a shared victory.

As we delved deeper into our reflections, we also took stock of the quieter, more personal moments that had shaped us. The late-night conversations that turned into laughter-filled exchanges, the quiet walks where we shared our innermost fears and dreams—these were the threads that had woven the fabric of our relationship. They were reminders of the intimacy and trust that had deepened over time.

We reminisced about the times when our individual goals had seemed so separate, yet we had managed to weave them into a shared vision for our future. Ethan's career aspirations and my personal passions had often seemed like diverging paths, but together, we had found ways to merge them into a harmonious blend. It was a dance of compromise and understanding, each step bringing us closer to the life we had envisioned.

There was a sense of profound satisfaction in recognizing how our personal growth had intertwined with our collective journey. The lessons we had learned were not just about navigating life's ups and downs but about understanding ourselves and each other on a deeper level. We had grown not just as individuals but as a couple, finding strength in our unity and resilience in our shared commitment.

As the evening drew to a close, we sat in comfortable silence, reflecting on the future that awaited us. The horizon seemed to stretch endlessly, filled with possibilities and new adventures. We had built a strong foundation, one that would support us as we continued to navigate life's twists and turns. There was an unspoken understanding between us, a recognition that while we had come a long way, the journey was far from over.

In our reflections, we found a renewed sense of purpose and excitement. We were eager to embrace the future with the same enthusiasm and commitment that had defined our past. The lessons we had learned and the growth we had experienced were not endpoints but stepping stones to the next chapter of our lives.

The room was bathed in the soft glow of the evening light, a fitting backdrop to our reflections. As we held each other close, there was a deep sense of contentment and joy. We had come so far, and the road ahead was filled with endless possibilities. Our journey was a testament to the strength of our love and the resilience of our partnership.

With a final, lingering embrace, we prepared to step into the future, knowing that whatever it held, we would face it together, with the same courage, love, and dedication that had brought us this far. The reflections of the past were not just memories but a celebration of the life we had built and the endless potential that lay ahead.

The night settled softly around us, the kind of quiet that felt like a gentle exhale after a long day. Ethan and I were nestled on the porch, wrapped in blankets, the stars above us a silent witness to the introspection unfolding in the stillness. The world outside seemed to fade away, leaving us in our own cocoon of reflection and connection.

We talked about the milestones that had marked our journey—the triumphs and trials that had sculpted us into who we were today. Each story we shared was like a brushstroke on the canvas of our lives, creating a vivid picture of how far we had come. Ethan's voice was tender as he recounted the early days of our relationship, the tentative steps we had taken together, and the dreams that had seemed so fragile back then. There was a warmth in his words, a gentle reverence for the path we had walked side by side.

Our conversations meandered through the years, touching on the moments that had tested our resolve and the victories that had made us believe in our strength. We remembered the late nights spent talking about our future, the planning and dreaming that had brought us closer. The early struggles, once so daunting, now seemed like distant echoes, reminders of the resilience we had cultivated. There was a shared sense of pride in recognizing how we had turned those challenges into opportunities for growth, both individually and as a couple.

I spoke of the lessons I had learned—how each experience had shaped my understanding of myself and my place in our partnership. The growth wasn't always easy; it came with its share of tears and uncertainty. But as I looked back, I saw the beauty in the struggle, the way it had forged a deeper connection between us. Our conversations were not just about reminiscing but about acknowledging the strength we had found in each other, the ways we had supported and uplifted one another through every twist and turn.

As we shared these reflections, there was a profound sense of gratitude that enveloped us. We were grateful for the love that had been our constant, for the unwavering support we had provided each other through every hurdle. It was clear that our growth had been a joint endeavor, a testament to the partnership we had built. The satisfaction of looking back on our accomplishments was tempered by the knowledge that the journey was ongoing, that there was still so much to discover and experience together.

We talked about our hopes for the future, how the lessons from our past would guide us as we continued to build our life together. There was an exciting anticipation in the air, a recognition that while we had achieved so much, there was still more to strive for. The future felt like a canvas waiting to be painted, and we were eager to see what new chapters awaited us.

Our reflections also brought us closer, reinforcing the bond that had been the cornerstone of our journey. Each word, each memory shared, was a reminder of the depth of our connection, the love that had weathered every storm and celebrated every victory. The sense of togetherness was stronger than ever, a beautiful reminder of why we had chosen to walk this path together.

As the night wore on, we sat in silence, letting the peacefulness of the moment settle around us. The stars above seemed to twinkle in agreement, a silent celebration of the love and growth that had marked our journey. We knew that the path ahead would continue to unfold with its own set of challenges and joys, but we were ready to face it together, armed with the lessons of our past and the hope of our future.

The evening wrapped us in its serene embrace, and we held each other close, feeling the warmth of our shared reflections. There was a deep sense of contentment in knowing that our journey had been rich and rewarding, that we had created something beautiful together. As we looked ahead, we did so with a heart full of gratitude, ready to embrace whatever came next with the same love and commitment that had brought us this far.

# Chapter 30: A Love Everlasting

As the final chapter of our journey unfolds, Ethan and I find ourselves immersed in a profound sense of fulfillment. The path we have walked together has been rich and varied, filled with moments that have tested and strengthened our bond. Now, as we stand on the threshold of what lies ahead, there is a serene satisfaction in knowing that our love has not only survived but thrived.

Our reflections on the past are marked by a deep gratitude for the experiences that have shaped us. We have weathered storms and embraced the sunshine, each phase of our lives adding layers to the story we share. The challenges we faced were not merely obstacles but opportunities that allowed us to grow and deepen our connection. We have built a life together that is a testament to our commitment and love, a life that feels both richly rewarding and profoundly meaningful.

With each passing day, the anticipation of the future grows stronger. The excitement of what's to come is not tinged with uncertainty but filled with optimism. Our journey has taught us that love is not just a feeling but a continual act of choice and effort. It's in the everyday moments—the shared laughter, the quiet understanding, the unspoken support—that our love finds its true expression. We are eager to continue this dance of life, knowing that the rhythm we've established will guide us through whatever comes next.

The sense of peace that envelops us is not just about contentment with the present but also about the confidence in our future. We have crafted a narrative that speaks of resilience, joy, and unwavering devotion. Our story has been one of evolution, where each chapter has added depth and nuance to our relationship. We stand together, hand in hand, ready to write the next pages with the same love and dedication that has brought us this far.

In this moment, the weight of our past achievements feels light, like a cherished memory rather than a burden. We have built a legacy of love that we are proud to pass on. Our lives have been intertwined in such a way that we cannot imagine one without the other. The experiences we have shared, the dreams we have realized, and the obstacles we have overcome all contribute to a narrative that feels complete yet ever-expanding.

As we look ahead, the horizon is not just a line in the distance but a canvas waiting for our continued creativity and passion. The future holds endless possibilities, and we approach it with the knowledge that our love will continue to be our guiding star. There is a comforting certainty in the way we face tomorrow together, knowing that the strength of our bond will carry us through whatever challenges or joys await.

Our love, like a well-tended garden, has blossomed into something truly extraordinary. It has been nurtured by our shared experiences and tested by the trials we've faced. The blooms of our affection are vibrant and resilient, a testament to the care and attention we have given to each other and to our relationship. This love, cultivated with patience and devotion, is something we cherish deeply and look forward to celebrating in the years to come.

In the quiet moments, when we are simply present with each other, there is a profound sense of peace. It is in these times of calm that we truly appreciate the journey we have taken together. The laughter and tears, the highs and lows, all weave together into a tapestry that is uniquely ours. We are grateful for every thread, every color, every pattern that has created this beautiful design of our lives.

As we close this chapter, we do so with a heart full of contentment and a spirit ready to embrace the future. Our love story is far from over; it continues to unfold with each new day. We face the future with excitement and hope, eager to see what new adventures and experiences will enrich our lives. Hand in hand, we move forward, knowing that the love we share will remain our constant source of strength and joy.

In the end, our story is one of enduring love—a love that has grown and flourished, that has weathered the tests of time and emerged stronger. As we write the next chapters of our lives, we do so with the certainty that our bond will continue to guide us, inspire us, and bring us closer together. With peace and contentment in our hearts, we step into the future, ready to embrace whatever comes next with the same unwavering love that has been our constant companion.

The quiet hum of the evening settled around us as we sat together, side by side, reflecting on the life we've built. The room, filled with the soft glow of lamp light and the faint aroma of the dinner we'd shared, seemed to cradle our contentment. We had journeyed through so many chapters together, each page etched with memories both sweet and poignant. Now, as we looked back, it was clear that the richness of our shared experiences had created a tapestry woven with threads of love, patience, and understanding.

The moments of joy and laughter stood out vividly, like bright stars in the night sky of our past. We remembered the quiet, stolen glances that had ignited the spark of our romance, the spontaneous adventures that had become cherished memories, and the everyday rituals that had deepened our bond. Every shared experience had contributed to the mosaic of our relationship, painting a picture of a love that had grown stronger with each passing day.

But it wasn't just the moments of triumph and happiness that had defined our journey. We had faced our share of challenges, too. There had been times of doubt, moments when the road ahead seemed uncertain and the future foggy. Yet, through it all, we had found strength in each other. The trials we encountered had not been roadblocks but rather stepping stones that had guided us toward a deeper, more profound understanding of one another. It was through overcoming these obstacles that our love had solidified into something unwavering and true.

Our journey together had been one of continuous evolution. We had grown not just as individuals but as a couple. The early days of our relationship, filled with passionate discovery and the excitement of new beginnings, had given way to a more mature and resilient love. The path had not always been smooth, but each twist and turn had shaped us, preparing us for the life we now embraced. We had learned to navigate the complexities of our relationship with grace and empathy, building a foundation that would support us through whatever lay ahead.

As we envisioned the future, it was with a sense of wonder and anticipation. The dreams we had once whispered to each other in the quiet of the night were now tangible possibilities, waiting to be explored. We talked about the places we wanted to visit, the experiences we wanted to share, and the goals we hoped to achieve. Each conversation was filled with hope and determination, a reflection of the optimism that characterized our outlook on life.

The future felt like a blank canvas, ready for us to fill with new memories and adventures. We approached it with a sense of excitement, knowing that whatever challenges might come our way, we would face them together. Our love had been our constant companion, guiding us through the highs and lows, and we were confident that it would continue to be our source of strength and inspiration.

There was a serene joy in the way we looked at each other, a deep understanding that the love we shared was something rare and precious. It was a love that had been tested and tempered, one that had withstood the test of time and emerged even more vibrant and enduring. The peace we felt was a testament to the journey we had taken, a journey that had brought us to this place of contentment and fulfillment.

Our hearts were full as we imagined the days to come, each one an opportunity to continue writing our story. We knew that the chapters ahead would be filled with new experiences, new challenges, and new joys. But we faced the future with the same unwavering commitment that had brought us to this point. Our love had been our compass, guiding us through every twist and turn, and we were confident that it would continue to lead us forward.

In the quiet moments, when it was just the two of us, there was a profound sense of peace. We were content with the life we had created together, grateful for the love that had carried us through so many experiences. As we looked back on our journey, we saw not just the story of our relationship but the story of two people who had found in each other a love that was enduring and true.

Our story was not just one of romance but of a deep and abiding partnership, built on a foundation of mutual respect and unwavering support. It was a love that had grown and evolved, adapting to the changes and challenges that life had presented. And as we moved forward, hand in hand, we did so with the certainty that our love would continue to be the guiding force in our lives.

As we closed this chapter, we did so with a heart full of gratitude and a spirit ready to embrace the future. The love we shared was a testament to the journey we had taken, a journey that had brought us to this place of peace and contentment. And with that same love as our guide, we looked forward to the next chapters of our lives, ready to continue writing our story together.

The soft twilight bathed our living room in a gentle glow as Ethan and I sat side by side, the comforting silence between us punctuated only by the occasional crackle of the fireplace. It was in these quiet moments that we felt the weight of our shared journey most profoundly, each flicker of the flames casting shadows that seemed to dance to the rhythm of our intertwined lives. Looking at the life we had built together, I was struck by the beauty of how far we had come, and how the simple acts of love and understanding had shaped our days.

Our home was a reflection of us—each corner imbued with the essence of our experiences, our laughter, and our shared dreams. Photographs of our adventures adorned the walls, each frame a silent witness to the milestones of our relationship. I glanced at the picture from our first anniversary, a snapshot of two people on the cusp of their journey, brimming with hope and excitement. And now, years later, that same hope had matured into a quiet, unwavering certainty, a testament to the strength of our bond.

We had weathered storms and basked in the sunlight together, each season of our life revealing new facets of our love. The challenges we faced had tested our resilience but also deepened our connection, turning moments of difficulty into opportunities for growth. Ethan's strength had been my anchor during the turbulent times, his unwavering support a constant source of comfort. And in turn, I had found solace in his arms, our love becoming a sanctuary from the world's chaos.

As we talked about our future, it was with a shared vision of what lay ahead, a future painted with the colors of our dreams and aspirations. We spoke of places we wanted to explore, of new experiences we wanted to share. Each conversation was an exploration of possibilities, a way of mapping out the uncharted territory that lay before us. Our dreams were no longer distant fantasies but tangible goals we planned to achieve together.

The excitement of these conversations was palpable, and yet there was a serene satisfaction in the realization that our love had already provided us with everything we needed. We had built a life rich in meaning and filled with joy, and as we looked forward, it was with a deep sense of gratitude for the journey that had brought us here. The love we shared was a constant, a beacon that had guided us through the darkest nights and the brightest days.

# THE WAY BACK TO US

We found contentment in the little things—the shared laughter over a simple meal, the quiet moments of reflection before sleep, and the everyday rituals that had become a cherished part of our routine. These seemingly small moments were the threads that wove our life together, creating a tapestry that was uniquely ours. It was in these moments that I felt the depth of our connection, a bond that had been forged through years of shared experiences and unwavering commitment.

As we contemplated the future, we did so with a sense of peace, knowing that our love had weathered the tests of time and emerged stronger. We had learned to navigate the complexities of life together, and our partnership had become a wellspring of strength and inspiration. The future was no longer an uncertain expanse but a canvas waiting to be filled with new chapters of our story.

Our love had always been our guiding star, and as we looked ahead, it continued to shine brightly, illuminating the path before us. We faced the future with optimism and excitement, ready to embrace whatever came our way. The journey we had undertaken was far from over, but we approached it with a deep-seated confidence in the strength of our bond.

In the stillness of the evening, as the last light of day faded into darkness, we sat together, our hands intertwined, hearts full. It was a moment of profound serenity, a culmination of all the love and joy we had shared. The quiet comfort of our togetherness was a testament to the enduring strength of our relationship, a love that had been tested and had triumphed.

As the night grew deeper, our reflections continued, each thought a testament to the life we had created and the love that had sustained us. We knew that the chapters ahead would be filled with new experiences, new challenges, and new joys. But whatever lay before us, we would face it together, our love a constant source of strength and inspiration.

And so, as the night embraced us in its quiet, we found solace in the knowledge that our story was far from over. Our love had been our guide, our anchor, and our joy. It had carried us through the highs and lows, and as we continued to write the next chapters of our lives, we did so with a heart full of gratitude and a spirit ready to embrace the future. Hand in hand, we looked forward to the adventures yet to come, knowing that our love would continue to light the way.